SHIMMY

ANNE CATEAUX

www.annecateaux.com

ISBN 978-1-7778770-0-2 (print)

ISBN 978-1-7778770-1-9 (ebook)

Cover artwork by Shirley Biggs

Cover design by Grayson Leier

Editing and layout by Amanda Bidnall

Poem "Children of Men" by Michele Coppinger

For Aidan, West, and all my four-legged children, thank you for choosing me as
your momma
Will and Nicole, you filled my home with so much love and laughter

Special thanks to
Shirley Biggs for her beautiful deer painting
Michele Coppinger for her touching and powerful
"Children of Men" poem

This book is for anyone who ever loved an animal and knows
they are still with you

1

THE FAWN

Sunday, November 23, 8:49 a.m.

EVAN THOUGHT the idea of taking the dog for a walk was nuts. Anyone familiar with Vancouver Island *knew* that light rain in November was like a shower of metal slivers hurtling out of the sky to slice you to the bone. Wind jacket or not, it was enough to ruin the prospect of a beach crawl adventure.

His mother's reassurances—"But sweetheart, it's only lightly raining, and the walk will do you good"—did little to console him. Evan couldn't help but notice that MJ was still snuggled in her hot-pink housecoat and fuzzy slippers. Obviously, *she* didn't need a walk. When he grumbled as much, she simply said, "Darling, I need to stay here and whip up a feast for you little men. Besides, Meagan will be disappointed if you don't go."

Puh-leeze, thought Evan. His mom wanted him out of the house so she could turn up her music and sing along to some hokey song. He couldn't understand her taste in music. She sang off-key and never seemed to know any of the right words. Frankly, it was annoying. After five minutes of her wailing away, the kids were begging her for mercy.

And Evan had reached a new level in his video game. As Master Chief, he was kicking some serious butt, and his ninja reflexes were out of control. Who knew what would happen if he broke his concentration and put the game on hold? What if he never achieved the same coordination or Zen-like state again? No. They were asking too much.

Gavin, Evan's ten-year-old brother, wasn't as subtle as his mother. "You come right now, or I'm going to tell Mom and Dad what you did to Holly last night!"

Evan hadn't counted on that tactic. Now he wasn't sure what to do. His first impulse was to reduce Gavin to a pulp, but he decided to counter with a threat of his own. "You tell them about that, and I'll rat you out for eating the chocolate bar Dad stashed away."

"Ha! Dad caught me. Sorry, big bro, can't use that one on me." Gavin shifted. "Aw, please, please, please come. Meggie and I want to show you what we found the other day." He dropped his voice. "We hid a human foot under some driftwood. You gotta see it before we turn it over to the police."

At twelve, Evan was older and wiser than Gavin. First off, he knew it couldn't be a human foot. Second, if it *were* a human foot, there was no way his brother or Meggie would ever touch it, not in a million years. Nope. No foot—no walk!

"Evan, I'm serious. If you don't come, I'll tell Dad how Holly's tail got singed."

Evan looked deep into Gavin's eyes and realized he had been outmanoeuvred. His brother had been waiting patiently for an opportunity to get one up on him, and he was now making good on the moment.

Evan huffed. How could he have known cat fur ignited so quickly? He wasn't sure what had shocked Holly more: the half second her tail was on fire, or the unceremonious dunk into the pond to put it out. In remorse, Evan had slipped tuna out of the house and let her gobble the entire can. He'd also tried to lure her inside so she could have the luxury of snuggling in his bed. It wasn't his fault she wouldn't come near him now.

Evan resigned himself to the fact that his sparkler and

firecracker days were over. He had to be responsible and think about the four-legged family members. But how would he explain how he'd gotten into Dad's locked studio to raid the stock of fireworks?

"Fine," said Evan grudgingly. "I'll go. But you'd better not talk about that foot all the way to the beach."

Gavin beamed and ran out of Evan's bedroom.

"He's coming! I *told* you I could get him to go!"

Evan put his game on hold and dragged himself into the kitchen. "Mom, if I lose my gaming groove, I'll never eat your pancakes again."

"I understand, honey. Should I stew the mixed berries or peaches?"

"Mixed berries, no sausages and only crispy bacon." He glanced back to see MJ jack up the volume on the radio and raise the wooden spoon to her mouth like a microphone. He covered his ears and yelled, "Wait up!"

Meagan Richards was waiting for them at the end of her driveway. As she dodged Gavin's hip check, she tucked her long chestnut hair into a knit hat and pulled on matching gloves. Gavin lit up when he saw her soft hazel eyes, and volunteered the back of his sleeve to wipe the tears watering from her eyes.

"Thanks, Gav, but this wind is nothing compared to yesterday's. My eyes stung so bad I couldn't see squat and ran straight into a tree! Look at the beauty of a bruise I'm sporting. Ever see such a shiner?"

Twelve years old, Meagan was tall and always moving. Gavin laughed as she danced around them and twirled in circles until she almost fell down.

"I hope you don't ride your ATV as crazy as you walk, child. You're a menace to the roads." The boys' dad, Joe Edmund, sidestepped the whirling dervish and caught her before she did a header into a ditch.

"Your mom said you gutted more fish than the pros yesterday. You beat the record again?" Evan asked. He didn't get lightheaded like Gavin did when he saw her. To him, Meggie was just one of the boys.

Despite the rain, which was coming down pretty hard, the kids were happy as they zigzagged across the road that wound down to the beach. Access was hidden behind mailboxes and blackberry bushes.

Red, the Edmunds' dog, veered into Miss Baker's flagstone path, but Meagan was onto him. "Red! Come here, boy," she cheerfully bellowed. Like a moth to a flame, like a hummingbird to a flower, he pranced merrily to her.

Joe watched enviously, shaking his head. He was relieved to avoid another encounter with Miss Baker. But he despaired that his prized German shepherd had forgotten all his training since he'd been "snipped." Now, Red shied away from Joe and gravitated to the women in his life. The dog was intelligent, hardworking and stupendously attractive. But he was also vindictive.

Oh well. Joe could not find it in him to get too upset. He breathed in the fresh west coast air and marvelled at how fiercely the Pacific Ocean crashed onto the shore below. Their little slice of heaven was nestled just outside the quaint village of Cedar. It was remote enough to be idyllic, but close enough to a big town that they could get supplies when they needed them.

"Slow down!"

But Evan, Gavin and Meagan had already raced down the steep steps to comb the beach for treasures. Joe looked east and admired the islands dotting the skyline. He squinted and could just make out the twinkling lights of Vancouver city. The snow-capped Coast Mountain range stood guard against the passage of time. Even on a day like today, it was breathtaking.

Gavin, meanwhile, was trying to keep up with Meggie and Evan. He ran along the beach, jumping over jellyfish and clumps of seaweed. The shore was made up of millions of pebbles, each one a different shape and colour, and broken shells added to the stone tapestry. He avoided the pounding surf as it hit the shore and slowed down only to leap over waterlogged trees and debris. He had just rounded the first bend, where the creek left the trees onto the smooth rock basin, when he saw the fawn.

"Red! Stop!" screamed Gavin.

Less than twenty feet in front of them stood a fawn. Frozen on a mossy stone ridge, the black-tailed, white-speckled fawn was dangerously close to the ocean's edge. Its dark eyes locked on them and blinked rapidly. Gavin noticed a white, half-crescent birthmark between its brows. The fawn was perfect and seemed so new. It looked steadily at the small group of children and did not seem to notice the fast-approaching dog.

"Red, stop! Come here, boy! *Stop!*"

The fawn finally noticed the wet, long-haired dog charging forward at top speed. Gavin, Evan and Meagan helplessly watched the terrified fawn leap high into the air and land with a loud splash in the water. Red skidded to a halt at the edge of the outcrop and barked insanely as the poor baby deer was pulled out to the middle of the cove.

⸻

Joe was meandering, admiring the trees, and was just about to pull a unique piece of driftwood from the rolling water when he heard the children screaming.

Running as fast as he could, he rounded the bend where the pebble beach gave way to smooth rocks. It took only a moment for Joe to realize what had happened. Red had frightened a young deer. Fearing for its life, the fawn had leapt into the icy water and was now being pulled out to sea.

Evan had Red by the collar and was struggling to control him. "Dad! Do something!" He managed to get Red's leash on, and secured it to the end of a fallen tree. But he watched in horror as the baby deer got swept out further. He searched frantically for anything that would help the poor creature.

"Dad, look! Herb's rowboat is up there!"

The nearest house belonged to a retired doctor and his wife. Herb and Joan had lived on the ocean for years and were the guardians of the beach. Running at a reckless speed, Joe narrowly missed wiping out on the steep wooden stairs. He banged on the solarium door until Mabel, Doc's live-in housekeeper, cautiously opened it. The sounds of Beethoven's Fifth Symphony could be heard from somewhere deep in the house.

"Mabel, where's Herb? I need his dinghy. There's a fawn in trouble in the bay, and I don't know how much longer he can swim."

Doc Herb came out of the powder room with shaving cream covering one half of his face and his razor suspended in midair. "Take what you need. The dingy is at the top of the deck. The oars are in the shed. I'll meet you down on the beach!"

Joe ran to the deck that overlooked the ocean. He untied and gently slid the dingy down to the beach.

"Gavin, grab the other end and pull!" Evan took the bow, and together they dragged the dingy to the shore.

The fawn struggled against the current pulling him to the centre of the cove. It made attempts to break free and swim toward the beach, but its thrashings grew weaker. The children followed along, never taking their eyes off him. Joe ran down the steep stairs and met up with them.

"Dad, you gotta help him!" Gavin took the oar out of his father's hand and threw it into the boat.

"Why won't he swim back?" cried Meagan. Tears ran down her pale face as she reached out to the water.

Joe was dragging the dinghy into the water when he heard the children's gasps. The fawn had drifted directly in front of them. His head dipped under the water, but he bobbed back up and let out a cry. He struggled frantically and went under again. Before anyone could utter a sound, he disappeared. He was gone.

Doctor Herb scrambled down the steep stairs to the beach. One keen glance told him everything.

"Go home, dear ones, and put on some dry clothes. There is nothing more you can do here."

2

THE AWAKENING

EVAN WOKE up tired and furious. He had not slept. The events of the day before haunted him all night long. He kept seeing the head of the baby deer as it went under and did not resurface.

His parents had tried to comfort him and Gavin. They explained it was okay to feel sad, that the little fawn was in a better place, but their well-meaning attempts to explain the cycle of life fell on deaf ears.

Had his family not insisted on going for a walk on such a crappy day with their stupid dog, none of this would have happened. He hadn't wanted to go, but did anyone listen to him? No. Now he had the memory of a helpless fawn drowning right before his eyes. Where was its mother? Why didn't it swim back after Red was out of sight and out of earshot?

Evan refused to look at his mom and dad when he made his way to the kitchen. On one hand, he wanted to rant and rave, but he knew nothing could change what had happened. The only thing he could do was get ready for school, walk to the bus stop and get on with his day. Gavin was still asleep. Typical, Evan thought. His brother wouldn't let anything interfere with *his* sleep.

When Gavin finally woke, he didn't comment on the previous

day's events. He stumbled from room to room and only muttered the odd word. It was his mother who noticed that his shoulders were low and his gaze blank. He accepted his lunch with a distracted kiss and made his way out the door to catch the 8:00 a.m. bus.

Evan was already halfway down the drive when Gavin caught up to him.

"Gonna say anything about it?" asked Gavin.

"Nope." That was the last of it as far as Evan was concerned.

Meagan was already on the bus, chatting away to the Coppy sisters, so the boys settled down beside their friend, Lukas William Gabriel III.

To his mother, he was Lukas. To his teachers, he was Luke. But to a select few friends, he was Coolio. It started in Grade 1. Evan had watched the famous movie *Cool Hand Luke* one rainy afternoon with his father. He'd taken a break from building his Lego Millennium Falcon model and joined his dad in the living room. At six years old, he didn't understand the entire story, but what struck him was how courageous and funny Luke was.

As Evan got to know Lukas Gabriel, he was reminded of the honest, persistent and pigheaded Cool Hand Luke. One day during lunch break, some bigger Grade 3 boys tried to suggest that Lukas was not welcome on the jungle gym. Lukas, being Lukas, did not agree and said as much. The tense showdown was broken up only by the arrival of the Principal. By then, Evan had dubbed Lukas William Gabriel III Cool Hand Luke—Coolio for short. It was a nickname his pal liked.

Evan took in his friend's attire. Coolio sported a Billabong T-shirt, Diesel jeans and an Alien Workshop toque. Flung over his seat was a DC hoodie. Coolio, at twelve years old, was a walking fashion billboard. Everything about him was cool. The girls loved his green eyes and short crew cut, and his cheeky smile often diffused the wrath of the adults when he sometimes went too far. Today, Coolio was so engrossed in describing that weekend's hockey game disaster that he didn't notice Gavin and Evan's sombre mood.

Evan was in Miss McGrade's Grade 7 class, while Gavin was in Mr. Shoreman's Grade 5 class. Usually, when the bus pulled up to the school, the boys raced off the bus and went their separate ways, but today they lingered behind and walked together to the south entrance. Meagan joined them but kept her eyes on the ground. The other kids were out of earshot, running to offload their gym bags in their lockers.

"You okay?" Meagan said, shuffling her feet.

"I guess," said Gavin, without much conviction.

"No!" hissed Evan. He looked at Meagan accusingly. He wanted to see signs of yesterday's trauma. He needed to know someone shared in his misery.

Anyone who knew Meagan Richards knew she loved animals. She had a dog, a cat, a gerbil, a cockatoo and a goldfish. And if she kept wearing her mother down, she'd end up with a pot-bellied pig for Christmas.

"Mom said the fawn's mother was probably already dead and couldn't protect him. He was all alone on the beach. I... I..." She couldn't finish her sentence. The tears started to fill her eyes, and instantly Evan felt like a schmuck. She felt just as sick as he did. And when he looked more closely at Gavin, he realized that his brother too, was far from okay.

His anger evaporated. Evan wanted to ease their sadness, but before he could say another word, the morning bell sounded. They had no choice but to run off to their separate classes.

The day wore on, painfully slow. During one of the recess breaks, Evan located Gavin with his three amigos: Cameron, Jake and Shawn. Meagan was defending her title as handball champion of Cedar Intermediate, and Evan decided not to break her concentration. Coolio roped Evan into covering net during a brief but fierce soccer match against the undefeated Grade 6 team. Even though the game was only fifteen minutes long, everyone left the field sweaty and out of breath. As they ran off to class, there were promises of a rematch the next day.

On the bus ride home, Coolio picked up his story where he had left off that morning. "Once the seven-man pileup got untangled, we realized the puck was still in play. Randolph Snider was sitting on the damn puck the whole time! He took a cheap, sloppy shot into our team's undefended net." Coolio's look of disgust was amusing to Evan. "I gotta tell ya, that's not how I thought we'd end our ten-game winning streak. The ref should have blown his whistle when our goalie was spinning like a turtle on his back. Oh, the misery! The shame of it!"

Coolio, as usual, was very funny as he recounted the story, but somehow the boys couldn't fully enjoy the moment.

When Evan got off the bus, he gave Earl the bus driver his usual high five, descended the stairs and waited for his brother. But right behind Gavin was Coolio.

"What's up?" Evan asked. Coolio's drop-off was not until the bottom of Pacific Drive.

"Did you forget I was coming over?" Coolio said. He was more than a little amazed. In all the years the boys had known each other, Evan had never forgotten an after-school hangout.

"Sorry, dude!" Evan had already been feeling bad, but now he felt colossally worse. The look on Coolio's face was somewhere between pitiful and comical.

"Forget about it," Coolio said, in his gangster voice. But despite his best efforts, he couldn't cover up his irritation.

Gavin piped up. "Something happened this weekend, and we aren't thinking straight."

This bit of news got Coolio moving, and within minutes, they were walking down the long driveway and warding off the one-hundred-pound shepherd.

"Let's grab some snacks and go up to the tree fort." Evan led the way into the house and shooed Red when the dog tried to follow them in. Even though it hadn't rained, he knew Red's footprints all over the tiled floor would not go over well with their mom.

"Hi, Mom," screamed both boys.

"Hi, darlings. I'm in my office."

"Mom, we're going up to the fort. No, we don't have any homework, and we won't eat the entire bag of Oreos. "

Evan, Gavin and Coolio wasted no time collecting their supplies. The knapsack was filled with cookies, Kool-Aid drink boxes, biodegradable pellets, airsoft guns and camo wear, including protective chest and eye wear. For two years, the Edmund brothers and Coolio had been fortifying their base camp. When the boys were born, Joe had committed himself to building a replica of the Ewok huts on the forest moon of Endor. Their *Star Wars*–inspired fortress was a series of platforms and shelters built ten feet in the air among the trees.

Gavin and Evan held their backpacks high. Red, smelling cookies, leapt into the air, trying to snatch the bag. By the time the trio made their way to the main hut, they were ready for a sugar fix and debrief. Coolio could see something was up but decided to hold his questions until Evan revealed what had been preoccupying him all day.

The boys climbed the sturdy ladder to the main platform, which was the hub for all the other huts. The covered fort was roomy enough for ten kids. In summer, the thatched roof and shuttered windows let in much-needed air, and in the winter they provided shelter from the torrential downpours. The platforms were connected by a series of suspension bridges and ropes for swinging from tree to tree.

It was a kid's paradise. But Evan and Gavin had only one thing on their mind.

"We watched a fawn drown down at the beach," Evan said.

Gavin added, "It was scared of Red and bolted for the water. It didn't come back to the beach. It drowned after going under three times."

Coolio nodded his head in sympathy. "No wonder you're bummed out."

That was it. No more, no less. Coolio seemed to understand what had taken place. Evan and Gavin were relieved not to have to tell the whole story.

"Ready? Coolio rubbed his hands together.

In unison they extended their hands and said, "Rock, paper, scissors!" Coolio's rock smashed Gavin and Evan's scissors, so he got to stay off the forest floor.

As Coolio climbed up the old-growth cedar to his vantage point, the boys swung down off the platform using the knotted ropes. They ducked for cover under the ferns and hostas.

Gavin turned to Evan. "Coolio seemed to get it."

Evan reloaded his M15A4 airsoft rifle and said, "Yup, he gets it."

"What if Meggie were here?" Gavin licked his finger and checked the direction of the breeze.

"We would still be up there, and she would be pounding on us to talk about our feelings."

"Good thing she has guitar practice tonight." Gavin shuddered at the thought and decided to put it all behind him. Coolio had the upper hand, and if he and Evan were going to outsmart him this time, they had to focus.

At one point during the game, while Evan was seeking cover under a large fern, Red crawled over on his belly and cautiously licked Evan's face. Since the fawn's drowning, Evan had avoided his beloved dog, but now he realized that Red was not to blame. He buried his face in his dog's thick, furry neck and whispered words of comfort. Red knew right away that he was forgiven, and after one last lick across Evan's mouth, he sauntered off to find and torture Holly.

The game seemed to be over before it started, but MJ assured them they had been out for hours and it was time to wash up for dinner. Monday was spaghetti and meatballs night, and while the boys slurped noodles and munched on garlic bread, they filled their parents in on their day. Coolio recounted the disastrous hockey game and embellished the seven-man pile-up.

MJ, for one, was relieved that her boys seemed to be back to their usual selves. The night was equal parts laughter, whining and negotiating to get out of their chores. MJ could see everyone was drained, so after the boys walked Coolio home, she insisted they call it an early night.

"But Ma," Gavin protested.

"No," MJ replied.

"That's not fair!" Evan shot back.

"No," she said again. She got up from sitting on the floor, where she had been reading and faced her boys head on. "It's only Monday, you had little sleep last night and you need to get up early for school tomorrow."

As their mouths opened to counter her argument, she raised her hands for silence and gave them "the look." This was the look that told the boys she meant business. Evan was the first one to shrug and walk away. He brushed his teeth and said good night to his dad. But Gavin wasn't ready to give in yet. He offered to clean up his room, but when that offer fell on deaf ears, he gave up as well.

MJ settled down beside Evan. "How are you feeling?"

"Okay, I guess." Evan's voice was heavy with sleep.

"I spoke with Meagan's mom today. She said that Meagan was still pretty shaken up. How was she at school?"

"We didn't talk much." Evan rubbed his eyes. "Can we not talk about this right now? I'm tired, and I want to sleep."

"No worries. What will it be? Head, back or arms?"

Following his prayers and back rub, he fell into a deep sleep.

Evan stood, screaming into the wind. "No!" Stop!" But the fawn kept swimming, further and further out. In the distance, he could see a giant orca heading straight for the helpless deer.

"Someone, help! Help!"

But the sound of the surf deadened his voice, and his cries were lost on the wind. Evan was gripped with fear as he watched the orca barrel down on the baby deer. Its dorsal fin cut through the water, and occasionally it disappeared altogether only to resurface closer to the fawn. From this distance, Evan could see that it was a huge whale, bigger than any he had seen before.

Suddenly the whale leapt up and started to hop through the water. As it approached the fawn, it slowed down and circled him. Several times it slapped its tail on the surface, and large waves rolled over the fawn. Evan heard cries coming from the baby deer. The wails echoed off the surrounding rocks and ridge.

Evan's heart was pounding so loud he couldn't think. No, please

God, no! He ran without thinking into the frigid water. The waves hit his face and soaked his hair. His feet slipped on the rocks, and his heavy suede coat pulled him down. He went under and gulped the cold, salty water. He couldn't breathe… He—

"Wake up!" Gavin shook Evan as hard as he could. Evan thrashed in his bed, but he couldn't untangle his legs from the blankets.

"*Evan!* Wake up!"

Gavin grabbed Evan by his wet PJ top and shook him as hard as he could. Slowly, Evan stopped twisting under Gavin's grip, and then he suddenly went still. He opened his eyes and looked *through* his brother, as if he couldn't see him. The dim moonlight cast shadows around the room.

"What… what happened?"

"You were dreaming. You kept saying, 'Don't hurt him, don't hurt him.' You wouldn't wake up. You really freaked me out."

Evan moved over so Gavin could sit on the bed. "Did I wake you with my yelling?" Evan looked around, now fully aware of his surroundings.

"No, I was already awake. I came in here to tell you about the deer at my window. I woke up for some reason. When I went to put my slippers on, I saw the deer just standing there looking at me. It's still there. Come see." Gavin peered down the hallway. "Lucky Mom and Dad are such deep sleepers."

"Great. I'm dreaming about a deer being eaten by an orca, and you're dreaming about a deer being a peeping Tom. We're a fine pair."

Gavin took no notice of his brother and pulled Evan from the bed. "Come on! I want you to see it before it's spooked away. It's a fawn, and it looks so much like Spotty."

"Who's Spotty?" Evan asked in amusement.

It was dark, but Gavin blushed deeply. "Oh. Well, that's the baby deer. Every time I think of him, I call him that in my head." Gavin had successfully pulled Evan into the hallway and was yanking him into his room.

"You're nuts. You drag me out of bed to stare at your window? You must…"

But Evan's words hung in the air. Standing at the window was a black-tailed, white-speckled fawn. Between his brows was a white half-crescent mark. The fawn stood very quietly, peering into the window. The moon lit the side of the house with a shimmering glow. The deer gazed at them and tilted his head at an angle.

"Holy. I've never seen a deer just stand there and look into a window." Evan grabbed his brother by his arm but did not take his eyes off the fawn.

"You're gonna think I'm nuts," Gavin whispered, "but I'm telling you *that is* Spotty. Look at him. He looks exactly like the fawn at the beach." Both boys walked slowly to the window. They held their breath and tried not to make any sudden movements.

The deer stood rock still. His huge ears dwarfed his head, and his caramel-coloured body looked soft. White spots covered his body, and his legs were spread out as if he were still a bit shaky on his spindly legs. But it was the mark that was most striking. Large and defined, it dominated his face and framed his eyes in a pretty way.

"It's him!" Evan sputtered. "But how?"

"I don't know. We saw him go under. Can deer swim underwater for a long time? Can they hold their breath?" Gavin was almost levitating off the floor in his excitement.

Evan pressed his nose up to the window and peered directly into Spotty's eyes. The fawn looked at him the way Red did when they were all outside, deciding which trail to hike. Their dog *knew* what they were discussing, and he would cock his head to one side and then the other. Spotty was doing the same thing.

Suddenly Spotty started to bleat. The sound erupted from his snout, and he seemed just as shocked by it as Evan and Gavin. At first it was soft and broken, but as he worked himself up, the noise got louder.

"He's going to wake up the house. We've got to get him to cut that out!" Gavin looked at Evan as if somehow *he* knew how to handle a baby deer. The boys ran to the back door and quietly slipped out without waking Red. They rounded the back of the house and were surprised to find the baby deer still there.

Spotty stopped pushing his neck out, and the bleating noise stopped. He stood very still and let the boys approach him. As they got closer, they realized that the shimmering light around his body was not the moon's glow. Rather, the dancing, sparkling light seemed to come from the fawn itself.

"You see what I'm seeing?" Gavin stayed a half-step behind his brother. "Did Spotty slip into a bucket of silver, glow-in-the dark paint?"

Evan inched slowly toward the fawn and put out his hand tentatively. Without hesitation, Spotty approached him and was just about to rub his snout into the boy's hand when he stopped and stepped away. Gavin gingerly went to put his hand on Spotty's head, but again the fawn stepped back.

"Wait till we tell Meggie!" Gavin was smiling from ear to ear. He couldn't believe that *their* deer was with them. "How does he make his fur sparkle? Look at his eyes." Gavin leaned closer and peered into Spotty's huge eyes. They looked like their mother's diamond ring, twinkling silver and white.

The shock of seeing Spotty was wearing off. The boy's teeth were chattering, and they could not feel their feet or hands. Their plaid slippers offered no protection against the cold flagstone walkway where they stood.

Evan was about to suggest that they go back indoors when he saw a movement out of the corner of his eye. Standing very close to them was a doe. She was grey and tan, and like the fawn, she glowed. The doe's ears stood high and twitched as she watched the boys with her fawn.

"Um, Gavin, I think we should back up slowly and move away from the fawn." Evan had his hand on his brother's shoulder and gently but firmly pulled him backward.

"She's sparkling too. Look how she shimmers. She's so pretty!"

The fawn hopped over to his mother and nuzzled his nose under her chin. She used her snout to prod him back into the heavy foliage. Then, as quickly as the magic and light filled the air, it was gone.

Gavin opened his mouth to speak, but Evan said, "Not here. Let's get inside before we freeze to death."

The clock read 2:22 a.m. Without even discussing it, Gavin got into bed with Evan, and they whispered about what had happened until early morning. When MJ found them, Gavin was hanging off the bed, and Evan's face was smooshed up against the wall. She thought it was sweet and decided to let them sleep another fifteen minutes.

When they woke up, it was like a firecracker had been lit under them. They hurried through their morning routine and flew out the door ten minutes before the bus was due to arrive. They raced up the road to Meagan's house. She was lacing up her sneakers on the front porch when she saw them.

"What's up with you?"

Before Evan could even formalize his thoughts, Gavin blurted out the whole night's events. To anyone else listening, it would have sounded like a far-fetched piece of fiction. But Meagan knew these boys. She knew truth when she heard it. She didn't ask any questions, but her smile warmed Gavin's heart, and Evan felt relieved that his friend was back to her usual, happy self.

"Evan, you must have skipped your thirty-minute hair ritual this morning." Meagan laughed as she tried to smooth down the ratty nest sitting on top of his head. Evan's jet-black hair curled wildly around his neck, and his deep, chestnut-brown eyes crinkled from his wide grin.

"Gavin, you shouldn't laugh. Your hair is no better." Meagan reached for his head, but he ducked under her arm.

Gavin was Evan's polar opposite in colouring. His white-blonde hair whipped around his green eyes, and the gold specks in his eyes were especially bright today.

"Come here, gorgeous, and I'll fix that mop." She laughed as she licked her hand and chased him around the garden.

Gavin enjoyed every minute of it, but Evan noticed that his brother's pale, freckled skin blushed bright red. Gavin tried to hide behind his taller brother, but Evan stepped aside like a boxer so Meagan could grab him. She took great delight in embarrassing Gavin.

Meagan glanced between the two boys and smiled. Despite their differences, they looked alike. It was their large white teeth and wide shoulders and, more than anything, their mannerisms. They laughed in the same belly-gut way, and they both talked fast.

The bus roared down the road, so they ran to greet it at the bottom of Meagan's driveway. The usual crowd was already hamming it up. The only kid who ever caused any real trouble was Ruth Cissy Blackhorne. She was a mean kid. There was no other way to say it. She was the anointed school bully and had been since kindergarten. Parent-teacher interviews, counsellors, neighbourhood intervention—none of it changed her behaviour. She existed to torture kids and adults alike.

She was sprawled across three seats but suddenly bolted up and leered at three scrawny boys.

"You stink! Take a shower, why don't ya!" She wheezed out a barking laugh and only stopped when Earl, who had already yelled at her a dozen times, stopped the bus and threatened to kick her off.

"Lovely. Ruth seems to be in top form today." Meagan's happy mood evaporated. She chose seats four rows up from her arch rival. "If we're lucky, maybe she'll pretend to get the swine flu again and skip school for a couple of days."

Evan could feel Ruth's stare boring a hole in his back, and it took all his willpower to ignore her. The only person who seemed completely immune to Ruth was Coolio. Oh, she tried to torment him with her taunts and intimidating size, but Coolio usually just laughed at her and told her to save it for high school. He loved to remind her that next year, she would be at the bottom of the food chain. He *wanted* to see her shoot off her big mouth to a pack of seniors. That image was vivid enough to get him out of bed every morning.

Gavin and Evan decided not to tell Coolio about the visit in the night. It wasn't that they didn't *want* to tell him, but somehow they knew the commute to school wasn't the right time. The kids parted ways when the bell rang.

"Don't forget: we need you in net for round two with the mighty Grade 6-ers." Evan rolled his eyes and assured his friend for the umpteenth time that he would be ready. Pulling out what he needed for the morning's class, Evan didn't notice when his prized Seattle Sounders soccer shirt fell out of his locker. It lay unnoticed on the terrazzo flooring when he walked away.

Miss McGrade surprised the class with a pop quiz on the fur trade in Canada. Evan was not prepared and needed the full hour to scribble down his answers. He had just handed in his paper when he heard Coolio out in the hallway. Requesting permission to go to the bathroom, Evan shot out to join his friend. He found Coolio and Ty Doucette, captain of the Cedar Intermediate Math Club, whispering near their lockers.

"What's up?" Evan said.

"Dude, I think you need to go to the bathroom." Coolio spun him around and pushed him toward the loo.

"You sound like my mom. I'll go if I wanna go." Truth be told, Evan was ready to burst, but he was not going to tell his pals that.

As they entered the boys' bathroom, Evan got a whiff of the urinal pucks. Charming, he thought. But the next thing he saw was his beloved Sounders shirt, stuffed into one of the urinals. A primal scream escaped his lips. He couldn't stop it. He didn't want to.

"*Nooo!*" In close quarters, Evan was like a caged animal. He paced in circles and kept pointing to his shirt. "If I find out who did this, I'm gonna… I'm gonna…" He found the right words and spewed them with as much venom as he could muster—just as Mrs. Rosaline walked in. Short, squat, her long grey hair neatly tied in a bun, their principal had heard every word of Evan's tirade.

"Would you mind telling me why you are all in here?" She turned her glare on Evan. "Mr. Edmund, precisely what did you mean by your words? Exactly *where* do you intend to shove your hockey stick?"

Evan had enough sense to know that Mrs. Rosaline did not, in fact, want to know where he planned on shoving his hockey stick. Self-preservation kicked in, and he kept quiet.

Coolio, on the other hand, jumped up and down on the spot like he desperately needed to use the facilities. He waved his hand wildly in the air like a child.

"Ooh! Ooh! Mrs. Rosaline, I know why he's in here." Coolio beamed, and he genuinely looked like he wanted to help. "Someone threw Evan's shirt in the yucky pee bowl."

Coolio didn't intend to sound like a four-year-old, but that was how he came across. Mrs. Rosaline walked over to the urinal. A huff escaped her lips. She cast her eyes to the heavens and silently counted to ten.

"Ty, please go to the office and see Miss Dickson. Request a plastic bag, and bring it to me." When the boy did not move, she clapped her hands. "Run along! You are missing too much class as it is."

Mrs. Rosaline asked the boys who was responsible. When Evan said he didn't know, she told them she would start an investigation. Clearly this would result in a misconduct for one or more children.

Evan had every intention of using his mom's biggest pot to boil his shirt. He didn't care if the disinfectant faded the bright lime colour. Better bleached out and unrecognizable than lost forever.

At recess, the boys gathered to hear about what had happened. Gavin sauntered over just as Coolio was describing how Mrs. Rosaline used the butt of a broomstick to place the soccer shirt into a plastic bag. Naturally, Gavin demanded that Evan start from the top, so the whole tale was retold again.

"There is only one person who would dare do this. Where's a circus when you need one? They could take her for the freak show!" As if to confirm his suspicions, Ruth and her Cro-Magnon friends walked by. They snickered at Evan.

"Lose something today? You should keep better care of your belongings. I'm sure your *mommy* will be most unhappy to learn about your crappy Sounders shirt." She got right up in Evan's face and hissed, "You should just burn it. It stinks, and fluorescent green makes you look like you puked on yourself."

Her mob burst out laughing. As they walked away, they gave Ruth high fives like she had just won a sporting event.

Gavin lunged forward, but Evan's hand shot out to grab his brother. "Cool it, G. If you get one more misconduct, Mrs. Rosaline will send you home for the day. Don't worry. I'll find a way to get her back."

The rest of the day was spent in usual boredom with the exception of Miss LeBoof's music class. They were learning a Beatles' song. LeBeef, as the kids liked to call her, was funny and cool. She could play every instrument and could make up rap lyrics on the spot. The kids liked to play Name That Tune. She could make out the songs no matter how badly they were whistled. She had a great sense of style and always looked like she had just stepped out of a fashion magazine. The boys tried to impress her, and the girls imitated her. Tuesday music class was something to look forward to.

When the boys got home, they didn't argue about finishing their homework. They wanted to go to the beach before dinner. They had already made arrangements with Meagan, so they knew they had to turn their charm on their mother—full wattage.

"You look nice today, Mom." Gavin stood at his mother's elbow.

"Something smells good. I know I'll eat my whole dinner tonight. " Evan rubbed his mom's back.

MJ narrowed her eyes. "What are you boys angling for?" For no less than ten seconds, they tried to look shocked and disappointed. When it seemed that would not penetrate her defences, Evan tried a simpler approach.

"Can we go down to the beach with Meggie? We'll be home by five thirty."

"We promise not to explore too far. Please, Mom? Pretty please." Gavin rubbed her back hard, hoping the friction might affect her decision.

"Yup. But don't climb the rocks on the east side of the beach, and fight the urge to bring home more seashells. The back deck smells like a cannery." In unison, they yelled, "Thanks, Mom," and flew out the front door.

Meagan was waiting for them at the end of her driveway. She had worn a figure eight in the gravel.

"What took you so long? Never mind. We only have an hour before it gets dark. I brought a flashlight, but technically, I'm supposed to be home before the sun goes down."

"Did you hear about what happened to Evan's Sounders shirt?" Gavin had moved to Meagan's other side as she took long strides down the road.

"Of course. I knew before I got out of class. The drums were beating seconds after it happened. I think Ty told Simon, Simon told Trent, Trent told Mick, Mick told me. When Coolio came in, he tried to talk to us, but Mr. Lanzilotta kept a close eye out, and every time Coolio slipped out of his desk, Lanzilotta gave him the evil eye."

Evan was having a hard time keeping up with Meagan's strides. Her long legs covered more ground than the boys.

"I know who did it, by the way."

"No way. You serious?" Evan grabbed her by the arm to slow her down.

"Of course. Do you think Ruth Cissy Blackhorne can keep her big mouth shut? She told Jennifer that if she didn't stop singing 'Diva,' she would put her hoodie in the toilet just the way she ordered Thumper Jones to put your shirt in the urinal."

"Who sings 'Diva'?" Gavin asked.

"You know. Beyoncé." She proceeded to sing it, and Gavin tried to sing along.

"Focus!" yelled Evan. "Who else heard Ruth say it? Was Jennifer on her own, or was there a huge crowd who could testify to this? Mrs. Rosaline could use some help on this one. She still hasn't solved the mystery of who put the entire bottle of detergent in the cafeteria's dishwasher."

"Nah. Ruth cornered her at the back of the class after everyone took off for gym." The look on Evan's face distressed Meagan. "Look, let me see what I can do. I want her gone more than you do. Remember? It took two years for my hair to get back to this length after she cut it off while I slept. Why my mother ever trusted that kid to stay over is beyond me. Ruth has it coming."

When they got down to the beach, no one was there. The sun was gleaming off the rocks, making the place look lovely. Some of their apprehension slowly slipped away. It was hard to believe that two days earlier, on this same beach, they had watched a baby deer drown.

"Okay, now we need to figure out what really happened. Could Spotty have swum underwater, around the point and then resurfaced somewhere we couldn't see him?" As he said the words, Evan knew it was impossible for any mammal to pull that off.

"What if Spotty had an identical twin, and that's who we saw last night?" Gavin picked up some flat stones and proceeded to make them bounce on the water like a pro.

"Let's go see if his body washed up on shore." Meagan's words seem to shock her even more than the boys. "If we find it, I refuse to go near it, but at least we'll know for sure he's dead."

They walked along the beach, much like they had that fateful morning. They combed the whole area, and after forty minutes of looking, they were certain there was no carcass on shore.

"Now what?" Gavin had stopped at Lookout Rock, the big climbing boulder, to get a better view of the ocean and surrounding area. The boulder was hard to climb, but the piled-up logs helped. With a little push from Evan, Meagan was perched up there too. They pulled Evan up and sat quietly, enjoying the scenery in front of them.

At first it seemed the big bird flying toward them was a blue heron or a bald eagle. But as it continued straight for them, they realized it was some kind of owl. Its wingspan was massive. The children gawked—and then screamed as it landed in front of them. It was only inches away, and yet the owl didn't seem the least bit troubled by them.

"Evan, I must be sleeping again. There's an owl sitting in front of us, and it's shimmering like Spotty did last night." Even in the blinding sunlight, there was no mistaking the wild predator sitting calmly, staring right at Gavin and glowing like a disco ball.

"It's the most beautiful bird I have ever seen." Without a thought, Meagan reached out to stroke it. But her hand passed through the owl, and the action seemed to distort it—like it was made of liquid instead of flesh and feathers. Her eyes told her the hand was inside the owl, but her brain told her it was grasping only thin air.

"That's impossible." Her moment of being awestruck was over. Now she was simply struck with horror.

Just as she was about to scramble off the rock, the owl leaned forward and said, "Hello. I am Carolynn."

3

CAROLYNN

ALL THREE KIDS jumped off the boulder and bolted for the stairs. Evan reached the bottom of the steps first and was just about to run up them when the talking owl swooped down and perched on the handrail.

"Don't be afraid. I won't hurt you. Funny—I thought you would be braver and smarter. I guess even Abigail can get it wrong occasionally."

"What are you?" stammered Gavin.

"What a question! What do they teach you kids at school these days? I'm a great horned owl, of course."

Meagan and the boys backed away from the stairs and stood together in a defensive position. Without taking his eyes off the owl, Evan leaned down and picked up a heavy, waterlogged stick. He pointed it at the owl. "How can you talk? Why are you shimmering? Why have you come to us? And who's Abigail?"

Evan's shotgun interrogation stopped. They all held their breath as they waited for the owl to talk again.

"How can *you* talk?" Carolynn asked politely.

"Because I can! I just can, is all." Evan's voice was so high it cracked.

"Well, I can just talk too. There was a time I couldn't talk to humans, but that was a long time ago. And there are few humans like you, who can see and hear us."

Carolynn flew down from the rail and settled on a big log at their feet. "Abigail is a lovely doe, and it is her fawn that found you. Abigail was without her darling for almost a full month. She fretted terribly for him. Now they are united. She came to me and told me of special children who inhabit the box dwellings and who seemed to know of us. She said her little one talked of three humans who were with him when he left the Mother Earth for the World of Light."

"Are you a ghost?" Meagan asked, so quietly the boys could hardly hear her.

"No, although I know of which you speak. Ghosts are apparitions that no longer inhabit their earthly bodies. They haunt particular locations or people they were associated with in life or at the time of their death. My guess is they do not know to seek the light." Carolynn hopped over to the middle of the log and invited the children to sit on the one directly in front of her.

After the children reluctantly settled, she carried on. "We live in the light. We are all we *were* and all we *can* be. We choose to live, as is our right and honour. We live in our world, which is within your world."

"I have *no idea* what that means," Gavin said, exasperated. "Are you dead? Where do you live? Why couldn't we see you before?"

"Ditto," Evan said.

"Double ditto!" Meagan echoed.

"Yes, I must remember you are not enlightened ones yet."

As Gavin made a move to get up and walk away, Carolynn laughed. "Okay, okay. Let me see if I can explain this in an easier way."

Gavin settled back down and crossed his arms over his chest. "You have one minute. Then I'm outta here."

"When I lived in the Earth World—"

"Before you died and when you were alive?" Gavin interrupted.

Annoyed, she said, "Yes, when I was just a plain old owl living in a barn."

"Then why didn't you say that?" Gavin didn't seem to realize he was arguing with a talking owl.

"I was alive a long time ago. I lived in the first barn erected by the coal miners in the Land of Wakesiah. That is what we called Nanaimo then. In those days, I watched the Coast Salish people catch the fish and hunt the forest. Today, countless humans live in box dwellings, and many of the trees I perched in are gone." Carolynn peered into Gavin's eyes to ensure that he understood her words. "When the sun disappeared behind the great mountains, I would fly the skies and look for prey. On these nights, I was drawn to the glow of the fires dotted all over the land. From sea to mountain slope, I would listen to the First Peoples tell their stories. Their children would listen intently and fall asleep in their mothers' arms. What I know of where I am today, and how I got here, is based on what I learned in those days." Her voice grew excited, and she fluttered her wings wide and let them settle again.

"Saghalie Tyhee made everything living, including you and I. Hundreds of years ago, he came to stand on the very top of that mountain that now peers down on us."

"Mount Benson!" said Gavin.

"Yes. It did not have that name then, but you are right, little one."

Gavin, proud of himself, leaned in close to hear the story.

"Saghalie Tyhee loved the world he made and stood quietly and admired his work. After some time had passed, he realized that it was very still and there was no sound. He decided to create animals. His mighty power crafted the beaver, the bear, the deer, the rabbit and the majestic eagle. His beautiful animals roamed the Land of Wakesiah and prospered.

"Years went by, how many I know not, and Saghalie Tyhee felt he needed to create a man. He clapped his great hands, and a thunderbird flew down from the clouded skies. In his talons, he held a human. The man's name was Soc-o-thock. He was the first male in the Land of Wakesiah. Soc-o-thock loved the valley, and his animal friends helped him because he was all alone.

"After some time, he called for his father. 'Saghalie Tyhee, I am lonely. Please send another to be with me so I may share in all that is here.' So his father made him a woman, and he and that princess made three sons. In time, those three sons took their families and moved to other parts of the island.

"My mother talked of those days. She talked about a time when only canoes crested the waterways. Then along came ships with large sails. The ships moved with the great coastal winds and carried many men. These men came from across the globe. They set up camps and took black stone from deep in the ground. In time, the ships changed again, and black smoke curled out of tall stacks that seemed to reach the skies. Change was constant, and the land gave up all it had for the newcomers."

Carolynn stopped and waited to see if the children had any questions.

"How long did you live?" Evan loved her plumage and wondered if he could find any marks to suggest how she died. Looking more closely, he noticed she was dark brown, with white spots on her neck and back. Her belly was creamy white. She had the most marvellous eyes.

"It is very hard to determine the passage of time. We do not sense it the way humans do. I lived longer than my mother and father. I lived longer than my brothers and sisters. I lived longer than the males I chose, and I lived longer than all the young I hatched. I watched human children be born and then watched them become tall, strong men.

"In those years, I hunted wood rats and flying squirrels. When food was scarce, I ate snakes and insects. One harsh winter night, I could not find prey. So much of the forest had been cut away. I searched all night. I flew west, climbing higher and higher to the glacier-draped mountaintop. It was there I froze to death."

The kids gasped. "How terrible for you!" Meagan hugged herself and looked like she was going to cry.

"Bummer," was all Gavin could muster.

"So then what happened? How did you get the way you are now?" Evan had never been more fascinated in his life.

"One minute, I felt only unbearable cold and pain. The next minute, I was bathed in light and warmth. I opened my eyes and found myself sitting high in an alder tree. Perched beside me were my beloveds. They all greeted me with deep, hooting calls. "Hoo-h'HOO—hoo-hoo." My young made loud, raspy screeches. They rubbed up close and gently ruffled my feathers. I have never been without them since."

"Wow. That's what my mom told me would happen when I die. Without the freezing part, of course." Meagan looked out to sea as if looking for something or someone.

Evan stood up reluctantly. "I forgot to wear my watch, but gauging by how fast the sun is going down, I'd say we had better get going, or else we'll be in trouble."

"Why did you say there are few humans who can see or hear you?" Gavin was trying to keep up with the kids and not trip over the logs as he looked up at Carolynn. She was flying just in front of them.

"We have lived among humans since the beginning of time. I was told that once in a blue moon, a human can sense us. Some can even hear us. In my time, I have never encountered ones such as you, who can hear me, see me *and* talk to me. It is a marvel!"

"But what do you think? Why are we so different?"

The owl looked at Evan but did not answer his question. Instead she entertained them by swooping and diving around them. She seemed to be putting on a show. Evan laughed out loud when she pulled a kamikaze move on Gavin, causing him to dive for cover in the ditch. Meagan pulled Gavin up and helped him brush off the leaves. He was red in the face but laughed a belly-gut laugh.

They were rounding the first corner on Pacific Drive when a car approached them. The kids moved off the road and stood in shock when the car drove right through Carolynn! She flew through the driver's-side window and emerged out the back, landing gracefully on the stop sign at the corner of Pacific Drive and Mahoney Avenue.

"Neat party trick!" Gavin ran and tried to jump up and touch her.

"Did you feel the car pass through you?" Meagan tried to hoist Gavin up the stop sign, but he did not budge. She finally gave up and continued walking. Carolynn flew only feet above their heads.

"I do not feel anything from the material world. Of course I can see it, and I can hear it, but I can't feel it the way I used to."

This went beyond the children's understanding, and they collectively chose to drop it.

Gavin stopped at the top of Meagan's drive and looked up. "Now that you are in our lives, what will happen?"

"You will meet the others," she said. And with that, she flew off with powerful thrusts of her wings.

4

THE OTHERS

THE YELLOW BUSES waited outside the school. The students had just enough time to write down the day's assignment from the blackboard before they had to put their coats back on for the day's excursion. Every year, the students got to visit a local wildlife sanctuary, wetland, museum, art gallery or poultry hatchery. This year it was the Nanaimo River salmon hatchery.

When the buses pulled up, the kids were instructed to proceed to the tourist building.

"Children, settle down now. Please give a warm welcome to Kara. She is going to explain what they do here at the hatchery and speak about the events the staff hosts year round."

Evan took a good look at Kara. She looked too young to be heading up a hatchery. She was slender, and the front strands of her long, flaming-red hair were highlighted emerald green. She wore a nose ring and black overalls with chains hanging from the lower pockets. Her bubblegum lipstick looked sticky and a grin that stretched from ear to ear.

"Hey, guys. You got lucky. The kids who came last week got soaked! We ordered up fine weather for your fascinating introduction to life at a hatchery." Her smirk suggested that she knew for most of these kids, a trip to the dentist was more enjoyable than a trip to the hatchery.

"You are standing in our visitor centre. Take a few minutes to check out our displays, aquarium and pictures. Oh, and for those of you who have not woken up yet, you are here to see fish. Salmon, to be specific. So run! Be free! Meet me back here in ten."

Kara walked off to talk to some kids who were pounding on the aquarium glass. Evan was sure the Vulcan death grip she put on Mick was less than comfortable.

"How crazy is this?" hissed Meagan, who appeared behind Evan. The picture in front of them showed a Chinook salmon in all its stages of life. "Every time I go to tell my mom about Carolynn, I *stop breathing*. She took my temperature this morning, for crying out loud! She thinks I'm coming down with something. I was up all night pacing. I spent most of the night on the floor, talking to Dakota. I told her that I knew she could hear me, and that I can now see and talk to dead owls!"

"What did Dakota do?"

"What do you think? She just licked my face and thumped her tail on the floor. She was so loud that she woke up my mom. I was put back to bed, and the next time my ma woke up, she found me asleep with Missy Kitty and Dakota on the living room floor. Evan, I don't think I can stand another day without telling someone." Meagan chewed her thumbnail, and Evan could see it was red raw. "Did you and Gavin tell your parents?"

"No. After we dropped you off last night, we decided to not tell them. At least not until we spend more time learning about Carolynn and her world. What I wanna know is what she meant when she said, 'You will meet the others.' I gotta tell you, I'm a bit freaked out about that. I've seen the roadkill on Yellow Point Road."

"Did Gavin sleep last night?" Megan asked, and then she shook her head. "No, scratch that. I know the answer. He slept like a baby, didn't he? So what do we do now?" She stopped gnawing and looked at Evan liked he was going to say something profound.

"We go to the beach again."

The rest of the hatchery tour included watching Kara do

something disgusting to the male Chinook salmon and then something equally disgusting to the female. At the first chance, Evan beelined for the exit. Right behind him was Meagan. They led the class around Napoleon Pond, and when the path headed back toward the visitor centre, they veered off to the left, down by Coho Creek.

"See if you can come down to the beach again. We'll see what Carolynn has in store for us. I mean, how many more dead Shimmies can there be?"

"What's a Shimmy?" Meagan asked, as she kicked riverbed rocks with her well-worn sneakers.

"Gavin started calling them that. You know, 'cause they shimmer. He says that the whole place probably shimmers. All I know is that when we saw Spotty in the middle of the night, he was magical, and the light danced around him." They agreed on a time to meet later and ran to catch up with the other kids boarding the bus.

Coolio held back for Evan.

"What happened today? I thought we had a plan." Before Evan's world had turned upside down, he and Coolio decided that they were going to hang together during the tour. Coolio knew the area inside out and figured they could slip away without being noticed for at least half the time. "I looked for you everywhere. Every time I saw you, you were chummy with Meggie. I decided not to break in, but hey man, if you wanted to ditch me for Meggie, you could have told me."

"It isn't like that. Meggie and I just had something to talk about. Look, there is *a lot* I gotta tell you. Can you meet us down at the beach after school?"

Coolio had been trying to act nonchalant, but his veneer was slipping. "Evan, you said you would come to my hockey game! Did you forget already? What is *up* with you?"

Shoot! Evan thought. He *had* forgotten completely. It was pretty tough to remember these things when a dead owl was about to introduce you to a family of other dead critters.

"Yeah, about that…"

But before Evan could say another word, Coolio huffed and slipped back two rows to sit beside Ty and Simon. He turned his back on Evan and started to tell a story really loud. Within minutes, the whole back of the bus was doubled over in laughter.

Evan rode the rest of the trip by himself, and when it was time to catch the bus home, he was shocked when Coolio sat up near Earl and proceeded to ignore him. Gavin was preoccupied and said little. Meagan had her yearly eye exam, so her mom picked her up early. How could something as mysterious and wonderful as this be causing such grief? Well, no worries, he thought. He only had to explain everything to Coolio, and then things would be fine—better than fine. He knew it.

MJ was in town helping the with the sixtieth annual Christmas charity art auction, so the boys wandered the property to find their father.

"Dad! Where are you?" Gavin had been looking for his father for at least five minutes. For a ten-year-old, that was an eternity. His bellow finally reached his dad, who was perched on the roof. He was sitting cross-legged and peering up into the trees.

"What are you doing?" Gavin asked in a hushed tone. He was afraid if he interrupted his father's intense concentration, he might come tumbling down.

"I'm watching a bird. A song sparrow has been chattering away up here for hours."

"Birds chirp all the time out here, Dad. Why is this one so special?"

"This time of year, song sparrows don't stick around as long as this one has. He's so beautiful." As if in appreciation of the compliment, the pretty little bird opened his beak and started to sing. His trill was sweet and high. He followed that with a *tweet-tweet* that made Joe laugh.

"Can Evan and I go down to the beach with Meggie? We promise to be home before five thirty. We're just going to skim stones." Gavin had his fingers crossed behind his back. It wasn't a complete lie. He did plan on skimming a few flat ones. He was, after all, the summer champion, and he had a title to defend. Why not start practising now?

"Sure, but no later. I figured we could get some takeout tonight. With Mom tied up till late, we might as well grab some Thai. I'm torn between the fried pineapple with prawns or pad Thai. You guys can help me decide."

The kids were grateful no one else was on the beach when they got there, and they settled themselves on the same log they had sat on the day before. Less than two minutes into the wait, Gavin got restless and jumped up, scanning the stones on the shore. He eyed some flat beauties and started to skip them across the water's surface.

"Good one, Gavin!" Meagan called out.

"For the record books," laughed Evan.

"Try two at a time," said Meagan.

They were so preoccupied with the brilliant stone-skimming display that they did not notice the soft glow that lit up behind them. They were up on their feet now, encouraging Gavin to throw three rocks on the next throw.

"Hello, humans."

Meagan yelped and jumped three feet in the air. Evan ran for the water's edge, and Gavin instinctively threw the three rocks in his hands at the collection of shimmering animals.

Carolynn was perched on the huge boulder, and at its base stood a doe, a fawn, a beaver, two raccoons and a family of rabbits. A blue jay circled above their heads. It was like someone had turned on a thousand-watt light bulb. Each shimmered a slightly different shade of silver or gold. The children were dumbstruck.

"Hello," stuttered Evan.

"Children, I would like to introduce you to my friends. Please say hello to Abigail and her fawn Hubert, whom I think you know. Our resident beaver is called Rad-knows-ways. Mr. and Mrs. Biggsy are raccoons. Our rabbits are all members of the Burrow family. And last but not least, we have Madeline, our wise and beautiful blue jay."

"Hello," they all said in unison.

Gavin eyed up the group. "What, no bear? No mountain lion?" When Meagan elbowed him, he quickly said, "Sorry," and went back to examining the eclectic group.

"Um, very nice to meet you," said Meagan. "Hubert, is it? Well, Hubert, we are so happy to see you with your mother. We were very worried about you." She moved closer and bent over at the waist until she was eye level with the little fawn.

"You're pretty. Can I keep you?" Hubert fluttered his eyes at Meagan and quickly looked at his mother. Meagan laughed.

"No, darling. We do not keep humans." Abigail stepped forward in an elegant way. "I want to thank you for your efforts to help my little one. It was greatly appreciated. You eased his fear."

Evan moved a step closer.

"Yeah, about that. I know Red scared him off. He *really* is a good dog. He just has a thing for deer. I don't think he would have hurt him, but you know dogs: the chase is the thrill. You know?" Evan grew quiet again and looked a little awkward.

Gavin was distracted by one of the bunnies, who was jumping up and down on his hind legs. Gavin squinted and peered more closely at him. It couldn't be, he thought. Could it?

"Reddy Bun-Buns? Is that you?" Gavin was on his knees in front of a fluffy, red-and-white bunny.

"Hi, Gavin! Hi, Evan. Boy, is it good to have you see me again!" Reddy Bun-Buns's nose twitched, and he sat up on his back legs. "You kids are so big now. Look, look! This is my mommy, daddy, my brothers Ed, Ted, Jed, and my big sister. Her name is Ever-Ready Freddy but we call her Fred." Fred was the spitting image of Reddy Bun-Buns.

Cheers exploded from all the kids. When she was ten years old, Meagan had rescued Reddy Bun-Buns after her dog Dakota snatched him by the scruff of his neck. The bunny had only been a baby, hiding behind her wood pile, when the dog somehow got a hold of him. The boys fell in love. Despite MJ's protests, they adopted Reddy Bun-Buns, who quickly became a beloved family member. He spent most of his days grazing on dandelions under Joe's makeshift bunny cage, and at night he roamed free in Mom's office. He was clever enough to use the kitty-litter box tucked away beside the water heater, and MJ grew to love him too. Reddy used to enjoy her belly rubs in the morning. The day he disappeared, MJ was so distressed. Everyone told her that he was probably living the life of Riley, and that she shouldn't worry about him.

Clearly his end had come sooner than they'd realized.

"Reddy, what happened to you? You've been gone a year, and we missed you every single one of those days." Evan was balanced on the back of his heels, taking stock of the fine-looking family his pet bunny had come from.

Before he could answer, Reddy's mother hopped forward and flipped her large ears to one side.

"He was minding his own business, hiding under a holly bush like we taught him, and what swoops down and snatches him? A seagull! A common, everyday, filthy gull. Just you wait," she continued, "until that creature shows its face on this side of the veil. I have a yearning to give it a piece of my mind. Taking one of my babies that way—the nerve! At least the rest of us died an honourable death: one served up for Sunday dinner, one a snack for a cougar, and a couple of my boys here didn't look before they crossed the road... Well, you know what kind of mess that makes. But to watch helplessly while my boy is torn apart by some halfwit birds... I just can't tell you how much it affected me. I was hopping mad!"

But before she could say another word, Mr. Burrow moved up beside his wife. Reddy slid up to her other side and proceeded to nuzzle her around her ears and nose.

"Mom, we *talked* about this. I am perfectly okay now. Better than okay, in fact. When I see those gulls, I will thank them. Didn't I get the gift that keeps on giving? Eternity with you?" Somehow his words sounded cheeky, but they pacified Mrs. Burrow. She allowed her boys and Ever-Ready Freddy to jump up on her back and nibble her ears. Kids!

"Why has your father stopped watching Formula 1 and NHL hockey?" the raccoon suddenly asked. Mr. Biggsy had a bushy tail, and his black-rimmed eyes contrasted wildly with his white face. He resembled a bandit, or a raccoon masquerading as a bandit. "Boys, an elder just asked you a question. Shouldn't you answer me?" Biggsy was not looking mischievous so much as a little persnickety.

"Sweetheart. They are only little humans. Show some patience." Mrs. Biggsy had moved up to her husband and was trying to cajole him with her voice.

"Either they know their cable bill is paid or they don't. Why can't they speak up?"

Before the female raccoon could say another word, Evan decided to help out. "I think our bill is paid. Dad hasn't been watching too much TV these days because he is really busy. Mr. Biggsy, how do you know my dad used to watch F1 and hockey? More importantly, why do you care?"

"Care! Are you kidding, boy? I've been following the NHL since its inception. I was *in Montreal* when there were only a handful of teams. A hundred years later, there are over thirty. It is the single most important sport in the world next to auto racing." Biggsy stood back and sized up the boy from head to toe. "You mean to tell me you do not appreciate the importance of these sporting events? You don't know what Grand Prix motor racing means to raccoons like me?" When the boys only looked perplexed, he huffed, swished his tail and stomped his little feet.

"Don't mind him," said Mrs. Biggsy. "He still thinks broomball does not get the respect it deserves." She looked sweet and intelligent. She stood up on her hind legs and looked slowly into each of their eyes.

Evan gestured for attention. "If you lived in Montreal, how did you get to British Columbia?" Evan wasn't trying to challenge him. He simply wanted to understand. When the Edmunds had moved from Toronto to the island, the flight took all day. Somehow, Evan could not picture the Biggsys flying coach.

"We train-hopped," Mr. Biggsy said. "Raccoons are very resourceful. The winter of 1918 was the worst we had ever seen. Trains were crisscrossing the country, moving troops from one place to another. This was World War I, and the Allies needed reinforcements. Mrs. Biggsy and I just kept moving west until we caught a steamship that was en route to Nanaimo to pick up shipment of coal. We found ourselves finally happy in the moderate climate here, with forests and rivers abundant with life."

Mrs. Biggsy carried on as if no one had interrupted her. Lovingly, she said, "Meagan, we have been watching you grow up before our very eyes. We knew you when you used to ride Dakota like a horsey." The boys burst out laughing.

"Evan, Gavin, we have been watching you since you wore water wings down here at the beach. Evan, remember the day your training wheels flew off your bike when you tried to ride down the skate bowl on your Little Red Rocket? Oh, and darling Gavin. Do you remember running around naked, yelling, 'The Force is with you'?" She sighed sweetly. "I miss those days."

"So you've been watching us, have you?" Gavin had finally caught on and was now paying more attention to these two old raccoons.

Mr. Biggsy stopped pacing. "Of course! Every Sunday morning, I could count on seeing your father sneak out of bed, turn on the kettle for a cuppa tea and settle in for the pre-show interviews. I would sit at your window and nibble on acorns. I could rely on your dad for at least one game per week… Oh, how I miss those nights!"

Carolynn swooshed her great wings and waited until everyone had their eyes on her. "May I introduce you to Rad-knows-ways?"

The children had never seen a beaver up close. He was larger than expected. His reddish-brown fur was luxurious, and his tail was flat from top to bottom. He stood balanced on his webbed feet, and his front webbed hand dangled in front of his protruding belly. He twitched his nose and looked at them with his little black eyes. He just looked… and looked… and looked…

"Stop staring at me!" Gavin burst out. "Oops. Sorry, but you kinda freak me out."

Rad-knows-ways waddled over to the children. "It's okay. You 'freak' me out too. So what can you do? Can you build a dam? How far can you swim? How big are your teeth?

The children just gawked.

"What? What did I say?" The beaver looked at Carolynn for guidance.

"Humans are rather different from beavers," Carolynn said politely. "How about we get back to that later? Children, do you have any questions for Rad-knows-ways?"

The beaver looked at the kids expectantly but no one spoke. After a few seconds, he slapped his tail on the ground in rhythm. He apparently liked the sound it made because he started to move his body back and forth, rumba-style. Meagan joined in, and within seconds, they were dancing together. They both fell into a fit of giggles because they knew just how funny they looked.

Madeline had gone unnoticed until this time. She flew down from a tree limb and perched on Rad-knows-ways's head. "I too have been watching you since you were little. Evan and Gavin, you have grown into handsome young men. Meagan, I must say, you are lovely and composed for one so young."

Madeline had a lilt to her voice. She sounded like she was from far away, and yet her accent was very soft—just a hint of something old-world. Madeline's crown was full and tall, and her plumage was a bright blue. Her face was white and trimmed with a black line. Her jet-black eyes peered deep into theirs.

The children enjoyed looking at her as much as Madeline enjoyed looking at them. The lavender blue of her feathers stood out against the grey of the boulder and pebbled beach.

"We are delighted you can acknowledge us now. Like Carolynn, I do not know why you can see and hear us. Clearly your experience with Hubert"—she cast a look at the little fawn listening intently to all the chatter—"sparked some kind of connection between our two worlds. Whether it was the"—she struggled for the right word—"*intensity* of the emotion you felt or simply the key required to open the door that was always yours to open, we may never know. Either way, it is a gift we can now share."

Rabbits, raccoons, deer, a beaver, an owl and a blue jay: they were all grouped together in one massive glow of gold and silver, and they all yearned to be near Evan, Gavin and Meagan.

Weird, Evan thought. Very weird.

"I was totally warped over what happened to Spotty. Sorry. Hubert, I mean." Gavin shook his head and addressed the little fawn directly, "Buddy, do you mind if I just call you Spotty? This whole Hubert thing is not working for me. No offence, Abigail." He stopped talking and proceeded to kick stones at his feet.

"None taken. Hubert, may the humans address you as Spotty?"

The fawn leapt high in the air and let out a bleating noise. "I love that name! Oh, please, Mom. May all the creatures call me that? Please!"

Abigail's gentle face suddenly looked a lot like MJ's. She knit her brows and cocked her head to one side. "Hubert is a fine name. I shall make allowances for the humans, but I assure you the rest of the animal kingdom will know you as Hubert. Do you understand?" Spotty looked contrite and hoofed the stones, much like Gavin did with his sneakers.

"Madeline, did you live here before you... Before you..." Meagan struggled for the right way to phrase it. "Before you passed over?"

"Yes, I did, my dear. You see, children, I am very rare in these parts. Stellar jays are a dime a dozen. Blue jays, on the other hand, seldom venture this far north.

"So how did you end up here?" Evan asked.

"I followed a family that moved from San Francisco to a large tract of land. They were your kin, Meagan. I followed them as they travelled by wagon, and when they took up tree farming, I never moved on. In fact, I crafted my nests in the hollows of the trees on your property. I stashed my goodies away for the winter and enjoyed your great-great-great-grandmother's hospitality. She often threw cracked corn and sunflower seeds on your lawn for me to swoop down and collect. What days," she said wistfully.

"Why did you follow them?" Evan asked.

"They sang to me, and I sang to them. They laid out seed and clean straw so I could make my nests. I never thought about it when it came time to go. I simply flew after them."

"Wow. I don't think Red would follow us that far," Gavin muttered under his breath.

"Why do you sound like you are from England?" Meagan asked.

"Your peopled hailed from Southampton in the English county of Hampshire. I gather I picked up my accent from them. Southampton was a port city, and your great-great-great grandfather was a shipbuilder. He left for America at a young age. Only after he met his wife and moved to the island did he decide on a life of tree farming. You must know that at one time, your family owned most of the land from here to Deer Point."

Meagan had always heard these stories and wondered if they were true. But her fascination had distracted her from more pressing matters. "Oh dear!" she exclaimed. "Look at the time. I gotta run. I didn't even notice the sun going down." Meagan started to move toward the steep stairs. Evan and Gavin registered, too, that it was past the time they were supposed to be home.

"Great meeting you all. Sorry we have to go in such a hurry. When will we see you again?" Evan yelled as he ascended the stairs.

"Don't worry. We will always be close by. Just call for us, and we will find you." Carolynn peered up at them and waved her left wing. She let out a loud hoot and then flew off.

The children were curious to see where the other animals would go, but they were already pushing their luck, so they jogged up the hill.

"With your parents at the Cedar art auction and my mom not getting home until dinnertime tomorrow, we can talk about all this tomorrow. Let's just keep our cool till then, okay?" Meagan was already running up her driveway. She threw them one last wave before she was lost behind the line of bushes.

"Come on. Let's get home before Dad realizes he's starving and comes looking for us." Evan said, pulling Gavin by the sleeve.

"Wait up." Gavin refused to move. "I have a question."

"Not now, Gav. I'm serious—we've got to boogie."

"I just want to know one thing. If the three of us can see the animals, why can't Dad?"

Evan stopped pulling and looked at him.

"I mean, think about it. Why are we the only ones who can see them? Dad was on the beach with us. He saw what we saw. He felt just as torn up about it as we did. Evan, what if Dad doesn't *know* he can see dead, talking, glowing animals?"

This possibility had not occurred to Evan. Maybe their father simply hadn't noticed what was in front of his eyes the whole time. Or maybe he thought fireflies were abundant this year… and out of season. Because if his dad were seeing what they did, the whole world would know by now. Discretion was not one of his virtues.

"You might have a point, Gav."

"So what do you suggest?"

"I think we arrange for Carolynn and the clan to visit us on the weekend when Dad is washing down his dirt bike. He's going to ride the pits this weekend, and for sure he and the bike will come home covered in mud. If he jumps ten feet in the air and runs for his pellet gun, then we'll know he can see them. If he carries on washing the bike, then we'll know he is clueless."

"Evan, we already know he's clueless. We want to know if he can see the Shimmies!"

Just as they started down the driveway, they heard the truck start up. Evan's suspicion was accurate. Hungry and out of patience, dad was coming to find them. They ran the rest of the way and hopped up into the cab.

"Going somewhere?" Evan asked with grin on his face. "I'm starving. I'm leaning toward Chicken Pad Thai tonight. Spicy! And with prawns. Spring rolls to start, followed by wontons…" Evan didn't stop talking until the first appetizer was put in front of him—and then he didn't utter another word.

5

PIGS REALLY CAN FLY

EVERY THURSDAY MORNING, the track and field team trained before school. Gavin and Evan competed in cross-country and relay racing. On these mornings, when they needed to be at school by seven, they got rides from either MJ or Isobel, Coolio's mom. Today it was Isobel's turn.

Coolio was still steaming. He nodded at Gavin but wouldn't even acknowledge Evan. During the brief drive to Cedar Intermediate, Evan noticed Isobel looking at him through her rearview mirror and then glancing at Coolio. She tried to make light conversation, but no one was responding. The car had hardly come to a stop when all the boys spilled out and ran for the gym door.

Isobel leaned forward in her seat to get a better view. No cajoling, no shoving, no hollering at the top of their lungs. "Huh, that's weird," she muttered under her breadth.

After school, when they got to Meagan's house, the boys beelined it to her fridge and cupboard.

"You gotta have something we can eat," Gavin said desperately. He went from cupboard to cupboard, pushing boxes aside, looking for something ready-made and tasty.

"I told you. We're only eating organic and non-packaged foods these days." She pulled apples and carrots from the fridge and started to slice the apples into wedges. She added a small bowl of caramel dip to the plate. Then she arranged some carrots and low-fat ranch dressing on a separate plate.

"You're killing me! Even Reddy Bun-Buns would need more substance by this time of day, and he is a blinking rabbit!" Evan joined Gavin in the search. Each thing he pulled out said "low sodium" or "Nature's Best." Where were the artificially enhanced, overpriced snacks? Surely Claire, Meagan's mom, hadn't completely abandoned her dependency on salty and sweet nibblies. She used to love salt and vinegar chips, Cheetos, pretzels. That wasn't something you could just turn off!

"Bingo!" Gavin bellowed. Clutched in his hands was a bag of baked potato crisps. He bit into one of them. "Hardly fresh, but they'll do. Hand me the caramel sauce."

"You're joking." Meagan watched in horror as the boys dipped their chips into the caramel sauce and *then* the ranch dressing. "Why don't you have some chips with your dip?" she said sarcastically. They only looked at her with pity, like she was missing out on a fine feast. Dakota barked once and sat at their side. Food was food. The drool pooled beneath her.

"Okay, look. As usual, we have precious few hours to talk in private. Let's think rationally and determine what we are going to do next. Right now, it appears we are the only humans in this hemisphere who can see, hear and talk to dead animals." Meagan very dramatically lifted her right hand and made a fist. She put up her index finger. "So *A*: Do we tell anyone about this?" She put up her middle finger. "*B*: Do we keep it a secret for the rest of our lives so people don't think we're nuts?" Then she stood up in one fluid movement, spun in a circle and waved her entire hand at them. "Or *C*: Do we forget this ever happened, pretend we can't see them, and carry on like we did before Sunday?"

"I opt for *A*. I say we tell Coolio." Evan tried an apple slice and was amazed at how good it tasted.

Gavin leaned back in his chair. "I say *B*. I remember what it felt like during my imaginary friend days. You guys were brutal to me.

I'm not telling anyone. I have a reputation to protect. You two are off to high school next year, while I have to suffer through two more years of middle school. If you think you're going to abandon me after telling the world about our unique gift," Gavin said scornfully, "you're crazier than I thought." Gavin stabbed a carrot into the ranch dip and flung it into his mouth. He didn't even chew it.

Evan grinned. He hadn't thought about Mr. Dee-Dee in years. Gavin used to go on and on about his imaginary friend all the time. Gavin was about three years old, and he'd been heavily into Power Rangers. Mr. Dee-Dee was an ordinary man who morphed into a Spandex superhero. Gavin had declared Mr. Dee-Dee was the sixth Power Ranger, capable of materializing at any time to save the bungling Mighty Morphins. Evan, Meagan and Coolio thought Gavin's wild imagination was priceless, and they went out of their way to torture him about it. Until one day, Joe Edmund lost it. He said that if anyone bothered Gavin about his friend again, Evan would no longer get to play with his miniature *Star Wars* figures or light sabers. His collection of *Star Wars* movies would be permanently put away. That did it. No one messed with Evan's *Star Wars* toys. He made sure that Coolio and Meagan zipped it when Gavin ran around the house claiming to be Mr. Dee-Dee's assistant. No amount of Megazord morphing or monster fighting could get Evan going. Eventually, Gavin shifted his loyalties exclusively to Luke Skywalker. He would run around the house, pretending to fly an X-wing fighter jet and yelling, "The force is with me! The force is with me! I will destroy the Death Star."

Maybe Gavin was right. Keeping quiet might be the wiser choice.

"Gavin suggested an interesting theory last night."

"Really?" Meagan said in mock disbelief.

"Hey, I've been known to come up with some good ideas once in a while." Gavin tried not to look offended. "What if my dad can see them too?"

Meagan handed each of them a glass of celery-beet-apple juice. "Wouldn't he have said something by now?"

"What, no Coke?" Gavin sniffed his glass and put it back down again, deciding he wasn't that thirsty. "What if he doesn't *know* he can see them? Think about it. He's probably knee-deep into his stuff, oblivious to everything around him. And the animals only knew we could see them when we acknowledged them. It's worth an experiment to find out."

"What are you cooking up?" Meagan took the full glasses away from the boys and dug two iced teas out of the back of the fridge. "Here, before your cheeks cave in."

"Thanks!" the boys said in unison. They knocked back half of the contents before she was settled into her chair again.

"We're going to invite the animals to our house on Saturday afternoon," said Evan. "We both have soccer in the morning, but after that we have no plans."

"Yes you do," Meagan said, nibbling on a carrot.

"No, I don't," Evan tossed back.

"Am I your secretary now, too? Evan, you have plans with Coolio Saturday afternoon. You said you would go to the skate park with him."

Awareness lit his face. "Oh, jumpin'! I forgot about that. Could you imagine if I missed another thing with him this week? He's already mad at me."

"Too right." Gavin was back in the cupboard, hoping to get lucky again. "Me want cookies! Cookies! Cookies!" he said in his best Cookie Monster impression.

"Okay, if not Saturday, then Sunday," Evan persisted. "The point is we will get Carolynn and her friends to come visit us at the house. We will make sure Dad is outside with us when they show up. Voilà! He sees them or not. Either way, we will know if we are the only ones who are plugged into Shimmies."

"That's a good plan, I guess." Meagan seemed distracted. She absently scratched Dakota's ears and fed him a slice of apple. Dakota rolled it around her mouth for a while and then unceremoniously dropped it on the floor and walked away.

"See! Even the dog can't eat your organic food. You'd better get some chemical cakes in you soon, Meg, or you are going to be severely unhealthy."

Meagan wiped the floor clean and disposed of the mess in the compost bin. "Look, I know we tripped onto something quite extraordinary. I love talking to Carolynn and her friends. Seeing Reddy Bun-Buns again is amazing, and seeing Spotty with his mom is such a relief." Her voice dropped to almost a whisper. "But I gotta tell you, I am a bit overwhelmed with what this all means." She sat back down and faced the boys. "What if we can see more than just the animals that passed away? What if we can see…" She cast her eyes down and fiddled with the zipper on her hoodie. "What if we can see people too?"

This had never occurred to Evan or Gavin. They exchanged looks and then started to fiddle with their own zippers. Meagan was suggesting something that got their stomachs turning. Sure, they believed in ghosts. They were Irish, after all. But the thought that they might bump into a human spirit late one night had them breaking into a cold sweat.

But Meagan didn't look afraid. She looked wistful. With a sudden jolt, Evan understood why. When Meagan was only four years old, her father died. He'd been helping a friend install a new chimney cap. The weather had been foul, but there was no end in sight for the miserable forecast, and the job had to be done. Her father had only just climbed onto the steep roof when a gust of wind came up out of nowhere. He grabbed the ladder so his friend, who was halfway up, wouldn't fall. They agreed it was too dangerous for roof work. Her dad waited until his friend got safely to the bottom and could hold the ladder for him. He was just about to start his descent when a large branch broke off a nearby tree and swung down on him. He was swept off the roof and landed on his back. He died later that day, in hospital.

Evan knew he should say something, but then Claire pulled up in front of the house. Dakota ran off to greet her. The kids went out to give her a hand with the groceries.

Gavin hooted when he saw cheese smokies. Claire was relieved that he had not taken a good look at the label. Emmy Lei's Tofu-Cheese Smokies… just like the ones Mother never made!

An hour later, dinner was finished.

"Gavin, can you handle one more?" Claire looked up from loading the dishwasher just in time to see Gavin open his mouth and release a deafening burp. The kids burst out laughing.

"Sorry about that, Claire. Um, I think the tank is full. Thanks for dinner. The dogs were really good."

Claire chuckled and went back to sorting the dishwasher. She couldn't get the boys to try her spinach salad but knew they would try her honey-almond bean curd squares. And if they didn't ask about the ingredients, she wouldn't tell them.

For the rest of the evening, the kids did their homework. Since MJ and Joe were not expected back until after midnight, the boys were sleeping over. Claire got the guest room ready, and by nine thirty, the lights were out. The boys fell into bed, exhausted.

"Do you think Meggie could be right? About the dead people, I mean?" Even though it was dark, Evan could tell that Gavin was chewing his thumb.

"Maybe, but we can't worry about that right now. I've decided that I *am* going to tell Coolio, so I gotta figure out how and when. Man, he is going to think I am off my rocker! But there has to be a way to make him believe me. You'll help, right?"

"I guess," Gavin whined.

"Don't worry, he'll buy it eventually. This one might just take a while."

With that, the boys stopped talking, and within minutes, there were no sounds but gentle snores.

———

They woke Saturday morning to brilliant sunshine. The island was so unpredictable when it came to weather. One day you almost needed a rowboat to get around, and the next you were stripping down to shorts and a T-shirt. All the way to the soccer game, MJ kept saying it would be a nice change not to feel miserably cold while they cheered by the sidelines. She left her forty-below boots and wool-lined raincoat at home, and was looking bright and cheerful in her fuchsia yoga gear with a beanie cap to match.

Joe teased her about the outfit. "Since you have the wardrobe, why not actually *take up* yoga? It's not right for all that stretchy material to go to waste!"

The boys left their parents to yak it up while they ran to join a bunch of their friends for a warm-up before the game. The sunshine had put everyone in a good mood, and when the game started, Evan joined his mom and dad on the sidelines to cheer his brother's team. They were up by one within the first ten minutes. Gavin had made a nice pass to his pal Cameron, and Cam sent it soaring over the goalie's head. But the opposing team was not discouraged and took control of the rest of the first half. Thankfully their goalie managed to save the ball rather spectacularly many times. When the whistle blew to indicate halftime he fell to the ground, exhausted.

During the break, the boys sucked on orange slices and listened intently to their coach as he worked out strategies with them. While the parents chatted with each other, Evan sauntered over to the concession stand.

Standing behind the counter was Davey Golding. Davey was eighty-nine years old, and he ran the concession stand. He was also blind.

A living legend and much loved by the people of Cedar, Davey was as strong as an ox and as cunning as a fox. Evan couldn't think of a time when he didn't see him at a soccer game, community event, school concert, or bobbing in his boat front and centre during a dragon boat race. Even though he couldn't see, Davey recognized everyone's voice and called you by your name. He also had two cute teenage girls working with him—and a knack for always making Evan blush around them.

"Mr. Edmund, what can I do for you today?" Davey's voice was low and gruff.

"How did you know it was me? I didn't say anything." Evan eyed him suspiciously.

"My boy, I would recognize that cologne anywhere."

Evan gasped. He always spritzed himself with a little Hugo Boss cologne in the morning. He didn't think anyone could really smell it. He heard the girls giggle and immediately his cheeks grew warm.

"Will it be the usual, my fair man?"

"Yes, please," Evan grumbled. He was determined to trip up Davey next week. He wouldn't wear any cologne.

Evan and Davey stood chatting for the remainder of the halftime break. It always amazed Evan how much the old man seemed to know. But Davey had a network that spread from one tip of the island to the other. Evan promised to pass on Davey's good wishes to his parents and ran off to see the rest of the game.

Gavin's team won two-nothing. This was cause for celebration since they had never beaten that team before.

Evan skipped out on the hootin' and hollerin' and made his way to field number four to warm up for his own game. His boys were in fine form. They talked big and played fast. Evan had little time to think about anything except how he was going to play his midfield position. His lungs were burning from all the sprinting, and he was a little relieved when the line was changed up. He spied his parents and Gavin on the opposite side. He was surprised as well to see Davey and one of the pretty teenage girls standing with them. Sitting quietly at Davey's feet was his guide dog, Taffy.

Davey was nodding his head in full agreement with something Joe had said, and cutie pie Tracy Wilson was grinning at something Gavin had said. Focus, Evan reminded himself. Now was not the time to wonder why Tracy was interested in watching his game. It was a highly competitive sport, and few errors were tolerated. But their goalie defended their net beautifully, and after many dives and leaps into the air, the team walked away with a one-nothing win. Evan sauntered slowly over to the mingling crowd at the end of the field and shyly took a position beside Gavin and Tracy.

"Congrats on the win, Evan." At fifteen, Tracy was taller than the boys by a clear foot. With long dark hair, amber eyes and freckles across her nose, Evan figured she was one of the prettiest girls in Cedar. But before he could respond, Gavin punched him in the arm and shoved his grinning face into Evan's.

"Ha! Did you hear? Pigs really *can* fly!" Gavin had an insanely goofy look on his face and was doing his happy dance.

"Cut that out! What's wrong with you?" Evan hissed at Gavin

under his breath, all the while looking at Tracy. By now MJ, Joe and Davey had stopped talking and had moved closer to the kids.

Joe looked down at Evan. "What did your mom say last year when you asked her if we could get a boat?"

Evan had to think about it for a moment, but then his head snapped up. "When pigs fly! Mom said, 'When pigs fly'!" Between Gavin's Christmas-has-come-early look and his mom's sheepish smile, realization dawned on him.

"We're getting a boat?" Evan's head whipped back and forth between his parents.

"Correction: we *have* a boat." Joe was clearly enjoying his boy's shock.

"No way. How cool! How? When? Why didn't we know about this? Mom, when did you cave?" He couldn't help himself. He joined Gavin in the happy dance.

"Last week, Tracy's parents mentioned to Dad that they were going to sell their motor boat and invest in something bigger. So naturally your father conned me into dropping by the marina to see it. One thing led to another, and before you knew it, we bought it. If the weather holds out, tomorrow Mr. Wilson will take us out to show us what that baby can do." Mom shocked them with a pathetic attempt to do the moonwalk before settling for her own happy dance.

"You're gonna love it," Tracy said. "It's fully loaded, and the arch is awesome for water skiing and tubing. Can I come with you tomorrow?" Tracy was looking at MJ, but it was the boys who yelled, "Yes!" in unison. Everyone was talking at once as they walked off the field to their cars.

⸺

When Evan and Coolio had made their plans for Saturday afternoon, they had been on talking terms. But since Wednesday, hardly a word had passed between them. As soon as he got home from soccer, Evan inhaled a hot dog and then rode his bike to Coolio's in the hope they could ride to the skate park together. He wanted to forget the awkwardness between them and get back to the way it used to be. He was surprised to find no one home. He swung back by the house to see if Gavin wanted to come, but his brother was heading to Cameron's house.

When Evan got to the park, the first thing he noticed was how busy it was. The fine weather had brought out all the boarders, and it looked like the Indy 500. It took less than a minute to locate Coolio, resting atop a flight of stairs overlooking the drain. He was sitting with Trent and Simon. The boys cheered when they saw Evan, but Coolio only tilted his water bottle at him.

"Ask me how stellar my morning has been." Before they could say anything, Evan said, "We won, and my parents bought Tracy Wilson's boat!" That got the reaction Evan wanted. It was unclear which event impressed the boys more, but the mention of Tracy's name piqued the most interest.

"I thought your mom was dead set against it." Coolio dropped the cold-shoulder routine and slid over to make room for Evan on the stair.

"She was. I'm not sure what happened, but somehow Dad convinced her that the boat was safe, easy to handle and a cinch to store in the winter." Evan pulled some Hot Rods out of his pocket and handed them out. He was determined not to lose momentum with Coolio. "So did you grind the rail?"

After a few awkward moments of stilted speech, the boys were showing off for each other, and soon the laughter was flowing. Talk turned to hockey, video games and Guinness world records.

Evan decided that this was the night to tell Coolio everything. Without thinking, he blurted, "Wanna sleep over?" He stared at his sneakers and waited to see if he was out of the doghouse.

"Sure. Why not? I gotta ask my parents, but I think they'll be okay with that. Let me buzz home and grab some stuff. Let's split before Simon does his replay of his header in the bowl last week."

The boys rode their bikes home, and when it was time to go their separate ways, Coolio yelled, "Meet you in an hour!"

Evan smiled while he pedalled slowly up the driveway. He had to hand it to Coolio. His friend didn't hold a grudge for long.

Evan found his mom in the kitchen. "You okay I invited Coolio to sleep over tonight?" Evan grabbed a handful of pistachios and started to munch.

"Wouldn't want a Saturday to go by without him." MJ had shelled her nuts and was crushing them with a mallet.

"What're you making for dinner?" Evan tried to scoop a nut, but his mother waved him off.

"Pistachio-crusted mahi-mahi fish with basmati rice, sautéed vegetables and flatbread." Before you complain that it sounds too healthy, dessert is a triple-layer chocolate cake topped with fresh whipped cream and strawberries."

Evan decided he could suffer through dinner to get to dessert. Just as he finished setting the table, Gavin walked in and dropped in his chair at the dinner table.

"I'm beat. Cameron and I ended up riding to Jake's, and then we played BMX tag. Cam tagged me fifteen minutes into the game, and after that I couldn't catch anyone, no matter how hard I pedalled. I may have size, but those runts have speed!"

Evan and Gavin compared their day and when Joe and Coolio walked into the kitchen, it turned into a rowdy session of boys competing for talk time. MJ and Joe kept up as best as they could but were relieved when the boys settled down to dinner. For almost twenty minutes, it was peacefully quiet.

The rest of the night was spent listening to music. While Coolio was getting ready in the bathroom, Evan whispered to Gavin, "Tomorrow we tell Coolio everything."

Gavin only shook his head. "I still think you're wrong, but it's your call. What I wanna know is how we're going to get Carolynn and the other Shimmies to come when Dad gets home from riding."

Evan scratched his head and looked out into the dark night. "I dunno. I guess we just call them and see if they'll come." Evan walked back to the bed and flopped himself down. "We have a busy day tomorrow. We have to somehow convince Coolio we can see dead animals, we have to get Dad to see them, and we have to help our parents launch our boat without sinking it. I tell ya, Gav, I'm going to need a day off school to recover from tomorrow."

Gavin rolled his eyes and reached for the remote. "Do you think Mom will hear if I turn the TV back on?"

"Yes, she will," yelled MJ from the living room.

"How does she do that?!" Gavin returned the remote control to the shelf and went to say good night to his parents.

When the boys woke up, their father was already gone for his Sunday morning dirt-bike ride. The sun was shining, but the wind was starting to pick up.

"Boys, I'm not sure about our little trip out on the boat today," said MJ. "The skies may look clear, but the wind will make launching the boat difficult, and with four-foot swells, we likely won't get very far from shore." Evan and Gavin thought it was incredibly cool to hear their mom talk like that. Sure, her news stank, but the fact that she was even talking about a boat was unreal.

"But Mom," Evan protested, "Mr. Wilson and Tracy will be waiting for us. We shouldn't let a few waves scare us off. Please, Mom? *Please?*"

"Let's see what your father says when he gets home."

It was approaching eleven o'clock when the boys wandered out of the house to throw the stick for Red. Evan had been rehearsing in his head how to tell Coolio about the Shimmies. Even in his mind, every angle he came up with sounded nuts. How could he tell his best friend that he could suddenly see and hear dead animals? How could he look him straight in the face and say, "Did you know raccoons have a knack for remembering NHL stats and that my new friend Mr. Biggsy can tell you who won every Grand Prix since 1901?" Oh boy, this was *not* going to be easy, thought Evan.

Just as he was building up the courage to say something, Meagan appeared at the top of the drive, and Red ran off enthusiastically to greet her.

"Howdy!" Meagan was wearing her dirt-bike boots and riding pants, and her jacket was covered in mud.

"You were out riding already?" Gavin noticed she had dirt smudged on her forehead too.

"My uncle and I took the quads up to the pits. We were the first ones there, so we really got to tear it up. Later, though, it got insanely busy, so we got out of there." Meagan picked up the stick and threw it into the bush for Red to fish out. "Besides, I wanted to be here when your dad got home." She winked at Evan and Gavin.

"Just in time. I decided to tell Coolio about Carolynn and the others."

"Oh, this should be interesting." Meagan slipped off her jacket and jumped up on the tail of Joe's pickup.

"What were you going to tell me?" Coolio noticed the odd looks between his friends, and he was not particularly comfortable with feeling left out.

"Okay, Coolio. You know how you got mad because you thought I was ditching you to hang with Meggie? And because I was acting really weird this week and forgetting everything?" A line of perspiration had appeared on Evan's upper lip.

"Yeah," Coolio said suspiciously.

"Well, there's a really good reason for it. I have wanted to tell you the whole week, but there was never a good time. It's going to sound really weird. You're gonna think we've all gone crazy." Evan noticed both Gavin and Meagan had their arms crossed against their chests and were looking at him intently. "Something really bizarre happened down at the beach."

"Yeah, I know," Coolio interrupted. "You all saw a deer drown."

"No. I mean yeah, but that's not all." Evan wiped his face with the back of his sleeve. "The next day we went back to the beach to see if we could find the body. Gavin and I saw a fawn that looked just like the one at the beach, so we hoped maybe it didn't die. We went down to look for him."

"Him?" Coolio was starting to look puzzled.

"Spotty is a boy fawn," Gavin volunteered.

Before Coolio could say anything, Evan rushed on. "We searched everywhere, but couldn't find anything, so we sat up on the climbing boulder. We were up there, just talking, when a freaky thing happened." Evan was pacing back and forth, and his hands were outstretched like wings. "Carolynn flew in and scared the heck out of us! She started talking, and then we screamed and ran in every direction. She flew down and blocked us from going up the stairs. She told us to calm down and just listen." Evan was now walking in circles and talking to himself. "She said she had been watching us, and so had the others, and that we were special 'cause no other humans can see them—"

"Hold up, Evan." Coolio stepped in front of him to stop his pacing. "Who is Carolynn, and how can she fly?"

"Carolynn is an owl. A really big owl," Meagan said.

Coolio looked at Meagan, then at Evan and Gavin. Then he burst out laughing. "How long did it take to make this one up? You really need to work on your stories, Evan. All these years hangin' with me, I'd think you would have learned something by now. The trick is to keep them believable. No flying or talking owls. Too funny!"

"And dead," Gavin muttered.

"Hilarious! No, seriously. You had me with the sweating and freaking out, but honestly, you gotta tone it down a bit. The Russian judge gives you a nine for delivery but only six for content." Coolio picked up the stick that Red had dropped at Meagan's feet and tossed it back into the bush.

"Coolio, we are not telling a story. This really happened. There are dead animals that live"—Evan waved his hands around to indicate "everywhere"—"and most people can't see them. Somehow the three of us can. It started with Spotty, the fawn that drowned. His mom Abigail was already dead and waiting for him. Then we saw Reddy Bun-Buns and his family. We met Rad-knows-ways the beaver, and Madeline—oh, she is so pretty—but the Biggsys know the most about humans. They're raccoons, and…"

Evan stopped talking. Coolio had backed up a bit and was looking at Evan with an odd expression.

"Ev, Ev, slow down. We're cool now. No need to take a trip to the funny farm just for my benefit. How about Meggie goes and grabs her airsoft gun, and we have a game before I leave for hockey?

You need to work off some of that nervous energy, and there's nothing like swinging from the treetops to do that."

At that moment, the sound of a two-stroke motor could be heard coming down the street. Evan realized that his dad was going to be home any second, and that Coolio was no closer to believing them.

"Gavin, Meggie, start calling for Carolynn and the others!" Evan ran out to the clearing and looked up into the sky.

"Carolynn, we need you!" Evan yelled.

"Rad-knows-ways, Mrs. Burrow? Please, we need you to come!" Meagan had jumped up onto the truck bed and was searching the ground all around her.

"Spotty, Abigail, we need you *now*! Where are you?" Gavin ran behind the carport and into the forest.

Coolio stood back and watched his friends in shock. He didn't think this was funny anymore. His friends' odd behaviour was starting to freak him out.

Joe turned onto the long laneway that led to his house. As he pulled up, he noticed the kids were all waiting for him, and that Red was running from kid to kid. Something was wrong. Evan and Meagan were frantically looking for something, and Coolio was watching them with apprehension on his face. Joe turned off the bike and hopped off.

Evan watched his dad dismount the dirty bike. Oh, where are they? he thought desperately. Then Gavin appeared from behind the carport.

"They came! They came!" Gavin ran over to where Evan and Meagan were standing. Looking past Gavin, the kids saw Spotty and Abigail emerge from the bushes. Not far behind them were the Biggsys, Rad-knows-ways and, hopping on and off his tail, the Burrow bunnies. Carolynn and Madeline swooped gracefully out of the sky and landed on the nearest tree.

"Thank goodness you're here." There was relief on Meagan's face.

"Dad, do you see anything? Anything glittery and shiny and really *odd*?" Gavin circled his father, pointing in every direction.

Meagan and Evan had calmed down and watched in awe as the animals joined Gavin in circling Joe. The swirl of gold and silver was mesmerizing.

Joe and Coolio looked at the three children and then at each other.

"Coolio, do you have any idea what this is about?" Joe asked.

"Nope. You got me. Um, if you guys are done with the theatrics, can we go play airsoft?"

Just then Evan noticed a movement out of the corner of his eye. He squinted against the sun in his eyes. Slowly moving out from the bush was a large dog. As it got closer, Evan realized who it was.

"Holy cow. Razor? Razor!" Evan ran to the big, lumbering, glowing dog. Right behind him were Gavin and Meagan.

"Hi, kids." Razor, an Irish wolfhound, stood smiling at them with a toothy grin. "I guess you didn't expect to see me, huh?" His tail was wagging, and he danced on the spot.

"Razor, you're back! We missed you so much." Meagan was down on her knees, laughing at the sorely missed dog.

Razor looked past the kids and saw his owner, Coolio. He barked insanely and raced to where Coolio stood frozen, looking at his friends. Razor approached Coolio at top speed, jumped up with both front paws and literally passed through their pale friend. Coolio never moved or showed any indication that his beloved— dead—125-pound dog had just passed through his body.

"I don't know what you think you're playing at, but you are all sick. What kind of sickos say they can see my dog, who's been dead for three years? I'm out of here." Coolio grabbed his knapsack and jumped on his bike. Before Evan could say a word, he was pedalling hard up the drive.

"Evan, Gavin—inside right now!" Joe had a thunderous look on his face, and it was clear he didn't want backtalk. "Meagan, I suggest you go home."

"I told you telling him was a bad idea." Gavin shouldered Evan as he passed.

"Why couldn't we have just kept our big mouths shut?" Meagan collected her jacket from the back of the pickup.

Carolynn and the others had gathered to one side and stood listening very quietly. As Evan walked past them with his head hung low, Madeline flew very close to his ear and whispered, "I am sorry, my little one. Clearly no one else can see us. Please do not be distressed. What harm has been caused can be undone."

"I doubt it," Evan muttered.

They followed their father into the house for what they knew would be a severe talking-to.

"Evan, let me do the talking now, okay? I think you got us into enough trouble for one day."

"I'm never going to open my mouth again." And with that, Evan sat down at the dining room table and put his head on his arms.

Joe had collected MJ and told her what he'd witnessed. They both stood rock still and waited for the boys to talk.

"I know what you saw looked crazy, and I know what you heard sounded nuts, but the best I can tell you is that it was a joke that went bad. Real bad." Gavin looked down at the tablecloth and traced a pattern in the fabric.

"Joke? That was no joke! You know how much Coolio loved his dog. You know how many years it has taken him to get over the loss of that wolfhound. What were you thinking?"

"Never mind what they were thinking. You two had better hop on your bikes and get your bottoms down there right now to apologize." MJ's cheeks had gone flaming red, and she was eyeing the phone with consternation.

"Mom, let us handle it, okay? I know we screwed up, but we need to go see Coolio. Please don't call Isobel and James. Please," Evan said in remorse.

"Fine. But you had better make this right, Evan. And no more playing with people's emotions."

Just as they left the property, the Shimmies appeared from all sides of the road and sky.

"Oh, no you don't. You're not going to tag along. I never asked to have this... this..." Evan grimaced. "This 'gift.' You can just go back to wherever you hang out when we can't see you." He rounded on them and screamed, "I never want to see you again!" He turned to Gavin. "I have exactly two minutes to figure out what to say to Coolio."

They looked around and found themselves alone.

As they approached Meagan's property, they were surprised to see her sitting on the ground beside a patch of wildflowers. Her eyes were red and swollen.

"What are you doin'?" Gavin asked.

"I didn't want to tell my mom why I was crying, so I'm waiting here for the waterworks to stop. Are you going to see Coolio?" When the boys nodded, she said, "Can I come too? He must think we are all such jerks. If only he could have seen Razor. What a surprise. He didn't even look sick anymore. He looked just like he did before he got the cancer." Meagan was up on her feet now and brushing off the dirt.

When they got to Coolio's house, they noticed that he had dropped his bike and backpack at the foot of the stairs leading up to his porch. He was nowhere in sight, so they rang the doorbell. James opened the door, and by the look on his face, he knew what had happened.

Evan spoke up immediately. "James, can we please speak to Coolio? It's really important that we talk to him."

James stepped outside and shut the door. "Look, kids, I can see by the looks on your faces that you feel bad about upsetting Lukas. But honestly, this is not a good time for you to explain anything to him. How about you go home? I'm sure tomorrow Lukas will be prepared to listen to what you have to say. Okay?" With that, he went inside and firmly closed the door.

6

THE FRAGILE CONNECTION

COOLIO WENT OUT of *his* way to stay out of Evan, Gavin and Meagan's way. He avoided them at every turn. On the bus, in the schoolyard and at track and field practice, he stayed clear. He could not be lured into conversation. He refused to take calls or return texts. By the third day, the other schoolkids started to clue in to what was going on. They targeted Meagan to give up the scoop, but she refused to discuss it. Rumours swirled around them, but even Coolio wouldn't share what had happened. It was more than awkward—it was bizarre and unsettling to their group of friends. The schoolyard became a silent battleground. The students split their time between one end of the school, where Coolio hung out, and the other end where Evan, Gavin and Meagan quietly gathered. To make matters worse, the Shimmies seemed to have taken Evan's request to heart. Not once had they shown up to greet them. This upset the children more than they cared to admit.

By Friday afternoon, Evan and Gavin were exhausted from keeping their guard up. The bus couldn't arrive home fast enough. As they stumbled up the lane, they were greeted by the sight of their parents loading the pickup with a camp cooler, suitcases and their bikes.

Evan reached them first and peeked into the cab to see what else they had packed. "Where are we going?"

"Tofino, my novice surfers." Joe beamed at his boys.

"All right!" Gavin jumped up and down and high-fived Evan.

"When did you decide this?" Evan wrapped his arm through his mother's and rested his head on her shoulder.

"When we realized you were both having a really lousy week and could use the break. Go grab whatever we forgot to pack. You've got exactly ten minutes."

As they headed out of Nanaimo and the highway started to hug the coastline, MJ went through her usual to-do list for a trip to the breathtaking Pacific coast town.

"Hiking, followed by a dip in the hot springs, a little bike ride to the beach, and then a scrumptious meal at my favorite restaurant. What do you think, boys? Do you think you can keep up with your old mom? Rain or shine, we are going to soak it all in… literally. Ha!"

It was almost seven o'clock by the time they reached Tofino. It had rained steadily, and at the highest peak of Mount Joan, it was snowing. Joe was relieved to pull into the hotel and call it a night. Despite the rain that fell off and on, the Edmunds enjoyed the breathtaking scenery and the warm welcome the locals extended. Unlike in summer, when the town swelled to ten times its size, the winter months were all about toughing out the weather and then getting cozy with a book beside a fire.

Saturday's hike was in the rain, and after a delicious meal at their favourite restaurant, they settled in for a night of Star Wars Monopoly. Sunday morning they all suited up and made their way to Chesterman Beach to tackle the waves with their longboards. MJ managed to catch a few waves, that got her rowdy applause from her men. The sun made a brief appearance, but the wind howled. Even in their hood-to-boots neoprene wetsuits, by midday they were exhausted and cold. They packed it in and made their way back to the hotel to enjoy hot showers and a quick meal to tide them over on the drive home. It was only when they pulled into the driveway that Evan allowed himself to feel the anxiety he had held at bay since Friday.

Meagan had saved two seats on the bus for the boys and hardly waited for them to sit down before she barraged them with a million questions about their weekend. Unlike their action-packed getaway, Meagan had to settle for a movie and a sleepover at her auntie's.

"Did you see a whale?"

"No."

"Did you see a black bear?"

"No."

"Did you see a bald eagle?"

"Yes!" Evan and Gavin said in unison. The boys' eyes popped, and together they said, "Jinx! Black magic! Under a roof-coke!" This was one of their odd rituals—no one remembered how it started or why, but everyone honoured it. Not doing so came with strict consequences.

"Good," said Meagan. "Now you can't talk to each other; you can only talk to me. So what are we going to do about the Shimmies? I miss them, and I know you do too, so don't tell me otherwise." Meagan tossed her long hair over her shoulder.

Suddenly her head snapped back, and she let out a scream.

"*Ouch!* What the…" Meagan spun around to see who had grabbed her hair. Ruth Cissy Blackhorne had quietly moved up and was sitting in the row behind them.

"Next time, don't flick your hair in my face!" Ruth had a sneer plastered on her mug as she pulled Meagan's snapped-off hair from her fingers.

"That's it! You're gonna get it now, Blackhorne. I'm gonna tell Earl and Mr. Lanzilotta." The bus had pulled into the roundabout and had come to a stop. Meagan ran to the front of the bus and gestured wildly to Earl.

Evan leaned over the bench and got as close to Ruth's face as he dared. "You know, Ruth, one of these days you're going to get yours, and I just hope I'm there to see it."

Before Ruth could retaliate, Gavin closed in on her. "You ever try that again, and I guarantee there won't be a hair left on your head. Another misconduct for me, and I will only lose recess privileges. Another misconduct for you, and you're out of here."

Evan looked at his brother and grinned. "Good point, bro. Maybe we should see how far we can push her before she snaps." He turned to Ruth. "You seem to have only two comebacks for everything: you hit, or you yell nasty words. Either one will get you kicked out." Evan looked at her pack of Neanderthals. "Goons, you'd better keep her on a short leash or else your ringleader will be taking *a long* break from school."

With that, Evan and Gavin got off the bus. Kids of all ages offered their praise at how they'd handled the bully. Everyone but Coolio. He slipped past them and was through the side door to the school before Meagan had pushed her way through the crowd.

"Meet me after school at the beach. I have a plan." With that, Meagan ran off to locate Mr. Lanzilotta. She was still steaming about the stunt Ruth pulled, and she hoped to catch him before he had his second cup of coffee and would be calmly ready to face the day. She *wanted* him cranky and short tempered in the hopes he would rain down punishment on Ruth Cissy Blackthorne.

With the Christmas concert less than three weeks away, Mrs. Rosaline ordered extra music rehearsals for all the classes. The kids were thrilled, so when it was time for Miss McGrade's class to line up and walk over to the music building, they sounded like a herd of elephants stampeding through the school. Miss LeBoof had sheet music out on the music stands. None of the kids recognized the title.

Evan looked at the sheet again and read the title out loud. He raised his hand. "Miss LeBoof, who is this band? I don't recognize the song."

The whole class burst out laughing when LeBeef walked over to the brick wall and pretended to bash her head against it.

"Okay, no worries," she said, brightening. "I anticipated this. Put down your instruments and just listen." She walked over to her computer and hit the play button. There was a murmur as some of the kids recognized the song. The rest of them sat quietly and listened. The room was filled with the sounds of acoustic guitar and the solid vocals of the singer.

"That is a cool song, Miss LeBoof, but it doesn't sound very Christmassy, does it?" Ty fingered his cello.

"You are correct. That is why we are going to learn two songs before the concert."

The class erupted.

"You're kidding."

"No way!"

"We can hardly play 'Jingle Bells,' and we've been practicing that for three years!"

"Class, settle down. We can do it. We will do it, and you will be magnificent. I would never set you up to fail. We will perform this 80's hit song that your parents will love and then a classic Christmas song.'"

"Miss LeBoof, what did the song mean? Evan had the lyrics rolling around his head and couldn't quite make out why Miss LeBoof had chosen it.

"Ah. *Now* we have a question that deserves an answer. Well, Mr. Edmund, the song can mean many things to different people. To an adult, it can mean one thing, but to a child it can be interpreted in a completely different way."

"What way?" Evan pushed back.

Miss LeBoof picked up a lyric sheet and read the chorus. "Class, give me some ideas!"

"They're your parents?" volunteered Julia shyly.

"Yes! Good girl." Miss LeBoof smiled. "More! Give me more! Evan?"

"Um, I don't know. Maybe that it's time to grow up and take responsibility? That we're at an age to be judged?"

"*Yes!* See, I knew you guys could get this. Max, who do you believe the singer is talking about?

No dozer, Max latched onto the theme. "Parents. It's about my parents. No one feels the way I do about them or the way they feel about me."

"A gold star to Maximilian. See, it is all in how you interpret a song. You Grade 7s chose, through the brilliant guidance of your music teacher"—that got a chuckle out of them—"to see this as a beautiful song about the love you share with your parents. But that life is not easy. Far from it. And sure, it is a *stretch* for you to learn to play it for the holiday concert in three weeks, but it's a great song, and I know you can do this." She picked up her guitar and started to strum the opening bars. "Now let's get started."

In all the years Evan had been going to school, no one had ever treated him like an adult, much less like a bona fide musician. They were nowhere near making it sound recognizable, but the time flew by quickly, and they had fun trying. The kids sang or hummed the lyrics on the way back. When they passed Mr. Lanzilotta's class, Evan peeked in and waved at Meagan. He saw Coolio look up from his textbook and was midway through a salute when Coolio turned his head and looked out the window. Meagan caught the exchange and looked sympathetically at her friend.

With the start of December, the sun set early. There was no way they would get permission to go to the beach when it was almost dark and the skies were threatening to open up. The boys decided the less their mom knew, the better.

"Mom!" they yelled in unison from the front door. "We're going to meet up with Meagan, but we'll be home before dinner, okay?" Without waiting for a response, they bolted down the driveway. Neither of them knew if MJ had heard them, but they decided to play dumb if she challenged them later.

They met up with Meagan as she rounded the corner of her laneway.

"So what's the plan?" Gavin huffed as he tried to keep up with her.

She passed them, heading for the beach. "Simple. We go to Lookout Rock and call for them. They'll come. I know it." She sprinted off, leaving Evan and Gavin in her dust. She only slowed down when she reached the top of the steep stairs leading down to the beach. By now the rain had started, and the last of the day's light was slipping behind them. Meagan reached the rock first and scrambled up effortlessly. To the boys, it was as if she had grown wings.

"Carolynn! Madeline! Spotty! Please come. Please *come*!" The wind picked up and whipped Meagan's hair wildly. She called again and craned her neck in every direction. Seconds turned into minutes, but to Meagan, it felt like eternity, and she started to panic. She couldn't stop the tears that sprang to her eyes.

Shocked, Evan grabbed her by the shoulders as she swayed with each racking sob. He had only seen her cry like this once or twice before. His concern was only for her now. He hadn't realized how distraught Meagan had become over the loss of their new friends. Meagan searched the dark skies frantically, and when she couldn't see any signs of the Shimmies, she buried her face in Evan's shoulder. In desperation, he too started to call their names. "Rad-knows-ways! Mr. Biggsy! We need you! Come to us!"

Gavin tried to pull himself up onto the wet rock, but with each effort he slid off and fell back over the beached logs. He was making his third attempt when the glow appeared behind him. He slowly turned and stood face to face with a spotted fawn.

"It's about time, Spotty." Gavin sounded equal parts relieved and annoyed. "What took you so long?"

Before Spotty could erupt into his famous bleating, Meagan jumped down and broke into hysterical laughter and shouts of glee. They were suddenly bathed in the soft glow of the Shimmies—above, below and all around them. Carolynn and Madeline's wings swooshed within inches of their faces. Rad-knows-ways jumped up on a pile of logs and banged his flat tail loudly. The Burrows ran around the children and shrieked with delight. The Biggsys and Abigail emerged from the heavily treed area and approached the group as quickly as they could. The last animal to lumber onto the beach was Razor. His tongue lolled from side to side, and he wore a huge grin on his face.

The noise was deafening, the chatter was incoherent, and the children had trouble focusing on all their stories and questions at once. No one seemed to notice that the rain was falling steadily. With the exception of the light emitting from the Shimmies, it had gone pitch black.

Evan finally stood up on a log and raised his hands for quiet. "Where were you? Why didn't you come to us this week?" He hadn't intended to sound hurt, but he couldn't keep the disappointment from his voice.

The others looked to Carolynn. She floated down onto the rock. "But we were with you. We never left."

"Yes, you did. I looked everywhere for you." Meagan wiped the streaked tears from her face. "I snuck out of the house almost every night and searched my property for you."

"I couldn't help myself either. I looked in every treetop and under every bush. You were nowhere in sight." Gavin looked and sounded indignant.

"Children, children. Please let me explain. We knew your every movement. We never left your side. But you see, Evan, when you banished the group, it appears you lost your connection to us. Simply put, you closed the door, and by doing so, we were lost to you."

Dismayed, Evan looked from Gavin to Meagan. Carolynn's words rang true, but he was shocked at their effect on him. If their connection was that fragile, what did that mean for their future?

He realized, then, that his connection to Coolio was just as fragile.

"I am sorry for my words. I promise never to do that again. There is so much to talk about, but we have to get home. I half expect our Moms to coming flying down here any minute."

"Spotty, do you think you can light our way home?" Gavin was eye to eye with the fawn and almost fell over when Spotty leapt high in the air and bleated all the way up the stairs. The children laughed and chased after him. The Shimmies appeared all around them. The sense of the loss they'd felt melted away, and there was a bounce in their step. Each animal took turns asking questions. Razor wanted news of Coolio, and Meagan answered diplomatically that he was doing just fine. They parted ways reluctantly but agreed to meet the next day after school.

Wet and cold, Evan and Gavin slipped into the house in hopes of making it to the laundry room to strip off their soaked clothing. They weren't so lucky.

"Oi! Where have you two been? And *don't* tell me you were at

Meagan's because I've already spoken with Claire." MJ had asked them a question, but the look on her face suggested that she wanted to be heard rather than answered. "Honestly, boys! You dropped off your backpacks, ran out before telling me where you were off to, and showed up an hour later in the dark, soaked to the skin. What have you got to say for yourselves?"

Evan looked nervously at Gavin. Gavin looked at his mom's feet.

"We just went for a walk, Mom. "

"A walk? I can't even get you to walk on a hot sunny day, but you were suddenly inspired to stretch your legs during a storm? Evan, you should know better." She turned to Gavin. "And what do you have to say for yourself? You have a paper due tomorrow, and Mr. Shoreman made it perfectly clear that comparing the universe of Pokémon to the French and British Seven-Year War is not acceptable."

Gavin geared up for a debate, but the look on his mother's face made him think twice.

"You'll both be lucky if you don't come down with pneumonia. Now go get changed and wash up for dinner."

The boys kept a low profile and managed to keep a lid on their excitement until it was time to go to bed. Waiting at Gavin's window were Spotty and Abigail, and Carolynn was perched on a branch a few feet away. Gavin ran to Evan's bedroom and summoned him with an urgent wave of his hand.

They opened the window and leaned out.

"I told you they would see us tonight!" Spotty jumped from hoof to hoof and craned his neck to see both boys.

"Every night we have looked through your windows and watched over you while you slept." Carolynn puffed out her chest and spread her wings wide. "You are never without us, children. At this very moment, the Biggsys are curled up on Meagan's floor, and I wouldn't be surprised if Mr. Biggsy is singing her a song. He was quite a tenor in his day."

The thought of a raccoon singing a classical song struck the boys as hilarious, but they managed to keep their mirth in check.

They shared a few thoughts about the day and then quickly said their good-nights.

MJ found Evan sneaking back to his room, but she decided not to make a stink over it. Pick your battles, her mother always said.

While brushing his teeth the next morning, Gavin looked up to see Evan standing behind him.

"Okay, we fixed the Shimmy business. *Now* we fix the problem with Coolio."

"How y'gonna do dat?" Gavin garbled out through his toothbrush.

"We enlist the help of the Shimmies."

7

BROTHER WHO?

IT WAS A LONG WEEK. Between morning track practice, extra band classes and the nightly gab sessions with the Shimmies, the kids hardly had enough time to squeeze in their homework. Each night after their parents fell asleep, Evan and Gavin got up and ushered the Shimmies into the kitchen. While Gavin raided the pantry, Evan logged into his video conferencing account, where Meagan was waiting. A few times they almost got caught, but the keen hearing of the Shimmies tipped them off when they had to go into stealth mode. By Friday, they'd worked out the details of a plan to persuade their enormously angry friend to believe the madness. Each animal contributed to the strategy. "Mission Coolio" was underway.

Like most communities, Cedar had its handful of Christmas traditions. The only one that Evan and Gavin insisted on participating in was the Boar's Moor Yuletide Carolling Night. Normally restricted to adults nineteen years or older, the pub opened its doors one night a year to revellers of all ages. For over thirty years, the families of Cedar had walked, cycled or ridden their horses to the ten-acre estate, where they enjoyed the British pub fare and Christmas festivities. The second Friday of December, everyone raced home to don their loudest plaid, brightest scarves and funniest hats. The goal of the night was to out-dress, out-sing and out-eat all others. At the height of the night, the post-and-beam pub filled the countryside with screams of laughter and music, its stone hearth crackling away inside.

The park-like surroundings included lush gardens, intricate paths and a fully stocked pond. Christmas lights sparkled from every tree. Green, red and white spotlights lit the shrubs. Holly dangled from exposed beams, and wooden reindeer gazed unblinkingly.

After wolfing down their fill of roast beef, mashed potatoes and Yorkshire pudding, the children always explored the grounds and organized games of tag or hide-and-seek. With the exception of 2006, when torrential rains brought severe flooding and the night was cancelled, the weather was always nippy but dry. Bundled in their ski coats and woolies, the children would burst into the pub only when their mouths were dry or their teeth needed sweets. Then, rosy-cheeked and out of breath, they would disappear back into the night with squeals of delight.

The Edmunds, Gabriels and Richards always carpooled together. Coolio, with his powerful voice, would lead the kids in the three or four carols that were required entertainment at the pub, but the first moment he could peel out, he would pull Evan, Gavin and Meagan out the back door. For years they'd appointed themselves games coordinators and got the night rolling. Nothing delighted Coolio more than sneaking up on snogging teenagers to scare the devil out of them.

That was every year—but not this year. The Gabriels expressed their regret at not being able to go. The week before, Evan had joined his mother for a quick grocery run. When he rounded the bakery corner, he found his mom and Isobel standing close together and talking quietly. He could tell they were discussing him and Coolio, so he veered off to the meat department. He feigned interest in the cold cuts and pretended to be surprised when his mom came up behind him. She didn't volunteer anything, and Evan never asked.

This night, like always, the weather was cold but clear. The boys dug out their goofiest hats and added tartan ties to their plaid vests. Evan opted for his circa-1980 Vancouver Canucks trucker hat. It wasn't terribly original but popular with the old-timers.

Gavin wore a faux-beaver-fur hat. It wasn't until they stepped outside that he felt a bit embarrassed about it. The hat sat high on his head, the ear flaps hung low, and the bushy fur crown was reddish brown. He looked like a eighteenth-century Russian trapper.

Waiting to greet them by the truck were the Shimmies. Rad-knows-ways stepped up to Gavin, and his beady little eyes took in every detail of the hat. The boys held their breath.

"Who's your Mad Hatter? That's a lousy knock-off, Gavin. My cousin Peppy got made into a real Russian ushanka. You should have seen the flaps on that puppy! Beaver fur will cook your brains if you're not careful."

"Yeah, okay, good to know. Can't imagine a time when I'll own a real beaver hat, but if I do, I'll remember to put in ventilation. Thanks for the tip."

With that, Gavin hopped into the truck and waited for his parents to join them. MJ and Joe wore his-and-hers Santa hats, while Meagan and Claire had matching jingle-bell sweaters covered in fuzzy balls. They also wore elf shoes and hats to round out the look. But as they pulled into the pub's parking lot, they quickly realized that some of the townsfolk had way too much time on their hands. It felt more like Halloween than Christmas!

The Shimmies escorted the children to the main entrance and promised to wait for them when they came out to start the night's adventures. But despite the frenzy of the night, the kids found themselves distracted. They missed Coolio. They slipped out the front door and headed straight for the secluded duck pond.

"How was the bread pudding?" Mrs. Biggsy twitched her whiskers and licked her lips.

"Too filling. Besides, the only thing I wanted was the trifle, and that was already gone." Evan threw a stone into the pond and was satisfied with the plopping sound it made.

"I would have gone for the carrot cake. You youngsters are far too picky. In my day, we ate whatever we could get our claws on, including what came out of garbage cans." Mr. Biggsy swooshed his tail indignantly.

"Well, you *are* scavengers." Evan quickly added, "No offence, Mrs. B."

"None taken, my dear."

Meagan scanned the trees for Carolynn and Madeline and was startled when they silently flew up beside her.

"Hello, children!" they said in unison. Madeline perched on a bird feeder, and Carolynn settled on a bench carved from a fallen cedar.

"Hi!"

"There you are!"

"We missed you."

Anyone listening would have thought Evan, Gavin and Meagan had just welcomed a rock star into their midst.

"The others will join us shortly. Abigail is trying to convince Hubert that the wooden deer decorations are not real, and Razor and Rad-knows-ways are eavesdropping on the barmaid."

Meagan knew she would regret asking, but she couldn't help herself. "Why are they doing that?"

"It appears that the children of Cedar left far too many leftovers. Cook wanted to scrape off the good bits from the plates and make bubble and squeak for tomorrow's special. The barmaid got wind of it and became rather distressed—"

"Mental, more like it," Mr. Biggsy muttered.

"—and threatened to tell the proprietor." Carolynn hopped along the bench until she was within a foot of Meagan. "Razor and Rad-knows-ways thought the whole thing was very funny and decided to stick around to see how the five-foot fireball was going to handle the seven-foot ape."

On cue, the wolfhound and beaver appeared out of the dark at a breakneck speed. They skidded to a halt, fell to their bellies and burst into fits of giggles. Razor's eyes rolled back in his head as his tongue flopped from side to side.

"He never saw that coming, did he?" Rad-knows-ways clutched

his belly with his tiny paws. His webbed feet kicked wildly in the air, and he let out a loud hiccup.

"Speak up! What did you see?" Mr. Biggsy was far from amused. "Stop laughing, you hyenas!"

This was too much for Mrs. Biggsy, and she fell to the ground, laughing.

"Okay, okay. Don't get your knickers in a twist." Rad-knows-ways sobered up and managed to pull himself into a sitting position. "Little Bridget thought Claude's idea to recycle the leftovers was idiotic. She told him as much. He grabbed the full plate of leftovers out of her hand, but she pulled it back. He yanked it has hard as he could"—the laugh started to build again—"and the… the plate flew high into the air…" And he was lost to another fit of giggles.

Razor leapt up and took over. "It came crashing down on Claude the Slob's head! He shrieked like a baboon and started to call her *really* nasty words. Well, Bridget lost it. She grabbed the cordless Dust Devil vacuum and started to bash him over the head with it."

The wolfhound had a full audience now. Spotty hopped from hoof to hoof, and Reddy Bun-Buns ran in circles at their feet.

"She chased him into the pub where Old Davey and the Cedar Cinder Boys Band were singing 'Chestnuts Roasting on an Open Fire.' She grabbed the fire poker and cornered him between the piano and hearth. Boy, did he quake in his boots!"

"Then what happened?" Evan was sorry he'd missed the whole spectacle.

"Whaddaya think? Your old man asked Bridget, as nice as pie, if he could have a shot of whisky, neat. She said, "Of course, Joe." And, Bob's your uncle, she dropped the Dirt Devil vacuum on the floor and skipped off to serve your dad."

Rad-knows-ways had composed himself. "Claude the Slob slinked out the side door, and the last we saw, he was pulling cabbage and carrots out of his hair. You know, children, you really ought to stick around and finish your dinner more often. The entertainment is worth the price of admission."

"Blimey!" was all Madeline could muster.

Off in the distance, the sounds of children playing hide-and-seek could be heard. Evan couldn't help but marvel at how much their lives had changed in just a few weeks. If last year someone had told him he would be without his best friend, surrounded by dead animals, and gossiping about a barmaid, he would have thought they were mad. He gazed into the pond, lost in thought.

"Do you mind? You're staring."

Evan jumped at the voice. He had been so engrossed in his thoughts that he hadn't noticed the iridescent duck looking up at him from behind the reeds.

"Excuse me. Where did you come from?" Evan looked around to see if any of the Shimmies noticed the newcomer.

"If you must know, I came from over there. This is my pond. I was disturbed by all the noise you lot were making, and I swam over to ask you to keep it down. It's more than enough that I have to put up with you children once a year—now I'm bombarded with the shrieks of an oversized rat and a miniature horse!"

"For your information, Razor is a wolfhound, and Rad-knows-ways is a beaver." Meagan took a step closer to the water's edge. "Furthermore, this is *not* your pond. It belongs to the Calhouns, who own this pub."

"Maybe introductions are in order." Carolynn flew to the low-hanging branch that reached over the murky water. "My name is Carolynn." But before she could say another word, the Shimmy duck interrupted her.

"This is all very nice, but I think we should forgo the hospitalities and you should just move along. I have enough to tolerate these days without vagabonds like you disturbing my sanctuary." With that, he stuck his head under the water and shot his backside into the air.

Madeline flew down from the bird feeder, where she had been quietly observing everything.

"I think this wood duck is a tad rude, don't you, children? Odd that he doesn't seem shocked by your ability to see him or speak to him. You would think he would be speechless!"

"Speechless!" the duck sputtered as he came up for air. "Why speechless? It's not the first time I've spoken to a human."

That got everyone's attention.

"What do you mean? Surely, you must be confused. *Humans*, little *humans*. We talk to them, and they hear us." Mrs. Biggsy spoke slowly, enunciating every word.

Equally slowly, the duck said, "Yes. H-u-m-a-n." He ruffled his feathers violently. "I have had many conversations with an elderly man, at this very spot, while he sat on that bench."

"Impossible! We would have heard of this." Mr. Biggsy rose up on his hind legs and looked up at Abigail, who had also moved closer to the pond's edge.

"Are you Duke Mortimer, by chance?" Abigail craned her neck as far as she could to get a better look at the glistening creature. "The wood duck who terrorized the patrons of the Boar's Moor for almost two decades? Are you the duck Mr. Calhoun shot and cooked up for Thanksgiving dinner?"

Spotty let out a guffaw.

"It was humiliating," the duck complained. "Being served up on a platter with dried cherry sauce. A duck of my pedigree! Of my beauty! Just look at me. Where have you seen a crested head as iridescent green and purple as mine?"

"Why did you attack my peeps?" said Gavin, who had been pretty quiet until now.

"The question is not why I would attack them, but why I would *not*." Duke Mortimer, for all his high and mighty behaviour, was enjoying all the attention. "For eighteen years I called this pond home, and for eighteen years, filthy, loudmouth humans interrupted my mate's brooding, my feeding and resting. They had no business coming here."

Gavin pushed himself off the tree he had been leaning against. "I see. It's the man-versus-nature argument. I learned about this at school. Sorry, Mortimer. But it seems to me you've got the short end of the stick on this one. You *chose* to set up home at a pub. You should have moved your nest a pond or two down the road."

"There is no point arguing about it now, Gavin," said Meagan.

"Look at him. He's a Shimmy. I want to know who this human is you spoke to. Where can we find him?" Meagan was seldom impatient, but this was one of those times.

"Why, he is inside that wretched pub right now, singing like he has a poker up his bottom," Duke Mortimer said, disgusted.

"Now? Right now?" Evan got up from the grass, where he had been watching the events unfold. "Davey Golding is singing. You're trying to tell me that our friendly neighbourhood monarch can see dead animals?"

"Of course not, you slow child. He is as blind as a bat. He can hear me, and we discuss the weather, techniques for building wood boxes, and the stupidity of mallards. Dumb, drab fowl, really. They—"

Evan interrupted him. "You mean to say he doesn't even know you're a dead talking duck?"

"I never thought to ask, but now that you mention it, he does discuss pesticides and pruning quite a bit. He once asked what I used to reduce beetle larvae on the ornamental cabbage."

The children's mouths were gaping open, and Carolynn flew over to join the other Shimmies, who were huddled in a group. Everyone was so preoccupied that no one noticed a pig and donkey slide up beside them.

"Hi, Duke Mortimer. Hi, everyone-else-whose-names-I-don't-know-but-don't-want-to-be-rude-so-I-will-let-you-tell-me-who-you-are." The pig took a breath. "Of course, if you don't want to tell me your name, that's fine. I won't be offended. It wouldn't be the first time I was completely ignored by a large gathering of animals and humans. It's just that I would really like to know why you are talking to Duke Mortimer. He's my friend. Well, not really. But he does talk to me sometimes. He usually tells me to shut up." He took another breath. "In case you were wondering, my name is Barry Schmelling, and this is my friend Donkey."

Barry was not a large pig. His small head was attached to a thick body with short stubby legs. His curly tail and snout twitched in unison, while his large ears flapped back and forth.

Donkey, on the other hand, was quite large. He was also an

albino donkey. He stood almost as tall as Evan, and his eyes were deep black pools of liquid glimmer. He inclined his head slightly to the left and carried on chewing a long blade of grass.

"Great. More Shimmies." The sarcasm dripped from Gavin's tongue as he leaned back against the tree he had just vacated.

"Barry. Donkey. Your timing is lousy as always. No need to trouble yourselves with these creatures. They're just leaving." The duck let out a honk and then tucked his beak under his wing.

"No, we aren't!" Meagan slowly circled the pond to where Barry and Donkey were standing. "Hello, my name is Meagan. That's Evan and Gavin over there. They usually call me Meggie. It is very nice to meet you."

"Me too! Nice to meet you." The pig let out a squeal.

"We wondered how many more Shimmies we would encounter. Please come meet my friends." Meagan stood back as Barry and Donkey approached the assembled group. Introductions took longer than usual because Barry kept asking questions about how each animal had died. Evan found the whole experience quite unsettling.

"So, Donkey, what is your real name?" asked Gavin. Duke Mortimer ignored everyone and could be heard splashing behind the reeds.

Donkey had said very little up until this point, letting Barry do most of the talking. He was not quick to respond. Finally, he let the grass drop from his mouth and said in a deep voice, "It's Donkey."

"Yes, I know what you are, but what's your name?" Gavin looked at his brother, wondering if he'd missed something.

"Donkey. Just plain ol' Donkey." He went back to chewing on the mulched, soggy blade.

"Sorry, we just thought you might have a real name like all the other animals." Meagan didn't want to offend their new friend.

"He has a name. He just doesn't like it," Barry volunteered.

"Oh," was all the children could say.

When the pig saw that they were not going to press the issue, he decided to give them a hint. "His mom called him Jack." He looked at them knowingly, then frowned when they said nothing. "*Jack*. His first name is Jack."

They still looked confused.

"His last name is Ass."

"Oh!"

"So you can just call me Donkey." And with that, he wondered off to where the bulrushes grew.

"How did you die, Barry?" Despite Evan's revulsion, he couldn't help being curious. "Did you end up as someone's Sunday night dinner?"

"Jeez, Louise. Now you're making me think back. It's been a long time since I was in your world."

Carolynn, Madeline and the Biggsys all nodded with understanding.

"I lived on a farm not too far from here in Cedar-by-the-Sea. I was a piglet when I was brought to live with all the other swine. I came with my mommy and my brothers and sisters. We had abundant food in our trough, and all the mud we wanted to roll in. Those were the days!"

"Can you estimate when that might have been?" Carolynn had a penchant for dating the animals' time on earth.

"Hard to say. It was a long time ago. There weren't near as many people or buildings, and the cars were stinky. My owner drove a Studebaker. Does that help?" Barry seemed pleased with himself for remembering such a detail.

"It might. Was it a four-door sedan? " Biggsy cocked his head to one side and peered at the pig with intense concentration.

"Uh-huh."

"Side-mounted spare tire?"

"Yup."

"Tan exterior?"

"If you mean brown, yes."

"Three-speed gearbox?"

"Sounds right."

"Leather interior?"

"Could have been. I never got that close."

"That's a 1929 Studebaker Commander. They were rugged cars designed for poor roads in the early twentieth century. Loaded with torque! It was no Durant, but not a shabby car. You must have been alive during the Great Depression."

"It was Wall Street this and Wall Street that. A pig couldn't get a moment's peace with that raving lunatic going on about his money! Black Tuesday, Black Tuesday was all that nutter would go on about."

"Was this the farmer?" Evan asked.

"Nah, this was the funny-looking guy everyone called Brother."

"Big family?"

Donkey laughed at that. He had returned and stood behind Rad-knows-ways and Razor. "If you call over two hundred women, men and children a big family."

"The farm was called the Aquarian Foundation," Barry said. "People came from all over to be saved by this Brother. I never was sure what they needed to be saved from. They'd show up by the boatload. Old women, young women, tired old men, all wanting to be taught something."

"They were taught something, all right. They were taught how to get robbed blind!" Donkey's deep voice echoed in the night. For an animal of few words, he certainly could be loud.

"He called himself the Messenger. I can tell you, he sure was the Messenger of Death for us pigs!" Barry was worked up good and proper. "For one straight year, all he ate was pig. Pork pies, pork chops, pork dumplings, pork cutlets, pork roast, pork ribs."

"Don't forget crispy bacon, honey ham and sausage rolls," Donkey reminded him.

"One by one, I saw my family and friends disappear. I ran squealing every time a human came near me."

Feeling sympathetic for the little pig, Evan said, "So you died at the knife of the butcher?"

"No! I got hoof-and-mouth disease." He paused for effect. "They slaughtered me on the spot." Barry looked stricken for a moment but then composed himself. "I was happy to get out of that place. There were crazy men and even crazier women." Barry looked knowingly at Donkey. "At least I didn't suffer the way my pal

Jack here did. Now there's a story." Barry looked over at Donkey and waited for him to share the facts.

Donkey was none too obliging. He just gazed out over the pond.

"Oh, come on, Donkey. Tell the nice humans about the gold!"

Evan, Gavin and Meagan all moved in closer.

"They don't want to hear about that," Donkey muttered.

"Yes, we do!" they all said at once.

"Jinx! Black magic! Under a roof-coke!" Evan was the fastest this time, and he grinned at his now-silent partners. "So tell us about the gold, Donkey." Evan crossed his arms over his chest and waited.

"Well, if you gotta know, I came back from World War I after transporting supplies to the front lines in Italy. I was shipped by rail to the island after the end of the war. At the Royal Canadian Naval Base, I was used to drag logs out of the bush. I was content and was treated fairly." He spoke slowly and sleepily. "One day, a few of us were taken by truck to a livestock auction. I was sold to Brother Twelve and his followers. I was used to haul lumber to the sites where they were building their lodging and schools. From dawn to dusk, I did my chores and gave rides to the children. At night, I patrolled the livestock pen. I never stopped! It was a miserable existence."

Barry pushed his snout affectionately into Donkey's neck. "Poor old Donkey! Those Aquarians never gave him a moment's peace. Worst of all was that horrid Madame Z. She carried a whip! She used it on beast and human alike."

"I'm breaking the code, Evan. This is too important." Meagan leaned in. "That's just awful. You poor thing. I can't imagine anyone being so cruel to a lovely donkey like you." Meagan, distressed, looked beseechingly at the boys.

"Um, yeah, that sounds like it was brutal." Gavin was at a loss for words and looked at Evan for help.

"Couldn't you run away from those kooks?" Evan asked.

"I did! I made many attempts, but they caught me every time."

"Tell them how you finally did get away—and about the gold. That's the best part of the story!" Barry nudged his pal again.

"Long after the children were taken away from the compounds and the remaining colonists became disillusioned by the tyrannical Brother Twelve and the whip-wielding Madame Z, we animals were taken to Valdes Island. The religious leader and his woman had set up their home there. His quest to start a new-age religion was at an end."

The children and the Shimmies were spellbound. Imagine a donkey witnessing all that!

"Then what happened?" Gavin pressed. He hadn't forgotten about the gold.

"Word came that the local police were coming to arrest the pair for physical abuse and theft. For years the charlatan had been bilking old women of all their savings, and when these penniless fools went to the authorities, Brother Twelve knew it was only a matter of time before the authorities came for him."

Donkey shifted his weight and carried on. "One night, they went crazy! They smashed everything in sight. Not a window was left unbroken. They destroyed the barns and set the animals loose. I was taken deep into the woods by Madame Z. She held me still while Brother Twelve tied heavy boxes to my saddle. I could hardly walk, I was so weighted down." He seemed to physically collapse under the memory of it. "While Brother Twelve blew up the colonists' sailboat in the harbour, Madame Z put me on a tugboat and got ready to cast off. The night was clear, and the waters were calm. I had no idea where we were going, but I didn't have to wait long to find out. We sailed west across the water toward a little bay sheltered by many trees. There was no sign of other humans."

"Then what happened?" The suspense was killing Evan.

"That nutcase beached the boat, and they led me down a gangplank and pulled me up a steep hill. Beyond some blackberry bushes, not far from the shore, stood a massive weeping willow. Its roots rose menacingly out of the ground, and I found it difficult to step around them. The tree was so vast that once we got under the hanging branches, we were completely concealed from the outside world. It was dark and terrifying in there."

"Why did they take you there?" Meagan took a step closer to Evan and rubbed her arms vigorously.

"To hide the gold!" Donkey bellowed.

They all jumped, then laughed at each other's jitters.

"Brother lit some lamps and started ') dig. He dug until the sun was almost up. It was only then that they took those awful wooden boxes off my back. They wasted no time. They buried them deep in the ground and then covered them up with soil, rocks and driftwood. That Madam Z even ripped out bushes and planted them around the area. They set me free and disappeared out into the Strait of Georgia."

"They left you all alone?" Meagan was horrified.

"Happiest day of my life. I grazed in the area for years, until one day a human found me and brought me here."

The children looked at each other. "Here as in… the pub?"

"Yup. This used to be a working farm. Died right over there behind the holly bushes. I keeled over and never got up again."

"Jeepers! What a tale."

Gavin asked in a hushed tone, "Donkey, do you know where the tree is?"

8

MISSION COOLIO

EVAN BELIEVED their plan to convince Coolio about the Shimmies was foolproof. It was because he clung so intensely to this belief that he didn't let Coolio's behaviour affect him… much. If Coolio saw him coming down the hall, he turned around. If they were standing too close in the cafeteria, Coolio left the line. On one occasion, during dress rehearsal for the holiday concert, Coolio asked Miss LeBoof to move him to the other end of the stage. Parents, teachers and friends stopped asking what was wrong.

The night of the concert, the gymnasium was packed to capacity. The event kicked off with Mr. Shoreman's class putting on a very funny puppet show. They had made life-size puppets and a medieval Punch-and-Judy stage with bright red curtains. Their quirky rendition of Hans Christian Andersen's "Princess and the Pea" was fast-paced and had the audience in stitches. Gavin was the princess. Cameron played the old queen, and little Bethany Silver was the prince. The puppeteers could be seen leaning over the makeshift stage while a dozen classmates sat in front, hurling insults at the characters. At the end of the performance, the kids were thrilled when they got a curtain call. Gavin took deep bows and blew kisses to his adoring fans.

Next up were the two Grade 6 classes with a medley of movie and TV tunes. They loudly assembled on stage, knocking chairs and music stands into place. They screeched out themes from *E.T.*, *Jaws*, *Indiana Jones* and *The Flintstones* on their wind and percussion instruments. A couple of the boys got into a laughing fit after a three-year-old boy tried to jump up on stage during their wind-chime rendition of the *Harry Potter* theme. It was beyond them how he could even recognize the song. They botched it up so badly that some of the parents covered their ears.

Relief was felt all around when they blew their last note and stood up to take a bow. As they exited stage left, Mr. Lanzilotta's class stumbled on from stage right. Mrs. Rosaline could be seen straightening ties and tucking shirts back in to pants in the wing. Every year at least one class was slated to perform a few classic Christmas tunes. Mr. Lanzilotta lost the coin toss, so his students were saddled with "The Twelve Days of Christmas" and "Let It Snow." Their lacklustre performance only perked up when the students got to the last chords of "We Wish You a Merry Christmas." In the history of Cedar Intermediate, a stage was never cleared so fast.

At the one-hour mark, siblings in the audience started to get restless. They ran around the gym during the Grade 5 Rockettes dance routine. The teenagers at the back of the room cat-called and whistled during the music-hall cancan routine. The performers wore striped red-and-white Christmas stockings and elf hats. They kicked and bounced their way across the stage. Some of the smaller girls could be heard screaming out in pain as gangly boys trod on their feet.

MJ and Joe peered at the program. They were relieved to see that Evan's class was the second-last performance. They had to find out how Miss LeBoof's experiment would work out. Would "Wonderwall" be a huge success—or go down in a ball of flames?

The kids quickly set up on stage. The house lights faded, and a spotlight focused on Meagan, Trent and Mick. In unison, they strummed the opening chords to "Wonderwall." There was a murmur in the crowd as many of the parents recognized the song.

Ty joined in with his cello, and the Coppy twins filled in with the gentle sounds of their violins. Evan added his ukulele, and Simon came in strong on the drums. The rest of the class, using their recorders or tambourines, mimicked the lyrics. The kids had decided to make it an instrumental, not trusting their abilities to sing the words as well. When Miss LeBoof joined halfway into the song on the piano, many of the parents were openly singing the words. The gymnasium was electrified. The children marvelled at their usually reserved parents. Moms and dads laughed at each other when they messed up the lyrics, and Mrs. Rosaline *finally* took a deep breath. The song ended the way it started, with just the sound of the acoustic guitar. For half of a second, you could hear a pin drop. Then the crowd erupted in applause and cheers.

Evan couldn't believe they'd pulled it off, let alone nailed it! He laughed at Meagan, who still looked a bit nauseated, and cat-called Tyler, who was shaking his heinie at his brothers.

Mrs. Rosaline was no dozer. If she didn't get Mr. Lanzilotta's class onto the stage for the last song of the night, all would be lost. Within minutes, both classes were shoulder to shoulder on stage, and with a wave of her conductor's wand, Miss LeBoof had the kids singing at the top of their lungs. "Snoopy vs. the Red Baron" never sounded so good. The audience loved it.

Mrs. Rosaline presented Miss LeBoof with a bouquet of roses and wished everyone a joyous Christmas. Only then did the lights come up and the parents stretched their limbs.

School was officially out for two weeks. The hall was filled with the laugher and cheers of the students. No one was ready to leave, and the children made it difficult for the parents to round them up.

Gavin finally found Evan and Meagan out in the music building, where they were returning their instruments. Shockingly, no one else was there to overhear them.

"What did you find out?" Gavin said, absently strumming the guitar Meagan was trying to put away.

"Isobel confirmed that Coolio's got a game tomorrow night at 8:00 p.m. at the Nanaimo Ice Centre. They're playing Port Alberni, and she said the rink will be packed. Nothing like fifty years of 'friendly' rivalry, two nights before Christmas, to pull out the diehard hockey fans."

"Mission Coolio starts tomorrow at twenty hundred hours." Evan laughed. "I've always wanted to say that. Gav, your job is to get us a ride to that rink. Meggie, you make sure the Shimmies know their role in this."

"And your role is…?" Gavin looked speculatively at his brother.

"My role is to convince Coolio that Carolynn and the others exist. Or I will lose my best friend forever."

⸻

Getting a ride to the rink was a cinch. The next morning, MJ drew herself a hot, bubbly bath. She had just submerged herself to her ears when Gavin waltzed in.

"Ma…"

"Gavin! Get out! No. Whatever it is, it can wait. Can't you see I'm having a bath? My eyes have cucumbers on them, and I'm relaxing to the silky sounds of rhythm and blues."

"Yeah, but Ma—"

"*Out!*"

Gavin backed up when his mom fumbled for a wet facecloth to throw at him. "I just want to ask for a ride to Coolio's game tonight." His delivery was high-pitched and rapid fire, but he was delighted when his mother said, "Yes! Now go!"

He found his brother behind the carport with the Shimmies. Mr. Biggsy was explaining to Evan that he could achieve a lower-end torque and higher speed from the bike if he followed his instructions. Evan knew better than to question the wise, old raccoon and just did as he was told.

"Transportation secured, *mon capitan*."

"Good! Carolynn, did Meggie talk to you?"

"Yes. While taking Dakota for her morning walk, she called us to join her. She filled us in on when and where to be waiting in the rink. Madeline suggested she follow the Gabriels to the centre, and Meagan agreed with the strategy."

"Excellent. Where are Razor and Rad-knows-ways right now?"

"Razor wanted to stay close to Coolio, so at this very moment, he is trailing him and his father to the mall for some last-minute shopping."

"Now *that* would be funny to see. Gav, imagine coming out of Purdy's Chocolates and seeing a dog and a beaver hanging out near the food court. Too funny."

Joe came out around noon, reminding them of their errand to pick up their mom's Christmas gift at the BeLieve Gallery. Hidden there was a custom painting Joe had ordered for MJ. Artists Trixie and Brant had collaborated on a one-of-a-kind painting. With MJ thinking they were going to pick up milk and bread, they jumped in the truck and slowly pulled out of the driveway.

Evan looked back into the bed of the truck and burst out laughing. Red had jumped in. But what really made him laugh was the entire Burrow family, the Biggsys and Barry, all sitting around him. Evan couldn't see Carolynn, but he was sure she was close by. It was comforting to have them so close. Gavin was discreetly waving at Reddy Bun-Buns, and they were making faces at each other through the window. Their lives changed the day they met the Shimmies. They would never really be like all the other kids again, but Evan was okay with that. Miracles were something you were taught to believe in but seldom got to see.

Trixie and Brant had suggested that the exchange take place at their home so that the boys could visit with their son Gray.

"Sweeties! How are you?"

Trixie was one of the Edmund boys' most favourite people. Full of life and good humour, she never failed to make them blush.

"You're *way* too cute. Joe, you gotta do something about the unfair advantage these boys have over the local yahoos. Geez! Compared to your boys, they all look like trolls! Not a pockmark on you. Shiny hair, strong teeth, sparkly eyes…"

"Trixie, they aren't race horses." Brant was one of the coolest fathers the boys knew. Nothing fazed him, and no one enjoyed Trixie more than her husband.

"Come with me, you *GQ* hunks," Trixie said. "Off to the

drawing room to see what waits to delight you." With that, Trixie swept through the hallway, dining room and into the grand living room, where an easel stood in the centre of the room. Covering the painting was bright-red silk fabric. With much fanfare, she whipped the silky curtain off the painting and quietly moved away to join her husband and son, who stood behind their guests.

Evan, Gavin and Joe moved in closer to look at the painting. Their eyes travelled the canvas from top to bottom. Then their heads cocked from right to left. They squinted their eyes to see the picture in a different way.

It was Gavin who erupted with the first gasp. It took a few seconds for him to realize what he was seeing subtly hidden in the painting. The scene was of wildflowers blowing on a rocky cliff. Several metres below, the ocean waves sprayed a rock wall. It was a collage of purple, orange and hot-pink flowers tangled in a patch of tall grass. The flowers were painstakingly detailed, but as their gaze adjusted, the boys could make out animal faces behind the petals and leaves. An owl, pig and dog were intertwined with blackberry blossoms, and peeking out from behind some trillium were two raccoons, a donkey and a beaver. The lady's slippers hid a family of rabbits coyly gazing out at the viewer. And painted at the tip of a purple iris was a stunning blue jay. The sun glowed, but cleverly textured onto its surface was Abigail's face. A little fawn curled up in one of the roses.

Trixie and Brant grinned madly at each other. They came around each side of the huddled Edmund men and peered at their faces.

"My drawings! My animals! I see them." Gavin was enraptured.

Trixie teared up, and she simply smiled and nodded her head. "If Gavin were my boy," she said to Joe, "I would yank him out of school and put him to work. With talent like his, he could be a star. Besides, who needs an education?" Trixie looked at Gavin with a twinkle in her eye. "Can you multiply one hundred by one hundred dollars? Can you tell east from west? If you mix purple with red, what colour do you get?" She beamed at him and winked at Joe.

During the past weeks, as the boys met secretly with the

Shimmies late at night, Gavin had idly sketched his beloved friends. With each passing week, his pencil strokes became bolder. He filled in his drawing with exquisite detail and even managed to capture the unique personality of each Shimmy.

"Gav, we quite literally took your sketches and copied them into the painting. You truly are a gifted young artist. Your renditions of the animals are fantastic. It's as if each one posed for you." Brant proudly surveyed the painting and shook his head in wonder as his eye settled on the wolfhound leaping through a wave.

The boys exchanged knowing looks and tried to suppress a giggle.

"Evan, see anything that might pique your interest?" Trixie stared pointedly at the lower right-hand corner of the canvas. Evan moved closer.

"No way! Trixie, you included my poem!"

"Once I stopped bawling my eyes out, I sure did. Your mother had better not be wearing mascara on Christmas morning. She'll look just like that raccoon there!"

Cleverly interwoven into the tall grass were the words:

> *Mother of mine, patient and kind*
> *Happy and light, but strong with might*
> *Just and firm, love confirmed*
> *Never a day devoid of kindness way*
> *Mother of mine, son's praise divine*

Evan reread the poem and smiled. Late one night, Madeline had visited him unexpectedly. He had been sleeping, but the glow from her presence woke him. She was perched on top of his headboard, peering down at him.

"Sorry to wake you. I was curious to see how you slept, and if your dreams might be evident to me."

Evan had rubbed the sleep from his eyes. "Was I dreaming? Could you see into my thoughts?"

"No, I could only see a peaceful young man slumbering away. You looked warm and snug. I do regret waking you."

"No worries. I was probably dreaming of my mom's triple layer chocolate cake." Evan had laughed and had gone on to explain how a couple of times a year, his mom got it in her head to bake an enormous cake. Though they were usually lopsided and decorated in a rainbow of icing, they never failed to taste marvellous. Madeline asked many questions about his mother that night, and it surprised Evan how much he enjoyed sharing stories about her. Long after Madeline flew off through the bedroom wall, Evan sat thinking about their conversation. By the light of the moon, he wrote his poem. It was only after Joe suggested each boy contribute something for the painting that he retrieved it from under his bed where it has fallen.

"She'll love it. What an incredible gift you've made. No doubt this one will go above the fireplace." Joe smiled and clapped his hands together. "Ha! Let her try and top this one! Got her this year!" Since the boys could remember, there had always been a fierce competition between his parents to outdo each other when it came to their gifts.

The three boys took off to roam the neighborhood and once they got back hugs and kisses were exchanged along with good wishes for Christmas day.

⊏⊐

On the drive home, Joe surveyed the mountaintops. "The sky looks awfully dark and menacing. They're calling for snow on Christmas day, but we might get it tonight by the looks of it."

"Perfect! We haven't used our toboggans in a long time. I've wanted to try out that hill across from Coolio's for years." Evan zipped up his jacket and pulled the hood over his head.

Coolio's game was fast approaching, so after a quick dinner of homemade pizza, they packed up the backpack and called Meagan to give her a five-minute heads-up. She answered on the first ring.

"Ready?"

"As I'll ever be. Nervous?"

"Nope… you?"

"Yup."

"Okay, I take it back. I'm nervous. I'm wearing my lucky Vancouver Canucks shirt. Gav is wearing a shirt and tie and a wool sweater. He said he wants to show Coolio just how serious he is. Coolio knows what it takes for that boy to get dressed up. I hope this works, Meggie."

Once she was in the car, nothing more was said on the topic. MJ kept the stream of dialogue flowing with questions about Christmas and ideas for how to spend the holiday week. By the time they got to the arena, Evan was feeling ill.

"See you back at this curb in ninety minutes. Gavin, go easy on the poutine. You know how those greasy fries upset your belly."

"No worries, Mom. Have fun at the mall. Don't get trampled."

They lined up to enter Rink 2. Already, the stands were crowded with family members and diehard hockey fans. Nanaimo supported all athletics, but hockey was still the number-one sport in town. From pickup hockey to the old-timers league and every level in between, the town really had only two official seasons: winter hockey and summer hockey.

The children made their way behind the home team's bench and squished themselves between two burly men. Neither seemed impressed to have children forcing their way in, but it was critical that they sit directly behind Coolio. Evan craned his neck to see if he could find the Shimmies. The teams were about to come on the ice.

"Look!" The boys followed Meagan's pointed finger. Sitting high in the rafters were Carolynn and Madeline.

"And there!" Gavin hooted with laughter when he spied Mr. Biggsy sitting on top of the visitors' team net.

"The rest of them are in the penalty box," said Meagan. "Spotty is loving this. Look at him running from side to side and looking at the crowd. Oops—Abigail is getting ready to rein him in. Wait for it, wait for it… Yup! Busted. Now she's making him stand quietly. What do you think, Evan? Do you give him more than five minutes before he goes berserk again?"

"Two, tops. That deer is jacked on adrenalin. Mrs. Biggsy is the

only one looking on serenely. You'd think she did this every day."
Evan tried to calm his nerves and enjoy the scene.

"With their adventures, she probably did." Meagan was relaxed
now and looking around for Isobel. "There's Coolio's mom. Geez,
the whole Gabriel family is here tonight. Okay, I'm nervous again."

The crowd suddenly erupted in thunderous applause as the two
teams emerged from separate ends of the rink. The first team to hit
the ice was the Cougars, led by their captain, number 11, Lukas
William Gabriel III. Their shirts were crimson, and the logo on the
back showed a cougar leaping into the air. Coolio skated around the
ice and warmed up with a few shots on their goalie.

Port Alberni's Killer Whales looked fierce in their black-and-
white jerseys. Orca whales crested their shirts front and back. They
pumped their fists at one end of the stands, where most of their
supporters sat cheering.

In an instant, all the Shimmies appeared behind the home
team's bench. The only one who had not moved was Mr. Biggsy. He
peered out from behind Tommy "Titan" Collins. Tom stretched his
arms out wide to catch his team's lightning-fast shots. The Cougars
were in for quite a challenge with Tom in net.

The whistle blew, and each player took their place on centre ice.
The rest of the players piled into their boxes. The entire Burrow
family was sitting on Razor's back and head. They jostled for the
best position to see what was going on. The whistle blew again, and
the game was on.

Over the noise, Evan tried to get Gavin and Meagan's attention.
"Okay, so we know the drill?"

"Yeah, yeah. Ouch. Watch it, Coolio—that defenceman is twice
your size!" Gavin was completely engrossed in the game. He
ignored Evan's attempt to engage him and stood up to yell at a
Killer Whale who was barrelling down on Coolio.

"I didn't know Mr. Gabriel was the coach. What is he going to
say when we try to talk to his son?" Meagan started to chew her
thumbnail.

"Don't worry about him. Stay focused on Coolio. We stick to the
plan. Second period, we take our positions." Evan knew he didn't

sound as convincing as he wanted to, but it was too late now to abandon the plan.

The rest of the period was a frenzy of players chasing the puck from one end of the rink to the other. Both teams had opportunities to score, but the goaltenders were fast on their feet and saved every shot. Coolio's line was rotated a few times in the first period.

If Coolio knew his friends were there, he didn't let on. He kept his gaze on his teammates and yelled encouragement from the bench. Just as the period was coming to an end, the Cougars got a penalty for high-sticking. A massive defenceman skated to the box with his head low.

"Defend your net! Keep an eye on the little guy. He's crafty!" Gavin was on his feet and yelling at no one and everyone. They had to kill a two-minute penalty, and the Whaler line was bursting with energy. Their team captain yelled instructions, and when the chance presented itself, he personally took the puck from centre ice into the Cougar's end. With seemingly little effort, he scored. It was one-nothing for Port Alberni's Killer Whales. The whistle blew, and the teams made their way to the locker rooms to regroup and get a pep talk from their coaches.

"Coolio will be in a foul mood now. Hard to say how he's going to react to us." Meagan had known him all her life, and she knew only too well what they were up against.

"He only has to listen for a few minutes. The minute he starts to waver, we go in for the kill."

"Funny, that saying," mused Gavin. "Anyway, I'm off to get my poutine. Want anything?"

Evan and Meagan marvelled at Gavin's cheerfulness. Not much got that boy down, and virtually nothing got in the way of his french fries smothered with cheese curds and brown gravy.

"Yeah, a Coke would be good, and a bag of salt and vinegar chips." Meagan shook her head and pulled some licorice from her jacket pocket. They watched Gavin stumble over feet and legs as he made his way to the aisle. He was swept up in the crowd that was headed for the concession stand.

"You know, Evan, we've spent so much time thinking about how to get Coolio to believe us about the Shimmies. But we haven't talked about what will happen once he does."

"What do you mean?"

"Think about it. Just because he believes us doesn't mean he'll be able to see them or hear them. Short of us translating for him every two seconds, he won't have a clue what they're saying, or even if they're with us. Won't that get annoying after a while?"

"True, I suppose, but I'd rather do a play-by-play for my pal than have him carry on hating us. Life without the Coolio is seriously getting boring." Meagan chose not to take offence at that. There was no denying that Coolio's charm and charisma were missed. They were down the funny amigo, and nothing else would fill the void they all felt.

They watched the Shimmies follow the Zamboni around the rink, and they laughed when Carolynn dove like a kamikaze into the front of the machine. Madeline sat on the front section like a hood ornament. The rest of the Shimmies slid around on the ice and seemed not the least bit bothered by the wet surface. The bunnies took turns rolling down the rink like bowling balls, knocking bunny pins flying. Evan and Meagan were almost sorry when the Zamboni finished its last circle and the crowd poured back in for the second period.

"There's Gav. Let's grab him before he tramples any more feet." Evan clutched his backpack and waved at the Shimmies to take their positions.

"Sorry it took me so long. The lineup was *so* long. Here's your Coke and chips. Can I have a sip of your soda?"

"Have the whole thing. My stomach is in knots." Evan pulled a notebook out of his bag and opened it to the last page. "Time to make a decision: present to past or past to present?"

Meagan didn't even ponder the question. "Present to past."

Gavin's hand shot out, and he chopped the air. "Past to present!"

"It's settled, then. The Shimmies make the decision." Evan looked up from his spot behind the home team's bench and looked for Carolynn. Before he could say a word, she appeared.

"I know the question you choose to ask. Humans are complex beings and logical thinkers. The presentation of facts in a chronological way brings order to a restless mind. I vote you go with past to present."

"That means Meggie to my right, Gav to my left. Shimmies, please surround us. "

The children were almost blinded by the intense light of the Shimmies. Rays of gold and silver engulfed them, and Meagan could almost feel the skin on her bare hands grow warm. Each animal took a spot directly behind their human friends. Carolynn and Madeline sat high on the wire fence that acted as a barrier between the team's bench and the spectators. Within a minute, the players emerged from the south entrance, and the audience cheered wildly. Again, the players took position on the ice, and the rest of the team fell into their boxes.

The whistle blew, and the game was on. Coolio skated like a demon up the ice. He took a shot on net, but it went wide. He followed it into the corner but got checked into the boards. He stood up and chased the puck behind the goalie. His team member took another shot on net, but Tommy "Titan" kicked the shot off his left pad and the puck flew into the air. The Killer Whales blocked the forwards from swarming the goaltender, forcing the play back into the Cougars' end. It went on like this, back and forth between the blue lines, for five minutes. Then an icing call brought a line change.

Coolio skated directly for the bench. He whipped off his helmet and squeezed half the contents of a water bottle into his mouth.

Evan stepped up behind him and clutched the fence.

"What are you waiting for, Evan? Now's your chance!" Gavin grabbed the notebook from his hand and pointed to the first entry.

Evan cleared his throat. "Coolio! Lean back. We have to tell you something."

Nada. Nothing. Coolio didn't even look over his shoulder.

"It's pretty loud in here. Let me try." Gavin climbed like a monkey three feet up the screen and bellowed as loud as he could. "Coolio! We gotta talk to you."

Several of the players glanced back at the kid hanging off the fence. Coolio, on the other hand, never took his eyes off the game in front of him.

But the ear-piercing whistle right behind his head got his attention. Meagan wiped her fingers on her jeans and cocked an eyebrow at Coolio as if to say, "Pretend you can't hear that, buster."

"Get lost!" It was the first time Coolio had spoken to any of them directly in over three weeks. Evan judged it was better than nothing.

"Coolio, listen. You gotta let us explain what's going on. What we told you about the animals is true. I swear on my heart. I swear on my brother's and parents' lives. Just turn around and look at us. We have proof."

Coolio didn't turn around, but his head didn't turn to the left when the players skated down to the Whalers' end.

Evan felt a little hopeful. He grabbed the notebook back from Gavin and looked at his notes. "Here, just listen. Um, I got it written down. Here is the first entry I wrote after we started to meet late at night with the Shimmies. We had them watch you, and we recorded everything you did." Evan pushed his face up against the fence and lifted the notebook up so he could read aloud. "Saturday, December twelfth, you woke up around 6:15 a.m. and watched James Bond's *Quantum of Solace* in the guest room. You then snuck into the kitchen and got a bowl of Frosted Flakes and a banana around 7:30 a.m. When your parents woke up, you had three pancakes, five strips of bacon and a glass of orange juice. You then—"

Coolio finally spun around to look at them, but the look on his face wasn't promising. "I don't even know what I ate yesterday, let alone weeks ago. You know I *always* get up early and watch a movie on the weekend, and guessing what I ate ain't all that hard since you've slept over a million times and know what my mom makes! So like I said, *get lost.*"

James finally noticed what was going on and shot the kids a menacing look.

"Okay, okay, you're right. Then how about this one: Monday, December fifteenth."

Rad-knows-ways came up behind Evan and looked at the entry. "Oh, oh, that was my watch! Tell it good, Evan."

"On Monday, December fifteenth, you asked Mr. Lanzilotta to go to the bathroom just after morning break. But instead of going to the loo, you snuck into the gym and found your Volcom hat, which you'd left in the change room. That same day, you passed a girl a note. Rad-knows-ways couldn't see what was in it , but the girl turned it upside down and burst out laughing. The teacher asked her what was so funny, but she only giggled and shook her head."

"I think it was a naughty picture, but she crumpled it before I could see." Rad-knows-ways was standing directly in front of Coolio and talking to him like he expected an answer.

Evan could see that Coolio was starting to get confused. He blocked out the sounds of the crowd and kept going. "Tuesday, December sixteenth, you had a math test. Mr. Biggsy said you rushed through the questions. You would have gotten a perfect score if you hadn't screwed up the letters that represented the vertex."

Mr. Biggsy appeared out of nowhere. "Tell that young man he was too impatient, as he is with most things in life. Rushing here, rushing there. He speed-reads as if the book will implode any minute. He brushes his teeth with such vigour it is a wonder he has any left. He—"

"My darling, I am sure your comments are accurate, but they are not necessarily timely. Let Evan continue." Mrs. Biggsy swished her tail and looked on with a charming glint in her eye.

"Where was I?" Evan checked his notes. "You got the test back, and you muttered that you knew the answer to that one, but Lanzilotta said if you did, you would have gotten it right. You made an airplane out of it and tried to shoot it to Jennifer, but just as you were about to hurl it, Mrs. Rosaline came in and asked to talk to Mr. Lanzilotta."

"The next day you stepped in cow dung," Gavin said, laughing. Coolio would have gone ape. His shoes came second only to his T-shirt collection in order of importance. "Reddy Bun-Buns said you wiped your shoe for like an hour in the tall grass. What were you doing, cutting through the cow field anyway?" Gavin genuinely wanted to know. He thought the chance of getting trodden to death by thirty angry Jersey cows was a solid deterrent.

"No time for questions now, Gav. That night, you went with your dad to pick up a turkey from the Douglas farm. The next morning you sang 'I Gotta Feeling'—"

"Anyone could have told you this. There are twenty-five kids in my class. You guessed at the rest, and I still think you're all freakin' nuts, and I'm *not* playing your game anymore." Coolio stood up with the rest of the line because they were about to go on the ice.

Meagan turned the page for Evan and pointed to another entry.

"Oh yeah, good one. Just the other night at the school concert you changed four times. You wanted your new Alien Workshop T-shirt, but it was in the wash 'cause you dripped salsa on it at your grandparent's house. And before you say I could have guessed that, you're wrong. Your mom just bought that shirt for you, and you've never worn it to school."

Coolio just huffed and put his helmet back on.

"Guys! Help me. What do I tell him next?" Evan scanned the pages. He knew Coolio was right. Even though he had pages and pages of notes, all the reports were superficial. A few sleepovers at his cousin's, a movie here or there, dinner with his grandparents, his usual tomfoolery at school. Hockey, hockey, hockey. There really wasn't anything that stood out as unique or out of character, nothing that could make Coolio stop dead in his tracks.

"Meggie, Gav... give me something here!" But they only looked at each other in panic and defeat. So much preparation had gone into tonight, but in hindsight, nothing they'd discovered was really that new. Evan could have guessed much of it himself.

Evan turned to the Shimmies and appealed to them. "Carolynn, Abigail, please. What have you got for me?" They looked just as defeated as Gavin and Meagan. Evan felt sick. He searched each of their faces—and found nothing.

Razor stepped up from where he was hidden behind Abigail and Rad-knows-ways. He jumped up and placed his front paws on the screen, where only feet separated him from his master and friend.

In a very wistful voice he said, "Tell him he whispered to me. I was just a puppy when I was brought home in a box. From the very beginning, Lukas kept me in his room every night. He would lay down on the ground and whisper in my ear. He did that every night until I died. His parents never knew what he did. Evan, you never knew what he said, and to this day only Lukas knows what he did the night I died." Razor looked at Evan. "Tell him precisely what I am about to say."

"Coolio, I've got one more for you." Evan spoke loud and clear and stared a hole into his back. "You said to Razor every night, 'You're my wolfhound. Defender of the Celtic...'" He looked strangely at Razor. "'Defender of the Celtic... my arse. You couldn't defend a kitten, but I love ya, buddy, and I'll protect you until the end of time.'"

Razor dropped down and hung his head low.

"You wrote that out on a piece of paper and buried it the night Razor died. It's probably still there, under the blackberry bushes near the front gate."

Coolio ignored his father when he yelled for him to get on the ice.

Coolio took off his helmet and stared into Evan's eyes. "How did you know that?"

"We've been telling you the truth since day one. I know this is really hard to believe. I don't know if I could believe you if the shoe were on the other foot. But Coolio, I swear to you I am telling the truth."

Coolio finally looked at Meagan and Gavin. He took in everything about them. What they were wearing, the white knuckles gripping the screen and the fierce determination in their eyes. If he didn't believe them, they would only keep trying.

"Lukas! On the ice *now!*"

Without another look back, Coolio jumped over the boards and skated to centre ice. The puck was dropped, and the kids suddenly heard the sounds of the arena again: the cheers, the chants and the pounding of feet on the wooden floorboards of the stands.

Evan looked around and saw hope in the eyes of his comrades.

"Razor, I know that was really hard to do," Meagan murmured.

"To share such a special secret must have felt like betrayal, but I think he might believe us now." She ached to hold the massive wolfhound and make him feel better.

Mr. Biggsy was clinging to the fence and watching the game intensely. "Never mind all that now. You help that boy win this game, and he'll believe you even if you tell him fairies live in his garden."

"That wouldn't surprise me these days," Gavin muttered, and took a gulp of Evan's pop.

"Evan, do exactly what I tell you to do, and all will be forgiven by this friend of yours," Mr. Biggsy said. "Come with me."

The racoon took off at a surprising speed. He passed through hordes of people as they pressed themselves up against the glass boards. The children tried to follow the Shimmies but fell behind when they got caught in a bottleneck at the rounded corner of the rink. They pushed and shoved their way through and came to an abrupt stop directly behind the opposing team's goalie.

Mr. Biggsy was on top of Tommy "Titan" Collins's net again. The Cougars were slowly moving the puck back to the Whalers' end.

"Evan, you must get Coolio's attention when he comes around the net. Tell him this young goalie has a bad habit of losing sight of the rebound. He is so focused on his save that he forgets to keep an eye on the puck as it circles around his net. It's a wonder there hasn't been a goal on him yet."

Evan nodded and kept his eye on Coolio.

"Tell him that when there is a rebound or he goes into the corner, *don't* take it out front. Take it around back and tuck it high and tight to the net. This goalie comes out of his crease about fifteen inches too far when the play is behind him, and then he drops to his knees. You got it?"

"Yeah, I think so."

As if on cue, Coolio came hurtling down the ice with his teammates spread across the blue line. They moved in for the attack, but a Whaler scuttled their attempt and sent the puck rebounding off the boards. Coolio chased it and dug in deep. While he was in the corner, fighting off two opponents and trying to kick the puck free, Evan yelled Mr. Biggsy's instructions to him. He was certain he got the instructions right, but had no idea if Coolio heard him—or would trust his advice.

Evan ran back to stand beside Gavin and Meagan and turned just in time to see Coolio free the puck with his skate and explode in a blur of speed. As he rounded the back of the net he literally twisted his body, flew into the air, and took a slapshot that sent the puck high into the top left-hand corner of the net. He'd scored! Coolio hit the ice hard but jumped up fast—only to be thrown back onto the ice by his deliriously happy teammates, who piled on top of him.

The game was now tied. The rink erupted with the wild screams of Cougars admirers. Even many of the Whalers fans clapped for such a stupendous shot. The buzzer went off two minutes later, and the game was over. Not a win but not a loss.

As Coolio skated off the ice, he looked to the left, where his friends were lined up in the opening of the door. His sheepish grin said it all.

"If it snows tonight, wanna toboggan tomorrow?" Evan held the door open for Coolio and kept his voice as nonchalant as he could.

"Sure. Bring those new sleds you got a few years ago."

"Will do. Night."

"Adios, amigos."

9

"DID SOMEONE SAY SNOW?"

THE SILENT WISH of every Vancouver Island child was answered resoundingly that night. The pretty snowflakes that fluttered in the wind at bedtime quickly developed into a blizzard, the likes of which had not been seen since 1961. The power went out at 1:23 a.m. Or at least that was when the clocks stopped working. It was the sound of the neighbour's backup diesel generator that woke Joe at 5:30 a.m. Old Betsy's reluctant sputtering shattered the thick blanket of silence. It was the kind of unnatural sound that wakes a man quickly with a feeling that something is terribly wrong.

The moment of clarity came when Joe shot his leg out from under the blankets and felt the bone-chilling cold. He stumbled to his closet. He habitually hit the light switch and only grunted when nothing happened. Groping in the dark for his clothes, he cursed under his breath when he couldn't find his flashlight. He had suspicions that he would find it in one of the boys' rooms.

Once Joe was certain his fire wouldn't go out, he made his rounds and located all the flashlights stockpiled in Evan's room.

By the time the boys woke up, the house was warmer. Joe had put cinnamon buns wrapped in foil on the barbecue to warm them up. They sat cheerfully in front of the fire with a glass of milk and sticky buns. The boys couldn't wait to haul out their snowboarding gear and trudge their way through the snow to retrieve their toboggans from the shed.

"Dad, when can we go out?"

"When something that resembles a sun comes out."

"But when will that be?" Gavin was less than patient.

"At this rate, around May."

"*Daaad*," Gavin whined. "I'm serious. When can we go tobogganing?"

"Help me make a tray up for your mom, and then wake her up sweetly with a song."

"Yeah, like we're going to do that." Evan laughed. "Sweet ain't my style. Now, if you want a funky little rap tune, I can accommodate."

"Never mind," Joe said. "Please get the brown sugar from the cupboard. Do you think she'll want yogourt with granola or Special K?"

"Cinnamon buns!" they said in unison.

MJ opened her eyes reluctantly. She had been having a lovely dream about a white sandy beach surrounded by turquoise water and a warm breeze blowing on her face. She tried to cling to the warm, fuzzy feeling but slowly realized she was being observed. She opened one eye first and then snapped the other one open in alarm. Peering down within inches of her face was a set of green eyes. She rose up on her elbows and almost bashed her head on the face that stared at her.

"Mornin', Mom!" Gavin leaned back and pulled his arm out from behind him. In the dim candlelight she could see a half-eaten cinnamon bun.

"Um, thank you, Gavin." MJ looked around. Evan and Joe were seated on the other side of the bed.

"Here's a hot cup of coffee, Mom." Evan gingerly handed over the steaming cup.

"Wow. Good thing I'm lying down. I would likely have banged my head on the floor. What's the occasion? Did I sleep through Christmas Eve day, and today is Christmas?"

"Nope," said Joe. "Just two excited boys who can't wait to get outside and test-drive their sleds. Since there is no power"—MJ groaned—"they figured they might as well get out of the house and do something thrilling. A blank TV is not thrilling."

MJ sipped her coffee and nibbled on her bun. "The day before Christmas, and we have no power, no water—except what's in the water cooler and rain barrel outside—and a fifteen-pound turkey to cook." She shook her head.

"Add to that no driveway. It's buried, like everything else on the property."

"That bad?" She scrambled out from under the duvet and immediately regretted it. She jumped from foot to foot until she located her slippers and housecoat. She peered out the window and gasped. "Where did the world go?" Where bushes and trees once stood on the curve of the driveway, there was now just a soft, round mound of snow.

"How are we going to get out?" She looked at Joe, expecting him to have an answer.

"We don't. Let's just hope we don't get a quick rise in temperature, or else this will all melt and flood the property."

"Mom, don't distress. This is amazing. Just think how much fun it's going to be to sled down Parson's back hill! We can build snowmen and make igloos. We can't wait to get outside in it."

"Well, as long as you're happy," MJ said sarcastically, "I might as well go back to bed and dream about taking a vacation in Fiji." With that, MJ hopped back in bed and grinned mischievously at her boys.

"The boys want to head down to Meagan's and then go wake up Coolio. What do you think?"

"What time is it?"

"According to my watch, 7:10 a.m."

"Yeah, I'm thinking no. How about you wait until a civil hour, like 8:30 a.m.? Besides, by then there might actually be light in the sky." She slid further under the covers. "The word for the day is *thermal*."

After spending an exhausting hour locating their winter gear, the boys were ready to head out.

"Ev, why were all the flashlights in your top drawer?"

Evan looked at his brother with an expression that said, *Help me out here, little buddy.* Gavin just shook his head. *You're on your own.*

"Um, I think I forgot I put them there." That is, when he wasn't creeping around the house in the dark, meeting with the Shimmies and talking online with Meagan.

Joe didn't pursue it any further. "Just remember: they're not toys. Please put them back where they belong."

"Yup. Sure. You got it." And with that, they shot out the door.

In the snow, Red sank up to his barrelled chest. He got only seven feet from the house before he couldn't go any further. He let loose a high-pitched bark at the boys, demanding that they get him unstuck. Evan and Gavin would have, too, but they were laughing too hard. Evan had face-planted, and he was now wiping the snow out of his eyes. Gavin had fallen on to his back and was busy making an angel. Fresh morning snow blanketed their view. There was no green, no brown, no colour other than white.

At precisely 8:30 a.m., they dragged their sleds up the drive. The path they cut allowed Red to follow them. It was a hard go up the long driveway, but once they got on the road, they found it easier. Where the white road rounded to the left, the pine trees leaned forward and the lower branches, heavy with glistening icicles, touched the ground.

Waiting for them at the top of Meagan's drive were the Shimmies. The bunnies were leaping off Razor's back and disappearing into the snow. They leapt up, covered from ears to tail.

"Good morning, children! Isn't this winter wonderland beautiful?" Carolynn let the wind lift her wings high, and then she dove down, swooping low over their heads.

"It's cool—I mean freezing—out here!" Evan agreed. "I've never experienced such cold on the island. Still, it's a perfect day for a snowball fight. I can't wait to nail Coolio. He won't know what hit him." To prove the point, he scooped a huge handful of snow, packed it tight, and whipped it at Barry. It sailed right through him, but the pig giggled as if he were being tickled.

"Do it again! Do it again!" Evan didn't wait to be asked again, and by the time Meagan rounded the corner of her drive, the Shimmies were being nailed with a hail of snowballs. She ducked just in time as two of them whizzed by her ear.

"I could hear you all the way up at the house. I told Mama you'd come first thing. The first one to get Coolio can be Snowball King for the day. I brought my Red Rocket, but the brakes don't work anymore. Let's hope I don't go sailing into the ocean!"

Dakota joined Red, and they started down the road toward Coolio's. Meagan asked the Shimmies if the snow bothered them. Naturally, they said no. They compared stories about their mornings and all agreed Christmas was going to be extra special this year. There was nothing like being snowed in to spark the imagination. So far, they couldn't see one downside to their situation.

The glow from the Shimmies created a bubble of light around them. Even though the sky was grey, they felt lighthearted and free-spirited. Their laughter and banter carried far over the silent treetops.

They found Coolio in his garage, digging out snowshoes, toboggans, crazy carpets and super-slider snow skates. He could only find one of his mini skis, and was relieved when his pals showed up.

"Hi, yetis. I see you're dressed appropriately for a day of outdoor activity. Can you help me find the ski that matches this one?"

"Happy to." Evan really meant it. He had missed his friend. Today would be the first time they had hung out together in almost four weeks. Since Grade 2, they had never gone more than a week without seeing each other. Life without Coolio was pretty boring.

Ten minutes later, there was still no sign of the ski, but Coolio didn't want to give up. Meagan had climbed under the workbench at the back of the garage and was pulling out lawn chairs when she heard a flutter behind her.

"Meagan, I believe I have located the item Coolio is looking for.

It's up there, behind a large black inner tube." Madeline was perched on the ladder that led up to the loft. She flew up to guide Meagan to the correct spot.

"Fantastic! Madeline found it!"

She scrambled up the ladder and disappeared into the loft. The kids all stopped what they were doing and gathered at the bottom.

"You're awesome, Madeline," she said from the loft. "We could have been here all day. What made you think to look up here?" When Meagan returned to view, she was holding the ski and looking up and off to the side. She laughed at some reply and came scampering down.

The boys gave Meagan a high five and added the ski to the pile. It was then Evan realized that Coolio had not moved. He just stood there, looking peculiarly at Meagan.

It hadn't occurred to Evan that Coolio may have developed doubts over the night. Meagan's actions required him to believe in the Shimmies, and by the look on his face, Evan wasn't sure he did.

"How did she know it was up there?" Coolio looked shy and a bit awkward.

"Madeline is a blue jay. She was flying around up there. She said she saw it in the reflection of a mirror resting in the rafters. Stand back. You can see the mirror from here. Madeline saw a purple ski sticking out from underneath the tube." Meagan was so excited and proud of her feathered friend that she didn't realize her enthusiasm was one-sided. Her voice trailed off, though, when an odd look came over Coolio's face.

Evan, Gavin and Meagan held their breaths. The Shimmies had stopped moving and stared intently at him. The moment of truth had arrived. If Coolio believed them, all would be fine. If he didn't, they would be turning around and walking out the way they'd come.

"Well, um, tell her thanks. I wouldn't have thought to look there."

They all let out a collective sigh and started to gather their belongings. At that moment, Isobel appeared at the door that connected the house to the garage. In her hands was a huge Thermos and backpack.

"Happy Christmas Eve! What a way to start the holidays, eh?" She was beaming from ear to ear. She had been very distressed by the falling-out between Lukas and his dear friends. Even though MJ, Claire and Isobel had discussed it many times, none of them could figure out a way to fix the problem.

Coolio started strapping all his supplies down to a sled. "Thanks to my mom, we have hot chocolate, marshmallows, camper cups, homemade cookies and blueberry muffins."

"And when you get too wet and cold, come back here for lunch. I already spoke to your moms. Thankfully the phones are still working."

The kids waved their thanks and headed up the drive. They took a right turn at Pacific Dive and headed for Old Man Parson's lot. It was a huge property that sat high above the Georgia Strait and boasted views of the mountains around Vancouver. Mr. Parson had cleared most of the trees and bushes and invited neighbourhood kids to enjoy his land. He knew it was perfect for mountain biking in the summer and sledding in the winter.

As they approached the bottom of the long hill, Gavin let out a squeal. "This is awesome! Look at how smooth the snow is. Beat ya to the top!" And with that, he lifted his legs high and ran as fast as he could in the deep snow. The dogs barked, the kids laughed and the Shimmies swarmed all around them. When they reached the top, they stopped to rest. It was so cold that that they could see their breath. They panted and tried to stand up straight to slow down their breathing.

"What's your pleasure, guys?" said Coolio. "We have six sleds. I think I'll stick to my crazy carpet. The last time I used it, I sailed through the bottom of the lot, cut through the bushes, and came to a stop in the middle of Pacific Drive. A few more feet, and I would have shot down the hill and into the ocean!" Coolio made sure that his gloves were pulled on tight. He adjusted his hat to cover the top of his forehead and then got himself into position.

"No brakes on mine, but if I reach the edge of the water, I'll roll off." Meagan positioned herself a distance from Coolio and pulled her goggles down over her eyes. When she looked over at the boys, she had a fiercely competitive look in her eyes. "Time to saddle up, Edmunds!"

Evan looked at Gavin. "Do we go solo on the new gliders or use the big wooden sled? Usually we go faster when we're both on. What do you think?"

Gavin didn't hesitate. "I'll take the rear. You steer. Let's show these babies how it's done." He let out a whoop and pulled the old sled into position.

Together they all said, "On the count of three... One, two, three, go!"

They dropped over the edge and shot forward at an unexpected speed. The wind whipped off their hoods and blurred their vision. They hung on for dear life as their various sleds sped over the bumps and dips in the ground. Gavin and Evan hit a knoll that sent them flying into the air. They both let out a yelp as their toboggan went airborne and hit a mound of snow. The snowbank exploded all around them, and they couldn't see where they were going. When they finally stopped, their eyes were sealed shut and their mouths were filled with snow. They cleared their eyes and looked for Coolio and Meagan. Coolio was ten feet in front of them, on his back, and laughing so hard he couldn't breathe. Meagan had gone the farthest and was tangled in some flattened bushes near the road.

She stood up and pumped her arms in the air. "I rule! I rule! *Sweet!*"

They walked up together and compared the levels they'd achieved on the thrill-o-meter. They concluded it was by far the best ride any of them had ever had. They spent the morning speeding down the hill or pulverizing each other with snowballs. On one of the runs, Gavin and Evan looked over to see Reddy Bun-Buns and Ever-Ready Freddy sliding down on their fluffy bums. They beat them by a mile! Rad-knows-ways showed up and rode his tail like it was a spinner saucer.

Coolio played club mix tunes all morning long. They danced, sledded and built snow forts to shield themselves from snowballs. They hardly noticed the dull sun trying to break through the dense clouds, and it was only after they had consumed all the snacks and drunk the Thermos dry that they realized they were soaked to the bone and freezing.

Coolio's voice took on a deep, southern Irish timbre. "What say you to some beef stew and crusty rolls?"

"Now you're talking!" Gavin grabbed as much as he could carry, jumped on his sled, and took off.

"Spin me, Evan!" Meagan let out a squeal as she flew down the hill, spinning the entire time. She stepped off and fell down, laughing.

"I think I should finally use these mini skis since Madeline went to so much trouble to find one." Coolio was busy putting his boots into the straps and didn't look up to see the expression on Evan's face.

"Good call. I bet they'll go fast. Remember to bend your knees. I'll bring down your stuff."

Coolio stood up, slapped Evan's back, jumped high in the air and shot off like a demon. Evan held his breath until his friend had reached the bottom in one piece.

"You are a good friend, Evan. Coolio is lucky to have you." He looked up to see Mr. Biggsy peering at him.

"We're both lucky. I'm just relieved that he believes us now."

"So are we, my dear boy, so are we. Now let me see how far you can take that sled. The hill is icy and slick now."

Evan pushed off hard and felt a thrill when his stomach hit the top of this throat. He caught up with his friends, and they chatted happily on the way back to Coolio's.

They agreed they had never had a better Christmas Eve day. Reluctantly, they said their goodbyes after the scrumptious lunch Isobel made. Their world seemed right again.

10

THE THREE BS: BUS, BOOKS, BORED

AS JOE HAD PREDICTED, they were snowed in for three days. And when the power returned on the fourth day, MJ was delighted to see a moment of disappointment on the boys' faces. Pioneering was more fun than they realized. On Christmas Day, neighbours went from house to house, sharing eggnog and treats and making sure that folks were fine. The Edmund boys, along with Meagan and Coolio, took turns building snowmen outside each of their homes. They even snuck in a game of road hockey. When a few of the older teenagers joined in, the game got quite competitive. The Shimmies watched enthusiastically, and Mr. Biggsy coached the younger kids on how to outmanoeuvre the bigger boys. They only stopped when they were called home for dinner. MJ pulled out old board games, and Joe made Jiffy Pop popcorn on the Coleman stove. Throughout the day, the Edmunds called their extended family around the globe.

Several days later, word got around that the snow removal crews had cleared most of town and were starting on the country roads. MJ made a grocery list and headed out to the truck.

"Mom, can you get some salt and vinegar chips and some hot chocolate?" Evan yelled from the front porch. "Oh, yeah—we need marshmallows too. Not the big ones, the little ones. Multicoloured if you can find them. I wouldn't say no to a Mars bar, either."

"Don't forget a bag of Oreos," Gavin added.

MJ just rolled her eyes and waved goodbye through the rear-view window.

Evan called Carolynn and asked her to trail his mom. "If she wipes out, come back and tell us, okay?" With that, Carolynn flew high over the trees and disappeared out of sight.

"It's just you and me, boys. How about we stock up the wood and catch up on some video games?"

By the sixth day of their holiday, the Edmunds were suffering a bit of cabin fever. It was Rad-knows-ways who suggested they go snowboarding up at Mount Washington. When the boys mentioned it, they were surprised at how fast their parents agreed. By noon that day, they were standing in a long line at the chairlift, smearing sunblock on their noses. The sun was high and blinding, and the view of the strait from the peak was breathtaking. When they stopped at the chalet for a drink and snack, they bumped into a few of their friends from school. Simon's family had rented a cabin at the base of the hill and spent their Christmas vacation boarding and tubing to their hearts' content. Apparently they hadn't been affected by the power outage. The boys took off with Simon and his older brother to try the west side of the mountain. After a quick dinner of fish and chips, they fell into the car for the long ride home.

It was past midnight when the boys got ready for bed.

"Only one week left of the holiday. I say we hit a movie tomorrow, get in another day of tobogganing, and see what time free skate is the at rink. That ought to eat up a few days." Evan glanced over at Gavin, who was sitting on the edge of the tub, his toothbrush suspended in midair. He had a far-off look in his eyes, and didn't hear a word Evan said.

"Earth to Gav. Where'd you go?" Evan waved his hand in front of Gavin's eyes, and when that didn't get his attention, he shoved him into the tub.

"What gives?!" Gavin pulled himself back up and glared at his brother.

"I was talking to you, and you were zoning out."

"Oh. Well, you didn't have to push me. My butt's going to be black and blue."

"It'll match the bruises on your knees from all your falls today. That was a YouTube-worthy wipeout on our last run."

Gavin had to laugh, even though the injuries from his colossal wipeout still smarted. He'd really thought he had the whole boarding thing down pat. He'd gotten too cocky and fallen while waving to a bunch of pretty girls going up the lift. He wasn't sure if his body or his ego was more bruised.

"Dad did warn you that your Casanova moves would get you into trouble."

"But did you see them? There were so many of them, and they were all smiling at me."

Evan rolled his eyes. "Okay. But what put the battle-ready look on your face a minute ago?" Evan asked.

"I was thinking about the buried gold Donkey told us about. I think we should try to find it." Gavin got up painfully and made his way to the sink. He started to brush his teeth, but he never took his eyes off his brother.

"We've been down this road a million times. Donkey doesn't know where it is. Don't you think Meggie and I haven't already thought about this? Gavin, he said it was buried under a big willow tree on some beach somewhere on the island. Where would we even begin?"

"I've been thinking about that. I say we start by checking out his story. Barry and Donkey said this dude was hardcore. He ripped off hundreds, maybe thousands of dollars. Let's start by checking out if this Brother Twelve was even real. If he was, maybe we can find out more about where he lived and where he might have buried the gold. For all we know, it's already been found." Gavin projected a ghastly spit. He wiped his face and looked at Evan for comment.

"Not a bad idea. If this guy was such a creep, then someone other than a pig and our mule must know about him." Evan scratched his chin. "Gav, I think it's time we learned how the transit system works."

"It's called a bus pass. Seriously? You've never been on a bus before?" Meagan looked from one boy to the other in complete amazement.

"No." Evan looked embarrassed, but he really didn't know what the big deal was.

"Talk about spoiled. Your parents act as chauffeur, chef and nursemaid."

"Hey! That's not true. What's a nursemaid?" Evan asked. "Gavin, stop fiddling with Meagan's Rubik's Cube." He looked Meagan square in the eyes. "Besides, it's not our fault if our parents won't let us walk two miles to wait in the middle of nowhere for some bus that comes every four hours."

"For Pete's sake. The pass lets you get on and off the bus anywhere in town. The bus comes out to Cedar four or five times a day. We just need the schedule, and then we can arrange to be at the bus stop just before it arrives. I know the library is on the route because I took it with my grandma once."

"Okay, so we just have to figure out how to get to the stop, when to get off, and then when and how to get back, right?" Evan looked like he was planning a trip to the moon. He had taken out a piece of paper and pen to take notes, but so far he had only scribbled a few lines.

"Yes, genius. Look, I won't let you get lost. You just do the talking when we get to the library, and I'll make sure we get there in one piece. Deal?"

"Deal," Evan and Gavin said in unison.

Evan felt better about the prospect now. But convincing their parents that they should be allowed to go to the library on their own was another matter.

"First off," said MJ, "you're wrong. The roads are not clear of snow yet, especially the back roads. Even if I dropped you off at the stop, I'm not sure how I feel about you kids travelling alone."

It was clear to Evan that asking to ride their bikes into Cedar to meet up with the number 44A bus had been a bad idea.

"But Ma, we'll be going with Coolio and Meggie. Meggie has done the trip a million times before with her grandma," he said, crossing his fingers behind his back. "Fine," he sighed, like he was making a compromise. "You can drop us off at 10:24 a.m. at the top of Gould Avenue, and we'll take the 44A downtown to the Front Street stop beside the theatre. Then we'll walk up the block to the library." Evan tried to keep his voice steady and casual. Instinct told him if he sounded too anxious, his mom would never agree to the trip. "We'll call you the minute we get there. Remember, Meggie got a cell phone this Christmas. We'll be just fine. And besides"—Evan looked at his mom with a stubborn lift in his chin—"didn't you tell us stories about how you and your friends took the bus everywhere in Toronto? *On your own?*"

Evan knew the moment his mom started to cave.

Her nose scrunched up, but after an eternity, she said, "Fine."

The moms had a three-way call to discuss the big outing. Rules were agreed to, and backpacks were filled with unnecessary supplies.

"Mom! We're not going for a week. I don't need a change of socks, seven granola bars, five bottles of water and my puffer. Come on. I need a pen and paper. That's it. I'm leaving this stuff in the truck." The look MJ shot him over the seat said, *Wanna bet?* So when the kids got out at the stop, he handed the bag to Gavin.

"Hey! Why do I get stuck with this? It's heavy!"

"'Cause I'm the brains of the outfit, and you need a job."

Before Gavin could retaliate, the number 44A rounded the corner of Gould Avenue and came to a loud halt in front of the kids. MJ yelled instructions from the front seat of her truck and waved goodbye.

Meagan took the lead and went up the stairs first. The boys watched her drop a ticket into the glass box, say good morning to the driver, and walk to the back of the bus. Coolio followed suit, tipping his hat to the burly old man behind the wheel. When Gavin got on, he asked a million questions. He wanted to know about the bike rack at the front of the bus. How did the bikes stay secure? What kind of mileage did the bus get? How long had the driver been working his route?

Evan grew impatient, but the driver enjoyed all the questions and took great pains to explain every detail of the inner workings of his vehicle.

"Sorry about my little brother. He doesn't know you have a tight schedule to keep. If you could just call out the Front Street stop, we would appreciate it. We'll go and sit down now."

"Sure thing, kid."

Evan bumped Gavin along, hissing at him to stop staring at the few other riders on the bus. From what Evan could tell, they were a mixture of students and old people.

"I did some research last night online," Meagan remarked. "This Brother Twelve was really a character. It looks like there are a lot of books about him. It shouldn't be too difficult to find something at the library." She had flipped open her little notebook and was scanning her scribbles. "He was originally from England, moved to Victoria, and at some point around the mid-1920s, he decided he was a mystic. Donkey was right about a few things. Brother Twelve did call his place the Aquarian Foundation. He built it close to where we live, and he ripped off a lot of super wealthy people."

Gavin's eyes lit up. "So if he was right about that, then he must be right about the gold. It's out there. I know it! We just have to find it."

Coolio, who had said very little up until this point, finally seemed to take some real interest in the direction of the conversation. "So, assuming this all turns out to be true, and assuming we somehow manage to find the hidden gold, will we be allowed to keep it?"

"What do you mean?"

"Think about it. Won't some historical preservation group want to get their hands on it? Or relatives of the dead people who were ripped off? Why would anyone let four kids keep it? Just think of the—what's that word you always use, Meggie?—the *unjustness* of it. We go to all the trouble of finding it, and then someone just strolls in and takes it from us! I think we'll have to keep this a secret. We tell no one." He eyed up each kid. "Let's make a pact. Deal?" He put his arm out with his hand facing down.

"Deal." Evan placed his on top.

"Deal." Meagan followed suit.

"Double deal. No one's taking my gold!" Gavin slapped his hand down hard.

After what seemed like a lifetime, the driver called out, "Front Street. Everyone for Front Street, here's your stop."

All day, the thick clouds had made the sky grey and dark. But just as the children stepped down from the bus, the sun broke through and shot rays of light across Nanaimo Bay. The harbour lay beneath them, and the sounds of the boats rocking against the docks filled the otherwise quiet morning. The night's rain had washed away most of the remaining snow. Left behind was the mud and debris that had fallen in the high winds. At the other end of the harbour, the kids could see a clean-up crew sweeping the sidewalks and removing the larger branches still blocking the paths down to the docks.

Meagan led the way to the building. When she arrived at the front door, she pulled out her cell phone and handed it to Evan. Per MJ's instructions, Evan called his mom precisely at the moment they were going into the library. After a brief description of their first bus ride, Evan reminded his mom to call Claire and Isobel.

They all nodded at each other and went in. Years of training on the dos and don'ts in a library kicked in. Each kid dropped their voice to a whisper, and they went straight to the bank of computers in the centre of the room.

"Use the keywords *Brother Twelve* or *fanatical religious leader on Vancouver Island* or something like that." Meagan could type faster than the boys, and she was already writing things down in her notebook. When they heard Gavin giggle, they looked up from their screens to see what was up.

Gavin stopped laughing and looked sheepish. "I was just checking out Simon's posts. He's hilarious. Look what he added this week." Gavin took one look at their faces and said, "Never mind." He went back to searching book titles.

It was Meagan who first noticed a white-haired lady politely standing behind them. She wore no-nonsense shoes, a plaid skirt topped off with a white blouse, and a green quilted vest. Her glasses were perched low on her nose, and tucked behind her left ear was a gold pen. Her eyes were sparkling blue, and her skin was powdery white. She looked ancient.

"Sorry, are we using all the computers? Would you like to use one?" Meagan started to collect her belongings to make room for the elderly lady.

"Oh no, my dear, you are quite fine there. My name is Mrs. Coppy. I'm a volunteer here. Is there anything I can help you with? If there is something specific you are trying to find, I might be able to make your search easier."

"Are you related to Tina and Ginger Coppy?" Meagan looked more closely at the lady, trying to figure out if she had ever seen her at her friend's house.

"I am indeed. I'm their great-grandmother on their father's side. I take it you're from Cedar? Do you go to school with them?"

"Yeah, we've known them since Grade 1," Coolio said. "I used to pull Ginger's hair and tie her laces together on the bus. You'll be happy to know I've outgrown all that now. Hi, I'm Luke, and these are my friends Evan, Meagan and Gavin." Coolio smiled sweetly at Mrs. Coppy and was rewarded with a huge grin from the old lady.

"I am glad to make your acquaintance. What brings you into the library over the Christmas holidays? Are you working on a school assignment?"

The kids exchanged quick looks. "Yeah, something like that. We're researching a guy called Brother Twelve. We got back some hits on the computer, and we were just going to start looking for the books."

"Yes, indeed. I know all about him. I was just a girl when the Aquarians made the news almost every day. I grew up on the farm at the top of Cedar-by-the-Sea, and no television show today can come close to the intrigue and mystery of what took place down there."

Mrs. Coppy's voice was creaky and wispy. Her eyes were blazing, but her weak voice and bent posture made it clear she was very old.

"May I ask how old you are, Mrs. Coppy?" Meagan asked reluctantly. It wasn't something one normally asked when meeting someone for the first time. But if Mrs. Coppy had first-hand knowledge of Brother Twelve, Meagan thought they might really have a shot at finding out some important facts today.

"I am very pleased to tell you that I am ninety years old come next Wednesday."

"No way!" Gavin yelled. The others hushed him, and he said sorry to no one in particular. "Wow! Ninety years old. My house isn't even that old. The trees might be, but not the house. Jeez, you're old."

Evan just glared at Gavin and gave him the universal sign to button it.

But Mrs. Coppy laughed. "Old and rickety, but thankfully I still have pretty good eyesight. Before I retired, I was a teacher librarian. I volunteer here a few days a week. It gets me out of my apartment. An old girl can only watch so many sailboats out the window before she goes loopy, if you know what I mean."

Gavin loved her instantly. He grabbed the backpack and then slipped his arm through hers. "Where to, Mrs. Coppy, to learn all about this crazy guy?"

Mrs. Coppy spent the morning pulling off the shelf every book that mentioned Brother Twelve, Madame Z, the Aquarian Foundation or even some of the wealthy members who lost hundreds of thousands of dollars to the Brother. She set them up at a table at the back of the library, and every so often she dropped another book on their pile.

"Now, children, it turns out the most detailed book is upstairs in the *restricted* area. You will be able to read it, but you won't be able to take it out of the locked room. Let me know when you are ready to head up there, and I will personally escort you in. I'm off to have my tea break now, but I will come find you in around twenty minutes."

When she was out of earshot, Meagan leaned over and

whispered, "How lucky are we to have Mrs. Coppy to help us out? She even volunteered to show us where her old farm was and where the foundation used to be. She doesn't drive anymore, but maybe we can get Tina and Ginger to help us out without letting them know what we're up to. I'll need to think about that one."

"Did you see the picture of her from the sixties?" Evan searched the table for a book. "Here it is. Around fifty years ago, a bunch of old ladies got together and created a book all about how Nanaimo got started. There are pictures that date back to the turn of the century. There are tons of pictures of the miners and the first schoolhouses. And see here." Evan scanned a black-and-white photo and then pointed to a tall lady standing in the back row. "There she is."

"I love her winged glasses. Look at that hairdo! Is that an ostrich feather in her hat?" Coolio leaned back in his chair and flexed his arms over his head. "My fingers are cramped from all the notes I've taken, and I'm hungry."

"No fear, my friend. Thanks to our mom, we have come prepared." After inhaling the granola bars and sipping some water, they turned their attention back to their notes.

"There's lots of talk of the money and gold he took, but it doesn't say where he might have buried it," Meagan murmured. "Some of the writers even think he took it with him. I think it's strange that Brother Twelve and Madame Z were never found. Could they have gotten all the way to Europe without being noticed?" Meagan scanned her sheets and drew an arrow between two entries.

"The gold never left the island," said Coolio. "We know that for sure because Donkey told you that. He is the only creature on earth that knows where it is, and we're going to find it."

Evan tried to hide the surprise on his face. Coolio had spoken the words without a shred of doubt. His complete turnaround about the Shimmies intrigued Evan. But he reminded himself not to dwell too long on it. They needed Coolio, and as long as he believed without seeing or hearing their animal friends, that was fine by Evan.

They were huddled around a picture of Brother Twelve and some of his followers when a familiar voice sent a chill up their spines.

"Well. Look who we have here." Ruth Cissy Blackhorne came out of nowhere and stood looking down at them. Behind her were a few girls the kids didn't know. Before anyone could react, she grabbed one of the books off the table and started to read the cover.

"*The Teachings of Brother Twelve*." Ruth flipped the book over and looked at the back. "A mystic or seaman—"

Before she could say another word, Coolio grabbed the book with lightning speed. "Piss off, Ruth! Did you get lost on the way to the wharf? I hear they're looking for some fish bait. Do us all a favour and be sure to fall overboard."

Ruth only laughed. "Down, boy! Did you miss your feeding time, Lukas? It's so not *like* you to ditch your *cool* exterior." She waved her hands at all the books. "Not going religious on us, are you?"

Meagan tried to gather up the books nonchalantly, laying her backpack over the evidence. Gavin and Evan had stood up and were moving toward Ruth menacingly. Ruth just laughed harder, and her friends joined in.

Shushing sounds came from behind some of the bookshelves. Clearly they had attracted the attention of the other library patrons.

"Go *shhh* yourself," Ruth yelled back at them.

Mrs. Coppy came barrelling in at an unexpected speed for a ninety-year-old woman.

"Ruth Cissy Blackhorne!"

The laughter stopped abruptly.

"You and your cousins have made enough of a disturbance. I am tired of the nuisance you always cause. I will not tolerate this." Mrs. Coppy's voice was strained, and her face was beet red.

"Your grandmother is waiting for you at the front door. If you do this one more time, we will have no choice but to ban you from the library."

Ruth muttered, "Like I care," but at least she was moving away from Coolio and the group.

"I'll be back to deal with you four in a minute." With that, Mrs. Coppy trailed behind the girls to make sure they made it to the exit.

"I haven't forgotten that I still owe that witch," Evan fumed. "Even though my Sounders shirt is clean, I can't bring myself to wear it. I owe her, and one of these days, I'm going to give her a dose of her own medicine." Evan glared at Ruth's back and ordered himself to calm down.

"Quick! Hide the evidence." Meagan started to grab the empty water bottles and granola bar wrappers. She had just stuffed them into her backpack when the old librarian returned.

Gavin was ready to jump to his team's defence when Mrs. Coppy raised her hand to silence him. "No need, Gavin. I know only too well what happened here. Ruth is no stranger to me. I have known her family for years. All in all they are a nice, decent family. But that one." Mrs. Coppy rolled her eyes to heaven. "Let's just say I've had my fill of stories about her from my great-granddaughters. When the twins were smaller, they used to come home with tales of abuse at the hands of Ruth. Since I don't hear those stories anymore, I presume the talk my grandson had with her parents worked."

The kids exchanged looks. It seemed Tina and Ginger had not kept their dad updated on Ruth's unrelenting bullying. Or maybe they were, and Mr. Coppy simply wanted to save his ninety-year-old grandmother the worry.

"It's a shame, too. Mrs. Blackhorne is such a lovely lady. She volunteers here a couple of days a week. She is blind to the behaviour of her granddaughters. Vipers! Each and every one of them. Too spoiled, I warrant."

They all nodded their heads in agreement. It was rare to hear an adult be so honest about a child.

"Back to business. Let's take the books you want up to the counter and get them checked out for you. I'll then take you upstairs to the restricted area."

The kids had never been on the second level of the Nanaimo library. Mrs. Coppy led them to the elevator and pushed the button to close the doors. When the doors opened, the children were a bit disappointed with how dull it looked. Shelves contained reference materials, and off to one side was a small room simply labelled *Restricted*.

"Mrs. Coppy, are the books in there really bad?" Gavin wondered if the library had a system like movie ratings: restricted, eighteen years or older, mature content.

"Oh no, my dear. The books stored in the restricted area are rare, or we only have one copy. The bulk of them contain historical facts and information on British Columbia. We have maps, first editions, and out-of-print material. If we can't replace it, it winds up in there."

She went off to talk to the serious-looking man who manned the counter upstairs. They quietly exchanged words, and after a few minutes, he handed a set of keys to Mrs. Coppy. She opened the door and led them in.

"You'll find information on Brother Twelve in this section, and you might as well browse through these books on Vancouver Island because they might contain additional information. There is no need for me to stay with you, but remember: you cannot take the books out. If you want a photocopy of anything, Mr. Cherry will give you a hand. I'll come back and check on you shortly."

Meagan sat on the floor and started to pull books off the lower shelf. She sat there for a long time, flipping through the pages of a big book. By now the boys were getting fidgety and just wanted to leave.

"Don't we have enough information, Meagan? I'm hungry again, and I want to go home." Gavin barely kept the whine from his voice.

"Me too. I can't read one more thing about this guy and his whip-wielding lady." Evan laid his head down on the table and started to blow bubbles.

"My mom gave me ten bucks. We can stop at the hot dog cart by the bus stop and grab a dog." Coolio fished the money out of his jeans and counted out the bills.

"Found it!" Meagan leapt up and ran to the boys. She laid the book down and smoothed out some pages. "Look at this map. It shows where Brother Twelve owned all his properties and which islands he had buildings on. It even shows you how to get there by boat. But look at this! Here's a picture of Brother Twelve—under a huge weeping willow!"

"You're kidding." Evan turned the book around to read the caption. "'Taken approximately one year before he vanished, it is believed that this photo was shot by one of his many followers while the Brother conducted one of his sermons.' Too bad it doesn't say which island it was taken on. But at least we know what the tree looks like now. Look at that crazy knot in the trunk. It looks like an old man's face—with hair growing out of its ears!" Evan turned the book around to show Coolio and Gavin. Sure enough, halfway up the trunk was a knot shaped like a wizened old man's face. It looked like it was grinning madly, while two oversized ears grew out of the side of the tree.

"Is that moss or leaves growing out of the ears?" Meagan had her nose within inches of the book.

"It looks creepy to me. But that knot ought to help us identify it more easily. I'm no tree expert, but there can't be too many trees that look like that." Coolio looked disgusted.

"Geez, guys! Look at the time. We gotta go. The one-forty-five bus will be arriving soon. Let's come back another day, and we can read through this book more thoroughly. I think it's the most comprehensive one we found, and it provides more accurate facts than all the other books combined." Meagan put the book back on the shelf and gathered up her belongings.

Mr. Cherry looked less than impressed when they burst through the door and took the stairs two at a time. Evan noticed that he went into the restricted area—probably to look for missing books. Mrs. Coppy was behind the main counter downstairs, busy sorting out returned books.

"Thanks for all your help today. We really appreciate it." Evan genuinely meant it. Their day had gone much easier with her help.

"You're the best, Mrs. C! I hope you'll be here when we come back in a few days."

The retired librarian looked quite smitten with the boy and

grinned from ear to ear. "You're a charmer, Mr. Edmund. I too hope I'm on duty when you next visit. I'm here every Tuesday and Thursday from 10:00 a.m. to 2:00 p.m. I then have to go home for my afternoon siesta."

They ran out the door and headed for the bus stop. Meagan pulled out her phone and hit redial. When she handed it to Evan, Gavin grabbed it midair.

"Hi, Mom. Yeah, it was great." Slight pause. "No, seriously, really enlightening. I want to come back on Thursday." Longer pause. "Okay, great! See you soon. Love you!" He handed the phone back to Meagan. "We're good for Thursday. She was convinced we'd only last twenty minutes." He rolled his eyes. "Parents."

Over the next week, they went back to the library two more times. Each time, they had the same bus driver. Walter—they were on a first-name basis by now—thought Gavin's questions were funny, and he looked out for the Cedar crew every day.

"Why do you kids need to go to the library so much?"

Evan explained that they were doing research on the early days of Nanaimo, and Walter offered some interesting stories about his ancestors, who were coal miner settlers. "They came all the way from Scotland in 1871. My great-great-grandfather was an explosives expert. Rumour had it he only had four fingers left by the time he died at the ripe old age of 83. Back in those days, that was pretty old! He was never one to talk about the mining days. He lost too many good friends in one accident or another. It was my great-great-grandmother who wrote detailed accounts of their life in Canada, and between her journal and letters to the family in Scotland, my father was able to piece together what life was like for them."

Gavin was intrigued by his new friend. "Why didn't he just ask his dad? He could have told him stories, I bet."

"Nope, he died during World War I. He was only thirty years old. Two months after he was killed, the war was declared over. My father was only a few months old, so he never knew him."

"Man, that is really sad."

"Sure was. My grandmother raised my father on her own and never remarried. Tough old bird, that one. She used to scare the bejeebers out of me. But I'm lucky. Old age is in my genes. She lived to almost one hundred!"

Gavin sat behind Walter most of the way to and from the library and liked telling him stories about school.

"Hope to see you soon!" Walter always called to the kids as he pulled away from the curb.

On their second visit back, Mrs. Coppy was off with a "dodgy" stomach, but the next time, she greeted them at the door.

Meagan took copious notes from the big book in the restricted area. She even managed to copy the map that detailed each island where the buildings, farmland and original docks had been situated. On the first day back at school, the kids were exhausted from so much reading and writing. They welcomed their math and phys ed classes.

By the end of January, they were back into a routine of school, soccer and homework. Coolio's hockey schedule was unrelenting, and between games, practices and extra endurance training, he was hardly ever around. Meagan picked up a babysitting job three nights a week, and between that and her guitar lessons, the boys only saw her at school. A whole month went by, and little progress was made to find the gold. They were disheartened, and worried they might never find it.

By now the winter had settled back to its pattern of rainy days and cold evenings. On odd days, the sun made an appearance but, typical to most island winters, it never stayed around for very long. No one expected "hoodie-only" weather until at least mid-February. The routine—a Shimmy greeting on their walk to the school bus, a brief afterschool visit to recap the day and quick glimpses during the weekend—was also leaving Evan, Gavin and Meagan lonely for their Shimmy friends.

⸺

"Let me get this straight. Coolio, you have no hockey tonight?"

"Nope."

"And Meagan, you don't have to babysit or... restring something?"

"That's what I said."

Evan scratched his head and dumped his pack on his seat. He watched the last of the kids climb onto the bus and find their seats. "So you mean to say that for the first time in, like, *forever*, we can actually hang out together?"

"It's a Friday night and our term tests are over," he said out of the side of his mouth. His eyes were on Ruth. She was shooting spitballs through a straw and had managed to plaster wads onto the backs of almost every kid in front of her. He was determined to ruin her fun. "Mom and Dad are bound to say yes to a sleepover. Watch this." Evan leaned forward and suddenly grabbed the straw out of Ruth's hands. Before she could stop him, he ran to the front of the bus and spun around to face the kids.

"Ruth covered all of your backs in spit wads!" He raised the straw into the air, showing the evidence to the victims. The disgust on their faces and the chaos that followed pleased Evan.

"Take your gobbed-up jackets, backpacks and baseball caps to Earl and scream, 'We're not going to take it anymore!'" He was rewarded with hysterical screams from the girls, fist pumping from the big boys and a steely determination for revenge from everyone else.

Earl was standing on the sidewalk, talking to Mr. Lanzilotta about the Canucks schedule, when two-thirds of his passengers pounded out of the bus and surrounded them. Their cries of frustration and demands for justice could be heard throughout Cedar.

Evan sauntered back to his seat, and as he passed a stunned Ruth, he flicked the straw back into her lap.

"Let's see how you get out of this one, Ruth." Evan grinned and sat down beside his brother. "Like I was saying, I'm sure Mom and Dad will say yes to a sleepover. I've been thinking for a while that we really need to go back and talk to Donkey. If he won't come to us, then we'll have to go to him."

Gavin laughed out loud when Mr. Lanzilotta stuck his head in the door and bellowed for Ruth to get off the bus immediately. The look of murder on her face did nothing to diminish the feeling of triumph.

"She's going to make you pay for that, Evan," Meagan said, very concerned. She opened the window to better hear Mr. Lanzilotta tear a strip off Ruth. Threats of expulsion and being banned from the bus for life did nothing to remove the look of sheer hatred from Ruth's face. There was no doubt she would be furious the minute she was out of detention.

"Forget her." Evan dismissed her with his hand.

"Do you guys think your parents will say yes to a sleepover—and can you bring your bikes?" Evan was intent on firming up the plans. "We could ride to the Boar's Moor Pub and back before anyone misses us. We really need to talk to Donkey again. Why he won't leave that blasted pasture beside the pub is beyond me."

Most of the Shimmies came when called by name. Even Barry Schmelling had come once when Gavin was desperate to talk to Donkey. But no amount of pleading could get his friend to leave the pub. "That's his home, and he doesn't like to go anywhere anymore," Barry explained. He had a habit of being cute and annoying at the same time.

"Sure. I'm overdue for some R and R. Give me an hour to finish my homework and work on my mother. I'll bring my Xbox controller and a bag of Hot Tamales." Coolio leaned out the window and yelled to alert Simon that he still had a wad stuck in the back of his hair. "The weather is really good for late January. If I bring marshmallows, will your dad build a bonfire tonight?" Coolio was in high spirits from all the commotion outside and the prospect of hanging out with this friends.

"Probably." Evan looked out the window and noticed Earl waving the kids back onto the bus. Mrs. Rosaline had appeared out of nowhere. She was no taller than Ruth, but her body language suggested she was ten times bigger. When she led Ruth away from the bus and back into school, students broke out into a cheer.

"Yup, you're gonna pay, Evan. Let's just hope she's in detention long enough for you to graduate from middle school with your head still in one piece." Coolio settled back into his seat.

As expected, MJ said yes to a sleepover. The boys walked down to Meagan's house and waited while she packed her overnight bag. Claire called twice to remind her to pack clean pajamas and bring MJ a jar of peaches from the pantry. Meagan locked up and told Dakota, through the front door, to "guard the house." As they walked down the driveway, Spotty, Abigail and Carolynn joined them.

"Are you gonna go to the pub, Evan? Can I come, can I come?" Spotty bounced from hoof to hoof. He looked between his mother and his human pal in anticipation.

"Hubert, you should always wait to be invited before inviting yourself. That isn't becoming of a young fawn." Spotty shrugged and looked past the doe to Meagan.

"Can I? Can I come? *Please*, Meagan?"

Abigail humphed.

"Sure you can," Meagan said. "You can all come. Carolynn, we found out some really interesting things about Brother Twelve. We are convinced that Donkey was telling the truth, and that the gold is still hidden. But no matter how many times we read through our notes, we can't figure out where to start looking. We have to talk to Donkey again. Maybe he will have some clues for us."

Carolynn flew slowly beside them and turned her spotted neck to look at the children. "He is expecting your visit. He is ready to tell you all he knows. But he fears that he will not be much help to you. He said he has already told you what he can remember." She let the wind lift her higher into the air and then drifted back to glide quietly beside them.

Coolio sped up the road and at the very last moment came to a skidding halt in front of them.

"How did you finish your homework so fast?" Evan had been prepared not to see his friend for at least an hour. Lanzilotta seldom let his class off the hook without at least forty-five minutes of homework every night.

"He gave us a codebreaker. They're usually really hard, but this time I figured it out in fifteen minutes. The theme was hockey. I mean, come on. How hard could that be for me?"

"Let's ride as fast as we can. My mom thinks we're hanging out at Meagan's until dinner. That will give us enough time to get to the Boar's Moor, talk to Donkey and ride back before we're missed."

When the kids got to the lane leading down to the pub, they cut through the woods so as not to be seen. The last thing they wanted was to get caught sneaking onto the grounds. They found all the Shimmies at the edge of the pond near the carved-out cedar bench. Donkey was busy chewing grass, much like he was the night they met him. Evan, Gavin and Meagan greeted all the Shimmies, and many different conversations were going on at once. It was Meagan who noticed that Coolio stood off to one side, staring at them. She suddenly realized that this was the first time he'd been in the presence of the Shimmies since the Christmas break.

"You okay?" Meagan tried to sound casual, but her voice was high-pitched.

"Yeah. I just wish I could see them and hear them the way you guys do." Coolio looked nervous. "Meagan, is he here?"

Her heart ached for him. She knew exactly what he was asking.

"He's at your feet, looking up at you."

Coolio looked down to his right side and said shyly, "Hi, Razor."

Meagan gently turned Coolio's shoulders so he was looking more to the left. The wolfhound took his head off his paws and sat straight up.

"Here I am! Here I am, Luke. Can you see me?" Razor peered up lovingly at his friend. For a moment it seemed to the dog that the familiar green eyes rested on his face, and that there was a second of connection.

"Tell him I like his new bike. What happened to his Mongoose BMX?"

Meagan translated, and Coolio grinned from ear to ear. "I outgrew it. Dad got me a Rocky Mountain Edge, dual suspension, aluminum tubing, front and rear discs... It brakes on a dime. Yeah, it's cool."

Evan looked over to where Coolio stood, and he could see

Razor was using Meagan to communicate. He wanted desperately to join them, but he knew they didn't have much time to find out what they came for.

"Donkey, we need your help to narrow down where that big weeping willow is. Let's recap what you told us that night." Evan pulled a notepad from his backpack and scanned it. "You said that once you were loaded up with the boxes, Brother Twelve and Madame Z sailed west. How did you know you were sailing west?"

"To the east was the mainland, and the crossing would have taken hours. You could see the grand mountains to the northeast, and that night we did not go in that direction."

By now Meagan and Coolio had joined them. In a whisper, Meagan relayed Donkey's words to Coolio.

"Okay, so we know which direction you took. Now look here at this map. There are three islands in front of Valdes Island: DeCourcy, Ruxton and Pylades. According to our research, Brother Twelve owned property here on Vancouver Island, just a few miles from the pub at Cedar-by-the-Sea; on DeCourcy Island; and on Valdes Island." Evan had rolled out the map on the ground and signalled for Donkey to join him.

"Everything you described was confirmed in many books we found. Brother Twelve and Madame Z went berserk and destroyed the colony on Valdes Island. Chances are, they sailed to DeCourcy Island and hid the gold there. Apparently many people have looked for it, but no one has found it. Does that make sense?"

Donkey looked down at the map and then at Evan.

"Nope."

"What do you mean… nope?"

"That doesn't make sense."

Meagan had been translating, but now she looked directly at Donkey. "Why?"

"'Cause if we only went to DeCourcy Island, that would have been a fifteen-minute tugboat ride. I was standing, crushed under those boxes, for at least forty minutes. We sailed through two islands and kept a straight line until we beached the boat."

Evan told Coolio what Donkey said. Coolio knelt down beside Evan and looked at the map.

"Gav, pass me that stick over there." He took the bare willow branch Gavin handed him and laid it on the map. "If what Donkey says is true, then he left Valdes Island, sailed through the channel between DeCourcy Island and Ruxton Island, and came ashore here."

"Holy cow!" Evan gasped. "They came ashore on Pebble Beach. Our Pebble Beach!"

Gavin looked wildly from face to face. He looked up to Mr. Biggsy, who stood close behind them and passed a knowing look to his wife.

"That would explain how Donkey came to live here," said Mr. Biggsy. "Didn't you say that once the Brother and his mistress disappeared, you roamed the land until you were found by a human and brought here?"

"Yup."

"Did you ever leave the land to travel by sea again?"

"Nope."

"There you have it. Donkey was on Vancouver Island when the gold was buried."

The children took turns keeping Coolio up to speed. Evan sat back on his bottom and contemplated what he'd just heard.

"We didn't expect that, did we?" Gavin said with a relieved grin. "No wonder no one ever found it. They've been looking in the wrong place. Well, at least that takes care of one of our problems. We couldn't figure out how we were going to get to DeCourcy Island. We're still too young to steal Dad's boat."

Evan laughed at that. It was one of the crazier ideas his brother had come up with.

"But if what you're saying is true, it would mean there is a huge weeping willow tree with ears near the beach," Meagan said. "And I gotta tell you, I grew up here, and I have never seen a tree like that in these parts." Her arms were crossed over her chest due to the cold. The sun sat to the west, and its rays filtered through the trees around the pond. It was a pretty day but still cool.

Razor and Rad-knows-ways suddenly bolted straight up and sniffed the air.

"Someone's coming." Rad-knows-ways balanced on his hind legs and peered intently into the brush that separated the pond from the pub.

Before the children could hide their bikes and dive behind some bushes, old Davey Golding, led by his guide dog, Taffy, emerged from behind the blackberry bushes.

"Who's there?" Davey didn't look particularly concerned, but he did stop walking, and Taffy sat obediently at his feet.

The kids were unsure what to do. They knew Davey couldn't see them, but it didn't feel right to deceive him. Just as Meagan was about to step out and announce herself, Duke Mortimer suddenly waddled up onto the pond's edge and greeted the old man.

"Good day, Mr. Golding. Fine weather we are having, wouldn't you say?" The duck looked quite spectacular. His burgundy chest was puffed out, and his eyes shone brightly.

"Ah, Duke. It's you. I wondered who was there." Davey let Taffy guide him to the cedar bench, where he settled himself down. He propped his white cane against the bench and pulled a Thermos from his peacoat. "The weather is fine indeed. As welcoming as the pub is, I had to slip out and come for a little walk. The Cinder Boys Band are huddled around their chessboards, and the smell of their brains working overtime had me making a speedy exit."

Duke cackled with laughter.

"Care to join me in a spot of tea?"

"Thank you, but no. I am busy eating some pondweed."

Davey let out a chuckle. "I know what you mean only too well. My daughter's idea of a healthy diet for me includes alfalfa sprouts, kidney beans and chickpeas, all tossed in a salad. If the taste doesn't kill me, the salmonella will!" Davey pulled out a bag filled with cookies. "She has me rationed to two biscuits a day. Not sure what she's afraid of. I can assure you that at my age, it won't be the sugar that will end my time here." He dipped his oatmeal raison cookie into his tea. "What new project are you working on today?"

"I'm gathering the partially submerged timber and wood debris and adding it to the winter cover I built."

"That sounds ambitions. Did you fly south like you said? I hear the short-term leases around San Diego are going cheap."

Duke Mortimer looked over at the Shimmies, who stood quietly on the opposite side of the pond, and acknowledged them for the first time. When he looked at the children, his expression was smug and superior. "No. I decided to stick around and see what interesting new developments might occur. Some characters have moved into the area." The duck looked suspiciously at the Shimmies and the children.

"I heard about that family from north island. Are they troublemakers? Mr. Douglas, the high school principal, said the three boys are as big as WWF wrestlers. He's not sure if he should be overjoyed and recruit them for his football team, or if he will be doing double-duty this term as an enforcer. Time will tell, I guess."

Davey and Duke Mortimer spoke of the proposed new housing development out near the marina, and neither of them had much good to say about it. Duke quacked on endlessly about man encroaching on the wetland areas and the negative impact it was having on its inhabitants. Davey agreed and suggested that local government were more interested in protecting their tax base than the environment. The children grew bored, listening to them drone on. Especially Coolio, who only heard one side of the conversation.

"Well, Duke. I must be off. If I'm gone too long, that little waitress Bridget will come looking for me. She watches me like a hawk. If I step one foot out of line, she tells my daughter." He got up slowly and rubbed the small of his back. He waved his hand high in the air and carefully wound his way through the path.

"Cheerio!" Duke yelled after him. Once he was sure Davey was out of earshot, he addressed the stunned audience. "See. I told you I spoke to humans. Well, at least one human. He is a fine, upstanding man, even if his singing upsets my delicate ears. I really must tell him to stop that."

Evan pushed his bike around to the spot where Duke stood preening his feathers.

"Wouldn't have believed it unless I saw it with my own two eyes. Davey really thinks you're a person. Not a duck."

"You'd think he would clue in. Mortimer, you stink." Gavin stayed on the other side of the pond and mounted his bike. "You have that duck smell. I can smell you from behind the bushes. How *can* a dead duck smell, anyway?"

"I *choose* to." With that, Duke splashed loudly into the pond and swam away.

Coolio checked his watch. "We gotta ride hard. Your mom's going to be home soon, Meagan, and we had better be back at Evan's place by then." They rode fast and cut across the broken cornfield beside the pub grounds. They pulled into the Edmunds' driveway and took a few minutes to catch their breath.

"Why can Davey hear the Shimmies, but I can't?" Coolio looked at Meagan, who turned and looked at the Shimmies perched around the back of the pickup truck.

"Carolynn, Madeline… do you have any ideas?"

It was Mrs. Biggsy who stepped forward with a theory. "Mr. Golding may have developed heightened senses because of his blindness. We have heard of other humans from time to time who could either see us or hear us, but none like you, who can do both."

Coolio frowned once Evan translated for him.

"Well, poking my eyes out isn't an option, so what else can we do to help me see you guys?" He looked all around, trusting his Shimmy friends were close by.

"I truly do wish you had the gift. I like you, Coolio. Some one-on-one time with me would greatly improve your puck handling and slapshot skills. There is a lot this boy could learn from me." Mr. Biggsy looked at Evan and demanded that he tell Coolio what he'd said, word for word.

When Evan did, Coolio laughed and simply said, "No doubt."

Carolynn could only repeat what she had said many times before. "It is possible a strong emotion like fear or sadness allows one to sense us." She shrugged her broad wings. "Or perhaps a human is born with the gift. We may never know."

The night was spent wolfing down ribs and wings and watching

Harry Potter and the Half-Blood Prince. By the time Meagan fell into bed in the guest room, she was too tired to think about treasure hunting. She left the boys to talk about hidden gold, sea captains turned mystic leaders, and talking animals. She nestled under the covers and was asleep within minutes.

Coolio's mind was restless, and he was too agitated to sleep. "Meggie's right. I have combed the beach for years, and there is no weeping willow. Maybe at one time there was, but it could have been struck by lightning and burnt down. We could have walked over the gold a million times and never realized what was beneath our feet."

"Or," Evan said sleepily, "we are way off on our calculations, and the tree is five miles down the coast."

"Only one way to find out." Gavin turned off the lamp beside his bed and puffed up his pillow. "We dig."

With that, he rolled over and fell asleep immediately.

11

FAMILY: FELIDAE. GENUS: PUMA. SPECIES: P. CONCOLOR. NICKNAME: COUGAR!

WHEN THE KIDS WOKE UP, the sun was breaking through the clouds. The first day of February suggested that the winter stretch was over. After putting back a dozen pancakes, they went outside to play a little soccer. They were just wrapping up a two-on-two game when Meagan's screaming broke the tranquility of the morning.

She had gone to retrieve the ball from the creek that ran at the top of the Edmunds' property. A noise from the left caught her attention. It was a large cougar, emerging from behind a holly bush. It was tawny brown with a reddish underbelly. It came out with its round head low to the ground and its ears flat against its skull. The cougar took deliberate steps out into the open.

It was stalking Coolio.

Meagan's heart was pumping so loudly she couldn't even hear her own voice. Her throat had gone dry, but she was trying to form the words "Run! Run!"

Coolio had his back to the powerful cat and was busy bouncing a rock from one shoe to the other. The deadly cat let out a low-pitched hiss and growled deeply as it strained it muscles, ready to pounce. Meagan's scream caught the boys off guard. Evan and Gavin turned just in time to see the cougar leap high in the air—

and Coolio turn and stare open-mouthed at Meagan, who was running wildly toward him.

The instant the cougar leapt through Coolio, the blood-curdling screams of Evan, Gavin and Meagan prompted Coolio to scream just as loud. The children stopped in their tracks. The cat sailed through Coolio, and its shimmering body skidded to a halt five feet away. The only one still screaming was Coolio. His eyes were bulging from his face, and he dropped into a defensive position.

"*What?* Why are you all running at me?" Coolio spun back and forth between his friends. His panting was loud and raspy.

The cougar was now circling him and making no moves to get any closer. It cocked its head from side to side and observed Coolio with deep interest.

"Sorry about that. Abigail thought attacking your friend was a good idea." The cougar was a she, and she suddenly sat down and started to lick her paw.

"Are you kidding me? Abigail thought a cougar *attacking our friend* was a good idea?" Meagan's adrenalin levels were peaking.

Upon hearing the word *cougar*, Coolio spun in circles again. "Where? Where? Where's the cougar?"

Evan reached out and grabbed him. "It's okay. She's a Shimmy. Oh no. Here comes Dad."

Gavin cut off Joe at the pass and explained that they were playing a game. He apologized if they'd freaked out their mom but assured him she could go back to her reading. It took some convincing, but Joe went back into the house.

"Abigail!" Evan yelled her name and was not surprised when she appeared from the same direction the cougar had come from. Within seconds, they were surrounded by the Shimmies. For the first time, they looked nervous. Reddy Bun-Buns and Ever-Ready Freddy hid behind their mother, and Razor's tail was tucked under his belly. Evan had never seen a guiltier-looking bunch in his life.

"Abigail, mind explaining?" But before the doe could speak up, Mr. Biggsy took centre stage.

"No point placing blame on the others. It was my idea to recruit Lisa."

Admittedly, the kids didn't have much experience with mountain cats, but the name *Lisa* simply didn't match the image.

"I thought if we could create a frightening enough situation, we might be able to *scare* Coolio into seeing us. I guess I was wrong."

Meagan explained the Shimmies' failed plan to Coolio. He had come out of his crouching position but still did not look relaxed.

"I thought about our conversation yesterday and figured if anyone could create a powerful reaction, it was Lisa."

The cougar inclined her head sweetly as if she had just been paid a compliment.

"Well, you still should have told us." Evan stared at Lisa and noticed how lovely her golden eyes were.

"You see, that is where you're wrong." Mr. Biggsy appealed to Evan to understand. "Your reaction was critical to Coolio feeling threatened. He had to *believe* his life was in danger."

Meagan quickly filled Coolio in on what the raccoon had said.

"I've never been so scared," Coolio admitted. "So if that didn't do it, nothing will, I guess." After a moment, he grinned. He looked at his friends and let his gaze roam over the spot where he guessed the Shimmies were. "That's the nicest thing anyone has ever done for me."

"What?" Meagan looked at him in shock.

"How do you figure that?" Evan exchanged a look with Gavin and wondered if delayed shock had set in.

"They *must* love me if they went to all this trouble. The Coolio effect is felt even by dead animals." With that, he crossed his arms, struck a pose and showed them his pearly whites.

Mr. Biggsy thought this was funny and nodded his little bandit face up and down.

"How do you know Abigail?" Meagan asked Lisa politely. It was time to treat their guest with more courtesy and acknowledge that she was a welcome Shimmy.

"I ate her."

"Oh dear!" Meagan didn't feel so courteous anymore.

"Don't despair, Meagan. Lisa cornered me down by the beach a few days before you met Hubert. I'll admit it wasn't pleasant at the time, but all is fine now."

"A cougar's got to eat, and I needed to fatten up for the winter. I was actually after Hubert, who was only a few weeks old and likely not much of a challenge to kill, but Abigail defended him to her death."

"Then what killed you?" Evan found these conversations extremely disturbing but unavoidable.

"A hunter who took offence when I tried to kill his goat. He shot me between the eyes."

"Ugh, sorry to hear that."

She shrugged her powerful shoulders and moved on to cleaning her other paw.

Gavin signalled for the other kids to join him a slight distance from their friends. "Not to be an uptight party pooper, but having a million Shimmies on our lawn is blinding me. I can't play soccer with this kind of distraction. How am I going to score on Meggie if Barry is standing in my way? Oh sure, I can run through him, but how creepy is that?" He glanced over to where the Burrow family was teasing each other. "The rabbits keep trying to roll on top of the ball, and Madeline's chirping is driving me nuts."

"Let them have their fun. I want to go down to the beach anyway. We can search it and the oceanfront properties on either side. Maybe there's a weeping willow hidden behind one of those garages."

They made their way to the beach, and their hearts skipped a beat when they looked out across the strait. This was their first time down since the previous November. The blue sky merged with the blue water. The kids looked across to the cluster of islands with new eyes. DeCourcy, Ruxton and Pylades stood in a long line, guarding their secrets with Valdes Island behind.

"There are only nine properties tucked away in this little cove. If we're caught, we can just say we're looking for Red." Coolio was in command, and the kids followed him willingly. They were happy to do something productive. Weeks of talking, planning and speculating had worn them down. With a gentle wind caressing their backs, they went to the first property at the closest end of the bay. They ran from tree to tree, carefully examining the ground for evidence of twisted or exposed roots. It was noon before they finished exploring each property. The bounce had left their step, and their eagerness had evaporated.

"Not one weeping willow. Not one. How could there be every other tree in existence but that one?" Meagan had pulled off her hiking boot and was rubbing her foot.

Evan massaged his sore neck. "Good thing Miss Baker didn't see us. She came close when she opened the shed door. Two more feet to the right, and she would have found us hiding behind her woodpile."

Gavin passed out the juice boxes and energy bars he had in the pack. "It's bad enough that our dog torments her. I can only imagine what she would have said if she found us!"

Gavin shook his head in a feeling of defeat. "Just 'cause we didn't find it doesn't mean it wasn't here at one time. For all we know, we're sitting on it."

That night during dinner, Gavin went from asking for the potatoes to announcing what he wanted for his birthday. For months he had been dropping hints about a new bike, then he asked for a computer, and finally he seemed to settle on a snowboard. So his announcement that night came as a complete shock to his parents.

"Mom, Dad…" MJ and Joe braced themselves. They knew that tone. "Can I have a metal detector for my eleventh birthday?"

"What's that?" Evan looked at his brother and realized he was quite serious. Gavin gave him a look that said, *Back me up.* Then the light bulb went off.

"That's a great idea, Gav. A metal detector. Just what we need."

"What are you boys talking about?" MJ shook her head and laughed. "Not once have you mentioned this. Do you even know what a metal detector is?"

Gavin rolled his eyes. "Of course. The name gives it away, Mom."

"Okay, smarty pants, but why do you want a metal detector?"

Evan held his breath and looked at Gavin out of the corner of his eye. But he needn't have worried; his bro had a quick reply.

"Pop cans, garbage, junk." Gavin put down his knife and fork, placed his elbows on the table and formed a teepee with his hands. "I can't sit back and let the garbage pile up any longer, Mom. I want to do something about it. The earth needs our help."

Evan thought Gavin was laying it on too thick, so when his brother tried to add more to his plea, Evan jumped in. "Besides, we can get cash by returning the cans and selling the metal."

Now *that* seemed to make more sense to Joe. "That's not a bad idea, Gavin. In fact, I've been meaning to clean up the back acre for a long time. A metal detector would come in handy for finding old barbed wire."

Gav winked at Evan and went back to eating his dinner.

On the day of his birthday, Gavin was not disappointed that he asked for a metal detector. It looked just like the one army soldiers used. Gavin had fun using his mom's wedding band to test it. Joe had suggested burying a fork, but Gavin had to make sure the unit could find gold. Evan and Coolio read the instructions and explained all the knobs and buttons to MJ. Joe particularly liked the digital readout and the fact that it could be set for different metals. Evan liked the fact that it could detect gold deep in the ground. It was lightweight and could be used underwater as well.

While Joe took Gavin and his three amigos—Cameron, Jake and Shawn—to a movie and go-cart racing, Evan stayed behind with Coolio and Meagan to map out where they would start searching the next day.

"Do you think Donkey got the tree wrong?" Coolio wondered. "Let's face it. What does a mule know about trees? Maybe it was a big old cedar." There were limits to how much he could accept. A talking, shiny, dead donkey was one thing. A talking, shiny, dead donkey tree expert was another.

"I don't know, Coolio. A weeping willow sure is different from any other tree."

"Yeah, you're right. I shouldn't lose faith in the funka donka!" Coolio started to rap. He bounced like a hip-hopper and started his rhyming game. "Monka, honka, lovin' my donka! Does he got fleas upon his honchies?"

Meagan joined in, and they danced around Evan. The rest of the afternoon was spent hanging in Evan's room, listening to their favourite music and checking out YouTube for the funniest videos they could find.

When Gavin returned with the boys, they devoured homemade pizza, and talk of gold, Shimmies and willow trees went right out the window.

⊏⊐

When the kids bumped into the Coppy twins and their great-grandmother, it promised to be a picture-perfect day. Both Evan and Gavin had won their early-morning soccer games, and they had plans to hook up with Coolio after his hockey game. They had ridden their bikes into Cedar, their pockets filled with loonies and toonies, and they planned to spend every last dime. After loading up on licorice, gummy bears and potato chips, they pedalled off to meet their friends. When they got to the skate park, they were surprised to see Tina and Ginger doing tricks on their BMX bikes. Coolio was encouraging them to take their bikes down the bowl, but the girls had enough sense not to take the bait. When Evan and Gavin showed up, Mrs. Coppy was just heaving herself off the park bench. She walked stiffly over to the kids to say hello.

"How goes the research into Brother Twelve? Are you any closer to solving the mystery of the lost gold?"

The boys exchanged quick looks. How could she know what they were after?

"All rubbish if you ask me. Who in their right mind would bury gold and never come back to claim it? I say they sailed off that night with whatever valuables they could scrounge, including the gold, and spent every last dollar between Canada and Europe."

The boys, relieved, smiled their easy smiles. "Yeah, they likely spent it on new horses and carriages. Stuff like that," Gavin said with confidence.

Mrs. Coppy actually giggled. It was odd to see a lady her age do that. "Gavin, Brother Twelve may seem like a character from a Sherlock Holmes movie, but I can assure you that in the thirties there were cars, telephones and even planes!" She smiled warmly at him. To one as young as Gavin, the thought of life eighty years before conjured up images of horse and buggies and ladies in feather bonnets.

When the twins came over to join them, they were surprised to learn that their great-grandmother had invited the Edmund boys to visit their home that afternoon.

"I want to show them where I grew up on the farm and the houses that used to belong to the Aquarian Foundation. It will help their research. How is your project coming along?" The girls looked confused but didn't push the topic except to explain that their father would be along in an hour to pick them up. Ginger suggested that they all come back for lunch, and then they could take a walk in the neighbourhood to see the infamous houses.

"There's nothing great about them. Just plain old houses. Daddy built our home just down the street from where the Foundation used to own land," Tina volunteered.

Ginger pulled out a phone and called Meagan.

"Meg, it's Gin. Wanna do lunch at my house? The Edmunds are in, and so is Coolio." She listened, nodding her head. "I can arrange that. Veggies, no tofu. Got some cracked-wheat something-or-other my mom wants us to try." She nodded her head again. "Yeah, sure. Say an hour. Just have your mom drop you off at the skate park. K. Cool. See ya."

Ginger winked at Evan. "Your girl's in. Wanna see me do a full rotation off the jump?" She pedalled off.

The hour flew by quickly. Mrs. Coppy sat happily on the bench and watched the children do one crazy stunt after another. At ninety, she had seen it all, and figured one more trip to the "emerge" unit at the Nanaimo hospital wouldn't add any more years to her life. She was quite fascinated by their moves, in fact. How the boys could keep their feet glued to a board with only four wheels was beyond her. The bowl, as they called it, was deep and deadly looking from where she sat, but they seemed to drop in and out the other side every time. After a while, she wished she had brought her knitting.

Claire dropped off Meagan at the precise moment Brian Coppy showed up with his pickup. Mrs. Coppy explained the new plans, and like any good father, Brian asked no questions. He simply loaded the bikes and boards into the bed of his truck. The kids piled into the double cab and buckled up. The chatter was deafening on the short ride home. Mrs. Coppy just turned off her hearing aid and peered happily out the window. When they approached the old family home, she put her arm on her grandson's and turned her hearing aid back up.

"Children! This is where I used to live. This is the farm where my father tended horses, sheep and pigs. He was also the best farrier in the area. When Brian's father managed the farm, he bought the lands beside us and added cornfields to the business. As you can see, the farm was perched high above the water, and if you look down, you can see the shoreline from here."

The boys could see that the new owners maintained the farm just as the Coppys had. In fact, Evan and Gavin had gone through the annual Halloween corn maze at least once since they'd moved to the island.

When they arrived at Tina and Ginger's house, they ran in to clean their hands and call their mom. After a smorgasbord of spicy barbecue sausage, grilled veggies and Greek salad, they made their way up the road to where the Aquarian homes stood.

"This one on the left was built by one of the Aquarian elders," Tina said. "He was ripped off thousands of dollars, and my dad said the court let him keep the land and house 'cause the Brother dude never showed up to defend himself. He and his wife lived here till they passed on, and since they had no kids, some distant relative sold the place back in the fifties." Tina sounded bored as she told the story.

"The two houses on the right were also owned by the religious cult, and they too were given to Aquarian members who could prove that Brother dude and Madame something-or-other stole all their money." Ginger was more enthusiastic than her sister. "Not sure when they got sold, but the new owners have done the most work to them. Don't you like that huge weeping willow tree in the front yard? We used to climb it when we were little." She looked to see if her audience was enjoying the story and was shocked to see Meagan, Coolio, Evan and Gavin staring at her with their mouths wide open.

"What did I say?" She took a step back and unconsciously slipped her arm through her sister's.

It was Meagan who came to her senses first. "Oh, nothing," she stammered. "It just seems so big for little girls to climb." She caught the boys exchanging not-so-subtle looks and quickly stepped in front of them. "Let's go down to the beach. How do you get there from here?"

Tina and Ginger looked back strangely at the boys as Meagan tried to lead them down the road, but after a few awkward moments they focused their attention on a shortcut through one of the Aquarian properties on the right.

Every time the boys started to huddle, Meagan broke them up. "Not now!" she hissed.

It was a blessing when Joe pulled into the Coppys' driveway. He made some small talk with Brian for a few minutes in the driveway until the impatient mutterings of his boys had him apologetically saying goodbye. He listened intently as Evan filled him in on their afternoon's activities. Apparently Joe already knew about the Aquarian Foundation and no, he didn't think it was something he should have shared with his boys. When he asked why they were grilling him so much about it, they backed off and changed the subject to hockey.

They had little time to formulate a plan because parents were waiting to divide them up once they arrived at the Edmund home. Isobel was taking Coolio to get a haircut, Claire was taking Meagan to her grandmother's, and MJ was bustling Evan and Gavin into their bedrooms to change for dinner. They had guests arriving for a night of crab and cards.

Coolio gave the universal sign for "call me!" as he got into his mom's car. Meagan gave her very personal and very secret hand signal, which meant "video conference me." Gavin just punched his brother in the arm and said at the top of his lungs, "We're rich!"

A few times that night, MJ asked the boys if they were okay. They were fidgety and distracted, and they hardly ate their meal—a first for a dinner of freshly caught crab. They assured her they were okay but admitted an early night was probably a good idea. They snuck their dad's laptop into Evan's room and quickly logged into the account. Both Coolio and Meagan were already on. They closed the door to block out the sounds of the rowdy hand of poker that was going on.

"How soon can we get back there with the metal detector?" Gavin pulled the comforter over their heads so the glow from the computer could not been seen under the door.

Meagan copied the boys and pulled her fuzzy pink blanket over her head. "Tina and Ginger's house is too far to ride to on our bikes. We'll need a car ride. Maybe I can ask them to hang out next Saturday, and one of us can slip out and check the tree without everyone knowing."

"Better make it Sunday. I've got a game in Victoria, and we won't be back until late."

"You can't have a game on Saturday! It's my birthday party!" Evan looked at Coolio in shock.

"Shoot, that's right! Man, I forgot."

"How could you forget?" Evan's indignation was hard to miss.

"What were we doing again?" Coolio truly looked puzzled.

"We're going bungee jumping with Meagan, Simon, Mick and Ty."

"Well, no wonder I forgot. Ev, you know how I hate heights!" Coolio's whine was thick and muffled as he tried to pull his Canucks hockey blanket over his head. It got stuck on his laptop.

"When will you be home?"

"Not till five thirty." Coolio really did look like he felt bad about missing his best friend's party. It would be the first time ever.

Evan cheered up immediately. "No worries. We don't dive till six o'clock."

"What? It'll be dark then!"

"Yeah, isn't that cool? What could be better than jumping off a bridge two hundred feet above a raging river and plummeting into the abyss below—at night? It'll be wild!" Evan's face was lit up full voltage.

"Dude, you are severely messed up. I'll show up, but don't expect me to sign up for your madness. I'll hold your head while you puke your guts up. That's the kind of good friend I am." Suddenly he ducked out from under his comforter. "I gotta split. I hear my mom outside my door. Figure out when and how we're getting back to that tree, and I'll show up with my shovel."

When Evan and Gavin turned off the computer, they were exhausted. Meagan wouldn't let them sign off until they'd talked through every angle of their mission. They needed the help of parents, the Coppy twins, and the weather. They all agreed that if they found gold on Evan's birthday, it would be extremely cool—a sign that it was meant to be theirs.

Gavin jumped off his brother's bed and turned to leave. His scream was short but piercing. Lisa was sitting quietly on the area rug in Evan's room. Evan rushed to the door and yelled to his parents that Gavin was fine and only bumped his big toe on the corner of the bed. He then turned on the cougar.

"What are you doing in here?" Shimmy or no Shimmy, a cougar in the centre of his room was unnerving.

"I wanted to see how you lived. Abigail told me you didn't sleep in trees, but I didn't believe her. Now I know she is right. Why do you need to go back to a weeping willow tree?" She cocked her head and peered intently at them with her enormous golden eyes.

"Geez, no cougar has ever come in our house before. This is weird. But, since you asked, we think there is gold buried beneath the willow tree down the road from friends of ours." Evan sat on his bed and looked admiringly at the cat. She sure was beautiful, but she was definitely intimidating.

"Why do you want the gold?"

"To help take care of our families…"

"I did that by killing prey for my cubs."

"Oh, that's nice." What else could Evan say?

Lisa shifted her weight from one hind leg to another. "Did you know the Latin name for a weeping willow is *Salix alba Vitellina-Tristis?*

"You don't say." Evan looked at Gavin out of the corner of his eye. His brother was just as stiff and uncomfortable as Evan.

"And human male is *Homo sapiens.*"

Gavin puffed out his chest. "I knew that one."

"How do you say *go away* in Latin?" Evan decided the educational part of the nightly program should come to an end.

"*Abeo.*" Lisa appeared to be grinning. She stood up on all fours, nodded her head, and disappeared.

———

First thing Monday morning, their problem was solved. Tina and Ginger called them to the back of the bus, and Tina held out an invitation.

"Evan, we want to invite you to our thirteenth birthday party on Saturday." Tina held the pink and peach polka-dotted envelope in midair and waited for him to respond.

"Wow. I didn't know your birthday was the same day as mine." Evan took it and turned it around in his hand. His name was written in a loopy scrawl.

"Well, you *would* have known—if you'd ever invited us to one of *your* parties." Tina winced when Ginger jabbed her in her ribs.

"Oh, don't mind her, Evan. Please say you will come. Everyone will be there. We even invited your crew of boys who are coming to your party. They'll come if you come. It doesn't start till seven thirty. We're going to dance, have a bonfire and set off fireworks around ten. It'll be fun."

"Sure, sounds great. Thanks."

Evan sat down beside Gavin and pulled out the invitation:

Come celebrate Tina and Ginger's 13th birthday!
Thumping music, chillin' by the campfire and magical fireworks

Be there or be square!
Saturday, February 18, 7:30 p.m.
5489 Fountain Way off Drummond Drive

"How did I not know the Coppy twins shared my birthday? Shouldn't I have known that by now?" Evan seemed truly perplexed by this fact, and he chewed his lower lip as he looked at the invitation again.

Meagan glanced over the back of the seat and looked at the invitation in his hand.

"Oh, good! You're going to come this year?"

"You knew?"

"Well, of course. I go every year."

"No, you come to my party every year."

"Evan, I go to *both* parties every year. The twins do the opposite of what you do. If you have a morning event, they do afternoon. If you do evening, they do morning. I have never missed either of your parties."

For some reason, this really bothered Evan. Was he so engrossed in his own celebrations that he never noticed that two of his friends, however distant, shared his birthday? The fact that Meagan knew this—and had likely even told him in the past—bothered him even more.

Gavin grabbed the invitation out of his hand. "You gotta get me invited to this party. Our problem of getting back to the tree is solved." He tapped it against his thigh and grinned foolishly. "I'm thinking we hide their gift in a hockey bag, which conveniently hides a metal detector and shovel. Bingo bango, lickety-split! A party and gold digging, all in one night. It can't get any better than that." Gavin almost levitated off the seat he was so excited.

"Leave it to me to get you invited. You guys fill in Coolio on the plans. We'll need his bag."

"Speaking of Coolio, where is he? He didn't get on at his stop." Evan looked around the bus to make sure he hadn't missed him.

"He said he had extra weight training this morning and we'd see him at school." Gavin was always plugged in.

"Good," Meagan muttered. "If we're going to dig for gold, we'll need his muscles too."

⊏ ⊐

In the end, it was Evan who held Coolio's head while he chucked into some bushes beside the suspension bridge. Everything was going fine with the bungee jumping until Simon, typically, freaked Coolio out. He was the last one to jump, and unlike all the other kids, he didn't let out a sound after he disappeared into the blackness below. Even the operators looked strangely at each other. Screams of fear, delight, laughter, whoops and catcalls were common. Dead silence was not. They stood around anxiously as the tension rope stopped bouncing. Slowly the cord, on a hydraulic system, rolled back up. The muffled moaning filtered up to them slowly at first. As the rope was hauled back up, they could hear a broken voice calling for help.

"My head!" My head!" Simon sounded like he was in pain.

Everyone stood at the railing, looking into the darkness as his outline came into view under the overhead spotlights. As he got closer, you could see that he was holding his head. Joe stepped up beside the three twenty-something operators and demanded to know what was going on.

"Don't know, sir. Maybe he hit his head, but I can't imagine how." The operator's voice was strained, and his words were whispered low.

"I told you this was a bad idea." Coolio was deadly white, wringing his hands nervously. He paced behind them and didn't even glance over the rail. "Who throws themselves off a bridge, anyway? He must have crashed into a floating log or hit a boulder. He could be a vegetable now!"

"Coolio! Relax. I'm sure he's fine." Evan sounded nearly as hysterical as Coolio, but the words seemed appropriate.

"Grab a hold of his ankles. Son, are you okay? Oh my God. Look at the blood!" Joe went equally white in the harsh light. Simon held his head in his hands, and blood was oozing out between his fingers.

Coolio couldn't help himself. He glanced over just as Simon was being lowered to the floor of the bridge. He took a step toward his limp friend and nearly fell over at the sight of him.

"Simon! Simon! Say something!" Coolio pushed his way into the surrounding crowd.

Simon moaned, opened his eyes and said, "Gotcha." He held up two squeezed McDonald's ketchup packages and winked at his old friend.

Coolio turned and hurled in the direction of the bushes.

"Evil. Pure evil. The things I could learn from you." Gavin high-fived Simon and then held his dad off from coming down too hard on the boy.

Joe was grateful that MJ's fear of heights excluded her from this year's activities. She was down in the café, enjoying her second latte. Simon was very lucky she wasn't up there at that moment. Simon sure wouldn't be strutting his stuff had MJ witnessed that!

Eventually Coolio calmed down and forgave Simon, but it took the drive to the Coppy sisters to ease him out of his sullen state. Only Evan knew that it was less to do with Simon's stream of apologies the fact that Coolio was getting excited about the possibility of finding gold.

When Meagan, Gavin, Coolio and Evan fell out of the car, the party was in full swing. Lights had been hung from every tree in the backyard. Ty had set up his player just inside the living room. Speakers were situated on either side of the open patio doors, and the back deck was crowded with girls who were dancing to a club mix. The boys stood along the sides and sipped cherry Pepsi.

"Make way, girls. Coolio has arrived." He disappeared into the centre and was lost in a sea of arms, all bumping to the sounds of the beat.

Meagan and Evan stood back and watched with amusement as the girls took this as their cue to drag the wallflowers onto the dance floor. Simon hadn't washed off the dried ketchup from his head and was trying to convince the Coppy twins that he had bashed his brains in. Tina rolled her eyes. "I think you've been brain dead for years," she yelled over the noise.

It was only when Gavin appeared behind them ten minutes later that they noticed he had been missing.

"The gift is on the table. The hockey bag with the metal detector and shovels are hidden in the garage. Just give me the signal, and I'll slip out. Coolio will leave five minutes after I go while you two stay here and distract the crowd." Gavin sounded focused and mature.

"Just don't get caught," Meagan warned. "If the owners of the house see their property being dug up, we're toast. Run the plan by us again."

"Ah, come on! I've done it a million times. I know it by heart."

"Humour us, Gav. We're getting nervous. It'll make me feel better." Meagan batted her eyes and smiled sweetly at him.

"Fine, I guess," Gavin muttered, annoyed. "I take off when no one is looking. I make sure that no one follows me. When I get to the weeping willow, I drop behind the bushes to the left of the tree and wait there until I'm certain no one is around." The words were flat and robotic. "I get under the branches where no one will be able to see me, and I pull out the metal detector. I quickly scan the area and locate the gold. Once I find it, I wait for Coolio to join me."

"Right. Remember: he'll give the bird call if anyone is approaching, and you are to lie flat on the ground. Only start digging once he's with you. Donkey said Brother Twelve dug for hours, so this might take the whole party. Meagan and I will relieve you an hour after you disappear. Let's just hope we locate it before Dad comes back for us."

Mr. and Mrs. Coppy stepped out onto the deck and announced that the burgers and hot dogs were ready. Kids ceased doing whatever they were doing and disappeared into the house. Coolio glanced nonchalantly to his friends and feigned interest in his shoelaces. Evan turned just as nonchalantly to give his brother the signal, but Gavin was already gone. Mission Gold Coast was on.

"Nothing. Nada." Gavin wiped the dirt from his hands onto his jeans.

"What do you mean? You didn't get any signals?" Evan tried to keep his voice down, but he was highly agitated.

"Just what I said!" Meagan hushed Gavin and signalled with her eyes that Tina was within earshot.

"Evan, I told you already. The metal detector didn't pick up anything. When Coolio arrived, we tested it by burying a dime really deep down. We easily found that. We had it on the most sensitive setting. If there was anything buried, it's gone. Or else we have the wrong tree."

"This doesn't make any sense," Evan fumed, talking more to himself than his brother. "All the pieces fit. A weeping willow on Aquarian property—his property! You can get to it from walking up the hill from the coast, and Valdes Island is right across the strait."

"Well, not directly across. It is just down a ways." Meagan's voice trailed off when she saw the look on Evan's face.

He looked at Coolio and Gavin. They looked back at him and Meagan. After a minute, it was Lisa who broke the silence.

"Hello, Homo sapiens."

A cougar on your front lawn or in your bedroom was one thing. A cougar sitting pertly on a dance floor, surrounded by teenagers dancing to "Super Freak," was quite another.

"What are you doing here, Lisa?" Evan could barely contain his anxiety.

"Lisa's here? Grand." Coolio was staring the wrong way, so Meagan subtly turned him around. Now he was looking at Mick, who was twisting in a grotesque way. *Dancing* was not the word that came to mind.

"I thought I would come and help you. You're going about finding the gold in the wrong way. Come with me."

Without looking back, she walked to the side of the house and disappeared around the corner. They looked at each other in bewilderment.

"We'd better all go." Meagan ran after her, and a second later, so did the boys.

They caught up with the cougar as she disappeared under the weeping willow branches that rested on the ground. It would have been pitch black in there, but Lisa's glow revealed the uneven ground and the spots where Gavin and Coolio had dug.

"What's the plan, then?" Evan was feeling very nervous. He was sure they were going to get caught or that someone had followed them. He kept pushing the branches aside to look.

"You need to call Donkey. Only he can confirm or deny if this is the right tree." Lisa jumped up onto one of the lower branches and stretched her body lazily.

"Why didn't we think of that?" Gavin said with a hint of sarcasm. "Wouldn't he know if this was the right tree? Of course he would. Trouble is, *he won't come.*"

"Why not?" Lisa didn't seem the least bit put off.

"He never comes when we call him. He never leaves his pub."

"If we start yelling for Donkey, we're going to alert the whole neighbourhood. Better we just—"

Lisa let out a deafening roar. It shattered the quiet of the night.

"What did you do that for?" Gavin took his hands away from his ears and stared accusingly at Lisa.

"That's why."

Donkey and Barry pushed their way through the branches of the tree. Together with Lisa, they lit up the snug little area like a hundred-watt light bulb.

"You called?" Donkey didn't seem at all surprised that he was there.

Barry ran from kid to kid and sniffed their clothes appreciatively.

"Hot dogs, hamburgers, barbecue chicken! Yum, yum, yum!"

"Barry, cut that out." The thought of a pig sniffing her was highly disturbing to Meagan.

"Will someone fill me in?" Coolio was learning that he had the patience of a saint, but watching his friends respond to animals he couldn't see was a tad frustrating. Not to mention his flashlight kept blinking on and off, and it unnerved him.

"Sorry about that. Donkey and Barry just arrived. Oh, and

looky here. Carolynn and the others just showed up too. What fun." You could have cut Evan's sarcasm with a knife.

The space was very tight now, the branches filled with a bird, an owl, a cougar and two raccoons. Mr. Rad-knows-ways and Razor sat on either side of Coolio. The rabbits took up their usual places on the beaver's and dog's heads, and Spotty and Abigail hung back between the swinging branches.

"Gang's all here. So much for a covert mission." Evan had hit a whole new level of grumpy. "We're going to get caught."

"No, you're not, Evan. Abigail and Hubert are standing guard to alert us if anyone comes." Carolynn turned her attention to the mule. "Well, Donkey, is this the right tree?" She settled her piercing eyes on his and commanded him to speak.

"Nope."

"What do you mean, *nope*? You didn't even look around." Evan was going from grumpy to right royally pissed off.

"I mean, this ain't the tree."

"How can you be so sure?" Gavin was trying to keep his cool too.

"It's too small, there are no roots lying twisted and snarly on the ground, and it's too far from the ocean."

Meagan whispered what was being said in Coolio's ear.

"No, he's got to be wrong. The beach is only a three-minute walk down the hill. And time must have distorted his memory of the tree." Coolio now sounded just as desperate as the other boys.

"Nope."

"Stop saying *nope*!" This time it was Meagan who lost her temper. "You're not even looking at the tree properly. How can you be so sure?"

"'Cause I remember that night like it happened yesterday. I remember how the sea air tasted, how the earth smelled, and how the wind blowing off the strait rustled the willow branches." He paused for effect. "And I remember there were *no houses*."

"Well, yeah," Meagan said. "Back then, there would have been just the three Aquarian houses. Today there are over a dozen on this street, but back then there would have been—"

"*None.* I said there were no houses. After they sailed off, I was left alone for years in a beautiful area that hugged the coastline. There were trees, a pebbled beach, and grassy knolls looking out over the water. It was years before I saw a human being. This ain't the tree." He turned around and walked out from under the cover of the branches. Barry looked nervously from kid to kid and then ran off after him.

"Sorry it didn't turn out the way you wanted, children," Carolynn murmured. "Don't despair. You will find the tree, and when you do, we will be here to help you."

12

MARCH MADNESS

THE WEEKS LEADING up to March break were crammed with tests, assignments and sporting events. The weather swung, in its typical pattern, from sunny and bright to rainy and miserable. Every morning the Shimmies escorted the children to their bus stop, and every afternoon they were the first ones to greet them upon their return. Carolynn sent scouts out every day to look for weeping willow trees in the area. The rabbits sent them on many goose chases because they couldn't tell the difference between a monkey tree and willow tree. It was finally decided they were better suited to pumping Donkey for additional information.

Coolio's team ranked number one in the divisional standings. He trained extra hours to hone his puck-handling skills and speed skating. Meagan had joined a weekend music workshop where she was learning about new acoustic styles. The Edmunds recorded the World Cup soccer games and watched them at night before going to bed. Dreams of making it to the international arena filled their heads.

One teacher described the Friday school let out for the March break as "the annual escape of the inmates." Screaming kids in the hallways, paper flung in every direction, cartwheels on the front lawn—it was pandemonium. MJ and Joe waited outside the school and honked impatiently as the boys mingled on the top step of the school.

"Come on! We gotta go. We're going to miss our flight." Joe waved back at some of the teachers, who were speeding off in every direction. As happy as the students were, nothing came close to the joy the staff felt.

Every year, the Edmunds rented a place on the water in sunny southern California. It boasted a stunning view of the ocean, a pool and hot tub shared by all the townhouse owners, and private steps that led down to the sandy beach below. Joe surfed, MJ walked the beach, and the boys swam to their hearts' content for one full week. While they laughed it up, Red was treated to a week at his favourite doggy spa and boarding home. A much-needed vacation for all.

When they arrived late that night at their apartment on the third floor of the complex, they simply dumped their bags in the hallway, found a bed and fell fast asleep. The long flight, fresh ocean air and pent-up energy brought on long, deep sleeps.

—

"Evan, wake up!" Gavin rocked his brother from side to side, trying to get him to budge. Evan moaned and told him to take a hike.

"You aren't gonna believe what's outside. Come on, get up!" Gavin hissed in his ear, trying to drag him from the bed.

"Stop that! Where're Mom and Dad?"

"Still sleeping. I want to sneak out and show you before they wake up."

"Why are you awake? You never wake up early."

"She woke me up. Come see."

Evan tried to open one eye. Dim light was coming through the curtains. He could smell the salt air and hear the crash of the ocean below.

"What time is it?"

"Dunno. I forgot my watch. Just get up. Once you see this, you won't go back to sleep, I promise you."

"This had better be worth it." He dragged on the clothes that were in a pile at the bottom of the bed and stumbled into the hallway. Gavin was already holding the front door open for him. He led him down the stairs and around the side to the back terrace, where he used a key to open the metal gate to the pool area. He ran past the pool and hot tub and used the same key to open the door to the private stairs that led down to the beach.

"If I fall down these steep stairs 'cause of you, I'm going to break *your* neck." Evan wished he had brought his sunglasses. The sun was now directly in his eyes, and he had trouble seeing the stairs.

"We're almost there." Gavin jumped the last two steps and landed smoothly on the hard sand. Evan shielded his eyes and stepped down gingerly.

"Now look!" Gavin grabbed him by the arm. Evan's eyes needed to adjust, so at first, all he saw was a blur of images and light dancing in his vision.

"I don't, I can't… Oh my God. Is that a whale?" Evan looked at Gavin's beaming face.

"Yeah, and not just any whale. Look closer."

Beached less than one hundred yards away was a huge grey whale. Its skin had grey patches, and white mottling spots covered it from head to tail. Two blowholes occasionally blew out water, but otherwise, the whale simply rocked back and forth as the surf came in and out. It let out the odd cry that sounded like a baby's cry. It also glowed—like a thirty-ton, sparkling diamond.

"It's a Shimmy!" Evan looked at Gavin and mirrored the smile on his face.

━━━

Denise had died on that beach many years before. She didn't know what decade, but she did know that humans had tried to help her. A pod of killer whales had separated her from her family. They had tracked Denise's pod for days. She'd hung back to protect her mother and her mother's new calf, but the effort caused her to grow weak, and eventually she was unable to keep up with her pod. She dropped back and, once separated from her kin, the orca pod systematically attacked her until she was unable to manoeuvre herself away from what should have been the final blow.

But just as the largest orca in the pod circled below for the killing shot to her belly, a disturbance had the whales darting in opposite directions. An earthquake hit within minutes. The ocean swelled, and Denise was caught in a rolling wave so huge she struggled to not tumble and toss. She had to fight to come to the surface, taking in gulps of air through her two blowholes. When it was over, she washed ashore and was unable to dislodge herself from the hard sand that had formed a basin around her. The sun was gone from the sky, and she thought she would never see the light of another day.

At daybreak, an elderly couple alerted the town that there was a beached whale clinging to life. Humans of all ages took turns dousing her with sea water and laying soaked towels across her battered body. Suffering from dehydration, malnutrition, internal injuries and depression stemming from separation from her pod, she slipped away late that afternoon.

The boys marvelled at how serenely Denise told her story. She was not sad or forlorn as she told her tale, just thoughtful.

"Do you come back here often, then?" Evan was particularly taken with the whale. All his life he had wanted to see, touch and look into the eyes of the gentle giant.

"Yes. I am drawn here every morning just as the sun rises. Over the years, I have met others like you who can see and hear me. I cherish those moments."

"You're kidding. You've met humans like Evan and I, who can see dead animals?" Gavin shook his head in wonder.

"Oh yes. Not many, mind you. They are often the very young or old. But yes, I have met humans from all parts of the world.

Somehow I understand them, and in turn they understand me."
Her voice was soft and high-pitched.

This baffled Evan. If this gift was more common than they
thought, why had they never heard of it? Why wouldn't more
people talk about it? When Evan muttered this question aloud,
Gavin snorted, used his finger to make circles in the air around his
ear, and mouthed, "Loco!"

When people started to show up for a stroll on the beach, the
boys decided it was time to get back to the apartment. They said
their goodbyes and promised to return the next day.

Evan took the steps two at a time on the way back. "Imagine—a
Shimmy whale! I can't wait to tell Carolynn and the others. I
wonder why we haven't seen other Shimmies outside our odd
collection. I always figured we could only see ones that lived near
home. I guess I was wrong."

As they entered the pool area, they heard their names. Their
parents were sitting on the porch that looked down over the pool.

"You're up remarkably early. I thought you'd sleep for hours."

"It's a whale of a morning. You never know what you'll see in
California." Gavin laughed at his own joke, waved, and disappeared
around the corner of the building.

"Mom, when we walk to town, can we stop by that historical
society place? You know the one. You always try to drag us in
there." Evan kept running and didn't wait to hear his mom's reply.

MJ turned to her husband, stunned. "Should I take their
temperature?"

The headquarters of the Encinitas Historical Society was in a
127-year-old schoolhouse that had been preserved over the years.
There were many fascinating stories about the town's origins and
the famous people who had called it home over the years—none of
which interested Evan or Gavin one bit. They wanted to learn
about Denise, and the earthquake that saved her and then took her
life.

MJ and an elderly gentleman, who volunteered on Saturdays,
were quickly engrossed in a conversation about the local artists and

photographers who had captured the spirit of the town through the years. The boys used one of the research computers to try and locate information on Denise, but they had a hard time using the search engine. Just when they were ready to call it quits and hit the ice cream parlour next door, an odd-looking man approached them.

"You look bored, confused and entirely out of place. Let me guess: your mom dragged you in here, and you thought you could Google your time away until you could hit Cones and Slurps next door."

Gavin eyed up the stranger. His badge said his name was Hiccup. He looked around sixty years old, wore his grey hair long, and had a scraggly beard and mustache. Under his royal-blue volunteer vest, he wore a T-shirt that read, "Jerry is not dead," and his high-top running shoes were different colours.

"We dragged her in here," said Evan. "We were hoping to learn about something in particular. Interesting name. Did the badge come with the vest?"

"No. The society refused to print the badge the way I wanted, so I had to flip for my own. Do you know it costs twelve dollars to engrave a name tag ? Highway robbery if you ask me."

"You don't say. What did the society want to put on your nameplate?" Evan's tone was deadpan. He was seriously interested to know.

"Bartholomew."

"How is Hiccup any better than Bartholomew?"

"It isn't, really. It's a state of mind I enjoy, and a condition I had as a child."

Evan decided this conversation had gone on long enough. "Do you know about an earthquake that happened in the area a long time ago, and when it was over, a grey whale was washed up on shore down near the volleyball courts?

Hiccup formed a teepee with his fingers and put the tips to his lips. He closed his eyes. He looked as if the very act of thinking hurt his brain.

"Yes, I believe I do recall something like that happening.

Earthquakes happen here all the time. Whales occasionally get beached, but an earthquake and a whale on the same day is rare." He continued to think, and then Hiccup smiled a yellow smile and twitched his head to suggest they follow him. He led them to a long counter in the back of the schoolhouse, where funny computers were set up.

"Ever work a microfiche before?" Hiccup sized them up and before they could answer decided it was unlikely. "What do you want to see? Newspaper articles that ran the story?"

"That would be great!" said Evan.

Hiccup turned on the machine. "I was around your age when it happened. My friends and I had gone down to Swami's beach the morning of the quake. We had just gotten there when a friend of ours said a whale was beached. We had to thumb a ride back, and when we finally got there, the cops were making everyone stand back so they could bring a crane in to lift the carcass. Total bummer that it died. Total bummer."

While he spoke, he walked to a cabinet and pulled out a folder from the top drawer. He took out what looked like tiny negatives all stuck together and placed the sheet on a glass tray. He played with a knob on the side of the machine and scrolled quickly through the images. Evan couldn't understand how Hiccup could make out the blurred pictures and words. They flew across the screen lightning fast. Suddenly it stopped, and Hiccup vacated the seat.

"There you go. Knock yourselves out." He walked to the front of the building to help an elderly couple who had just walked in.

Gavin sat down, and Evan peered over his shoulder.

06/17 1960—Encinitas Times

Locals Try to Save Gray Whale, Earthquake Claims One More Victim

The town was alerted to the plight of the gray whale by Edith and Harold Hughes. Long-time residents of the area, they left their quaint 4th Street bungalow for their ritual 6:00 a.m. beach walk. "I said to

Harold, earthquake or no earthquake, I am taking my morning constitutional." At 79 years of age, Ms. Hughes did not think some debris on the beach was worth worrying about. "Downed trees are one thing, but a whale is something different altogether!" Mr. Hughes was recovering from the exertion of pailing water on the baleen whale all morning. "Just a shame it is, a lovely creature dying that way. It should have been safe out at sea."

Scientists from the Whale Research Centre agreed with Mr. Hughes. Donald Swivel, director for the centre, said the whale's sonar should have alerted it to the hydrostatic pressure change, and its instinct should have had it retreating to open water. "It's a bit of a mystery as to why the whale ended up on shore. The state of the battered carcass leads us to believe that this twenty-year-old female was in poor shape before the earthquake hit."

Below the story was a series of pictures. The first one showed a dozen or more people standing around Denise. Some were pouring water on her while others covered her body with beach towels. Others simply stood back and watched. By the angle of the picture, Evan and Gavin could tell that it had been taken right where they stood that morning when they first saw the Shimmy.

The second picture showed the police directing a large truck onto the beach. On the back bed was a crane. The caption read, *Police and volunteers watch helplessly as the whale gasps its last breath. H. R. Henderson and Sons were called in to dispose of the carcass.*

The third picture was a close-up of the Hugheses. Harold had his arm around his wife, and she was dabbing her eyes with a tissue. *Local residents mourn the loss of this coastal gentle giant.*

Gavin sat back in the chair and looked up at his brother.

"Poor Denise. At least she knew there were people who tried to help her. I wonder what happened to her pod. If that happened fifty years ago, they would all be dead now." Gavin chewed his lower lip and then suddenly his face lit up.

"Maybe she's reunited with them now!"

After stopping for a double scoop of cookies 'n' cream on a

waffle cone, they helped their mother unload the groceries from the car rental. Joe was down on the beach, waxing his board and getting ready to brave the cold water. The waves were less than perfect, but Joe was itching to get in and test his new board.

"You boys ready to get wet?" Joe's grin was infectious. He let out a whoop and ran into the water. They all laughed when he ran right back out.

"Wowza!"

"Where's the tough guy I married? Not going to let some frigid water keep you from surfing, are you?"

With that challenge, Joe ran back in and dove under the first wave that hit the shoreline. He came up sputtering but kept swimming out until he found a good spot to climb onto his board and wave to his family.

The day was spent between the beach, pool, hot tub, kitchen—for snacks—and back to the beach again for a game of volleyball. Denise did not reappear, but that didn't stop Evan and Gavin from keeping an eye out for her. By the time the sun went down, the boys were exhausted and more than sun-kissed.

They settled into a happy routine of waking up early and heading down to the beach to greet their new friend. As the days passed, they learned more and more about her life at sea. They learned she was a February baby, like the boys. She was born in Baja, California, where the water was warm and salty. She arrived into the world, and immediately her mother pushed her up to the surface to take her first breaths. She nursed from her mother for months, and one day she and her extended family of twenty-eight whales headed north for the long Pacific journey to the Bering Sea, off the coast of Alaska.

As fascinated at the boys were with Denise, she was even more interested to learn about their life. She asked many questions about the other Shimmies, and about their school, friends and the sports they played. She marvelled at the idea that they could board a plane and fly high in the air. She never grew tired of hearing them talk, and laughed easily at their stories. To the morning walkers, they appeared to be two boys standing side by side, looking out at the ocean and telling wild stories.

When it suited her, Denise slipped back into the water, blew glistening water into the air and disappeared beneath the waves. Only then did the boys run back up to the townhouse and wolf down a hearty breakfast. MJ and Joe observed them with a new awareness. The boys seemed to have reached a new level of maturity. They had no interest in going to the amusement parks, zoos or arcade. They were happiest on the beach.

On the last morning of their vacation, Evan and Gavin descended the wood stairs more slowly than they had the other mornings. They were not ready to go home, and they certainly were not ready to say goodbye to Denise. But the sight that greeted them on the bottom stair had them running as fast as they could to the beach.

Countless grey whales were swimming in the water behind Denise. She was in her customary place on the beach, but directly beside her was an older, larger whale.

"Evan and Gavin, meet my mother. Her name is Marta."

Marta greeted them warmly.

"It is a pleasure to meet you finally. Denise has been talking about you non-stop. She has convinced us that when we migrate north next month, we should hang a right at the opening of the Salish Sea, pass the Gulf Islands and detour up to your bay. I would like to see your beach and meet Carolynn and the others."

Her voice was slow, and she enunciated her words very slowly. Barnacles covered her grey body except in those places where she had deep gashes from head to fin.

"It's very nice to meet you too. We wondered where Denise went when she left us. You sure have a large family!" Evan looked out at the bobbing whales and laughed when one of the smaller ones tried to roll over his mother.

"Yes, our pod has been swimming these waters for centuries. You are seeing only a small handful of them. Our numbers would overwhelm you."

Gavin was cheered to know that their beloved friend was not

alone. It had troubled him to think she might not have any of her kind. They had been afraid to ask in case it left her sad and lonely.

Marta introduced each whale to the boys. Grandparents, uncle, aunts, cousins, sisters and brothers took their turn to swim close and nod their enormous heads at the humans. The boys couldn't keep their names straight, but one of the last great whales to be introduced was Priscilla, Denise's sister. She was no longer a helpless calf but a full-sized adult.

"I was just a calf when the orcas attacked us. Denise was travelling ahead of us with some of the older relatives. She dropped back to try and protect me. You see, the killer whales didn't want my mother." Priscilla looked lovingly at Marta. "They were after me. There were so many of them. One male in particular was enormous, and his dorsal fin cut through the water like a knife. He tried to separate me from my mother, and the other orcas pushed me under the water to try and drown me." After all these years, it was still difficult for Priscilla to relive the memory. "Denise rushed to my aid and pushed me back up to the surface where I could take a breath. She nudged me between my mother's body and hers. For over an hour, the attack went on. The male knew that if he could weaken Denise and draw her away from me, they would have a chance of separating me from my exhausted mother." She sniffed. "You see me now as I was when I died of natural causes. I lived to the ripe old age of forty-five. You have met several of my calves. It is because of Denise and her bravery that I had such a rich life."

"Now, now, Priscilla. You make it sound so dramatic." Denise turned her huge head toward the boys. "You get home safely. And start to look for us around late May. I will miss you, my darling little friends."

Denise slipped back into the water, followed by Marta and Pricilla. She turned, and in unison, the entire pod blew spouts of water high into the air. They rolled on their sides and raised their short flippers before diving below the surface. Evan and Gavin watched for what seemed like a very long time, hoping to see them resurface. As if sensing their tension, the pod flew out of the water and breached onto their backs.

"Cool!"

"Wild."

"Go, Denise!

See you soon!"

The boys ran up to the rental in time to make one last trip for bags. The Edmunds beeped the horn to the neighbours out on the lawn and headed south on Highway 5 to San Diego airport.

13

SWEET, SWEATY REVENGE

RUTH CISSY BLACKHORNE came back from the March school break on a tear. Rumour had it her ski trip to Whistler had been a complete disaster. From the moment the Blackhorne family arrived at the ferry terminal until they pulled into their driveway a week later, the vacation was nothing but misery. It started when Ruth refused to get into the car because she could not find her Justin Bieber hoodie. Mr. Blackhorne had paid a reservation fee to ensure they had a spot on the 10:15 a.m. ferry, but when they arrived ten minutes before sailing, the man at the booth said they had forfeited their spot because they were too late. They would have to wait for the 12:45 p.m. sailing.

Duncan, Ruth's four-year-old brother, lost it. He threw his juice box at the man in the window and barely missed spraying him with grape juice. This almost had them banned from sailing BC Ferries for life. Between scream, rants, tears and moaning from Mrs. Blackhorne about how they were going to arrive in the dark, Ruth closed her eyes and rocked out to "Burn It to the Ground."

Ruth got carsick on the winding roads and, without warning, vomited all over Duncan. Duncan puked on the back of his father's head, and Mrs. Blackhorne passed out. Ruth's father pulled over and retched till there was nothing left but dry heaves. It took over five minutes to revive their mother, and Ruth refused to help clean up. The final insult of the day came when the hotel's front desk clerk informed them that their two-bedroom suite had flooded. The only room left was a one-bedroom junior suite. Would they be needing one or two rollaway beds?

The next morning's sun and freshly groomed snow promised a day of fun and adventure. After a hearty breakfast, they hit the slopes. By noon they all laughed about the previous day. That was until they went to the indoor pool. Ruth ran out of the change room as fast as she could and did a cannonball. She hit the water and sprayed it all over the people who stood waiting by the pool's edge. She came up sputtering and laughing. It took her a moment to realize that no one was in the pool, and that everyone was pointing at her.

"Ruth! Get out of that pool right now!" Mrs. Blackhorne had gone grey in the face. Her finger trembled as she pointed at Ruth's forehead.

"Young lady! Do you not see the yellow hazard cones? This pool has been contaminated."

"Huh?" Ruth looked at the beak-faced man and gave him her best drop-dead look.

"Your forehead, stupid. You got *poo* on your forehead!" Duncan was deliriously happy.

Ruth reached up without thinking and wiped her hand across her brow. The lump of poo clung to her index finger and her thumb. The vacationers gasped. A little blonde-haired girl wrapped her arms around her mother's legs and buried her face in her knees. "Eww. Mommy, she's got cooties!"

Ruth ran screaming to the change room and all but peeled her skin off with the amount of scrubbing she did. Thirty minutes later, the pool was deemed sanitary again. Ruth decided to skip it and head for the hot tub. She jumped in and leapt out, all in one fluid motion, tripping over the *out of service* sign propped up against the ladder. Cold didn't even come close to describing how freezing the water was. Mr. Blackhorne threw up his arms in disgust and demanded that they all head back to the room.

The next day, the weather was too windy for skiing. Mrs. Blackhorne had been sulking since the day they'd left, so her husband announced he would help make up for it by taking her to the spa for a Swedish massage, a pedicure and a French manicure. He decided Ruth could be trusted to look after four-year-old Duncan for a few hours, and no amount of wailing on her part could persuade her father to change his mind. Duncan cried even louder but dried up when Mr. Blackhorne handed him a twenty-dollar bill. They were told not to leave the resort and to be back in the room by 4:00 p.m.

Ruth lost her brother within five minutes of her parents' departure.

She wasn't concerned at first. She was certain he was hiding in the room. Not that she tried to look. She flipped through a magazine and made half-hearted attempts to call for him. It was only when she got hungry that she started to look in the closet, under the bed and in the bathroom. The only room key they had was no longer on the side table, and his sneakers were missing.

"I'll kill that kid." She grabbed her hoodie and raced out the door.

First she checked the fitness centre. Duncan liked to hang off the pull-up bar and swing his little legs back and forth. If he wasn't doing that, he liked to put knots in the headphone sets that dangled from the treadmills and stationary bikes. She ran into the pool area but found no one there. She came up empty in the games room, café and gift shop. She thought it highly unlikely that he would go to the spa, but just in case, she snuck into the reception area and ran from room to room until she was satisfied he wasn't there. She heard her parents in the steam room discussing the value of new versus refurbished X-ray units. They were both dentists and seldom went an hour without discussing proper dental hygiene, non-surgical treatments or hard-to-find dental technicians.

Ruth circled the grounds. She knew that the chance of her rotten little brother going very far without his coat was pretty slim, so she tried the indoor tennis court and wound her way through the huge convention area. By the time she circled back to the reception area, she was sure she had inspected every square inch of the place. The question now was whether she should fess up to her parents or call 911. She decided to simply slip back into the room and pretend that she had fallen asleep. It wasn't her fault if the goofball took off while she was catnapping.

But getting back into the room was a much bigger problem than she anticipated. At twelve, she looked fourteen but talked like she was ten. She lacked manners, and made demands rather than requests. The front desk refused to give her a key. She begged, yelled and finally just walked away. She took the elevator to the nineteenth floor and decided that she would sit outside the door and wait until her parents came back. Plan B was to say that goofball had locked her out and escaped while she slept on the carpet.

She figured it was a stroke of genius when she switched to Plan C. She asked the cleaning lady in room 1905 to let her back in her room. She explained that her little defenceless brother was in there all by himself, and that she needed to make sure he was okay. The middle-aged lady shrugged and opened the door.

Ruth looked around the cramped room. Her eyes settled on a lump under the blankets on the bed. Quietly snoring away, curled up in a ball, was Duncan. Ruth's first instinct was to beat him to a pulp. Instead, she went to the bathroom, filled a glass with warm water and put his entire hand into the cup. He never woke up when he soaked the bed with bright yellow urine.

It took Mr. Blackhorne less than thirty seconds to see the bed and realize that his five-hundred-dollar spa investment to inject some peace into his wife's day had gone right out the window. The pee stain fanned out from Duncan, who was still sleeping soundly on his belly. Ruth never took her eyes off the television and offered no explanation.

Mr. Blackhorne wondered what time the last ferry left for the island. If only he could teleport himself home.

Rain kept them off the hills for the next three days, and by Thursday, cabin fever had set in so badly that all they could do was plug in their ear buds. Ruth went to bed early, hopeful that the morning trip home would be uneventful. Sometime in the night she rolled over, and, without warning, the rollaway bed caved in and snapped shut. Her nose pressed against her knees, and her toes stuck out from the top of the bed. Her muffled screams were barely heard by her parents. They were reliving their nightmarish vacation in their dreams and, try as they might, they couldn't make the screaming in their heads stop. It was Duncan who woke up and calmly stood beside the folded-up bed.

"Watcha doin'?"

"You idiot! Help me out!" Ruth's rants sounded a million miles away.

"Not till you say pretty please." Duncan wrapped a blanket around his shoulders and sat down on his own rollaway bed.

"You little twerp. I'll pulverize you! Get me out of here!"

"That's not very nice." Duncan stuck his thumb in his mouth and picked up Pooky Bear from the floor.

"Duncan…" Ruth's breathing was laboured and heavy. "If you don't get me out right now, I will smash your Lego train station to a thousand pieces!"

Duncan started to cry. He jumped in between his parents and wailed in his mother's ear. Mrs. Blackhorne woke with a start and smacked her head against the headboard. She groped in the dark for the light switch and stared in disbelief at the scene in front of her.

"I want to go home!" Her wails were louder than her son's. When hotel security arrived, they called for backup.

⸻

Now school was back in session, and there would be hell to pay.

When Ruth saw the Edmund boys with their tan, golden highlights, sporting T-shirts that read *Gnarly, Man!* and *Stoked!* she lost it. Bitterness welled in her throat, and a feeling of injustice overwhelmed her. *She* was the one who was supposed to have a sun-kissed glow. *She* was supposed to be back with stories about riding the Peak 2 Peak gondola between Whistler and Blackcomb Mountain and hanging out in Whistler Village. Instead, the kids were circled around Evan and Gavin, waiting to hear about *their* vacation. She saw red.

"Your shirts are lame. No one talks like that anymore. You look like idiots."

"They're vintage. You can't *get* anything cooler than this." Evan flashed his pearly whites, which looked even whiter against his tan.

"You wouldn't catch me wearing that," Ruth sneered.

"Yeah, I didn't need you to tell me that." Evan laughed and was joined by the large group of kids within earshot. Ruth clenched her fists tight and looked around for Thumper and his gang. She caught their eye, and they came over.

"They're like sharks," Coolio whispered in Evan's ear when he saw them approach. "Don't let them smell any fear." Coolio leaned back and greeted the hammerheads. "Ruth, good of you to call over your fiends... I mean your *friends*." Coolio's cheeky grin had some of the girls giggling.

"Watch your mouth, Gabriel."

"I see you grew another foot, Jonesy. Are you sure you don't have a hormone disorder?" The look of genuine concern on Coolio's face was amusing, at least to Evan and Gavin. "I know you don't let getting an education stand in the way of nabbing your next meal, but if I were you I'd lay off the grease. It's really is messing with your wholesome beauty."

Thumper Jones stepped into Coolio's space, but Ruth shot her hand out to block him and nodded in the direction of Mr. Lanzilotta, who had just walked out the side door of the school.

"Let me guess, you played hockey all March break?" Ruth wasn't an ugly girl, but every time she opened her mouth, her face contorted into a fearsome look. She was certainly lacking in the girlish charms department.

"Sure did. Non-stop. Just call me a skating demon!"

Coolio pretended to take a slap shot. Gavin joined in and gave his friend a hip check. Coolio feigned a bounce off the boards, tumbled down at Gavin's feet, then shot back up and laughed as he threw his full weight back at Gavin. Evan watched as his brother pretended to take the hit to his gut and doubled over. He came up with a holler. He threw his full body at Coolio, but suddenly Ruth jumped between them and took the full hit.

She let out a scream, fell to the ground and pointed at Gavin.

"He hit me! Ouch! My arm! He broke it. Mr. Lanzilotta, he hit me!"

The crowd of kids scattered. By the time Mr. Lanzilotta reached the group, there were only Evan, Gavin, Coolio, Thumper Jones and Ruth left. She didn't move from the ground, and Thumper had a menacing look on his face.

Coolio wasted no time. "She's lying. Gavin didn't hit her. She jumped in front of him. He was going to hit me."

Evan moaned. He knew Coolio didn't mean for it to come out that way, but the damage was done.

"You know the school's policy on hitting. Let's go, the two of you. Ruth, go see Miss Dickson. Evan and Mr. Jones, get to your next class."

Mr. Lanzilotta led Gavin and Coolio away, holding an elbow in each hand. When they disappeared behind the steel door, Ruth jumped up, brushed the dirt from her pants and high-fived Thumper.

"*Sweet*. Boy, am I good or what? Maybe my dad is right. Maybe I should channel my energy into dramatic arts." She turned away, but Evan grabbed the back of her sweater.

"You're gonna regret that, Ruth. I swear to God, you're going to wish you never got out of bed today. You went too far this time." Evan's face had gone bright red, and he wouldn't let go of her.

"If you don't let go of me, I'll tell Thumper here to break a few more school rules." Evan could see that the goon was dying to do that very thing, and he knew now was not the time to seek his revenge. He was so mad he couldn't think straight. He picked up Gavin and Coolio's backpacks and walked away from his arch rival.

He was determined that this would be the last time Ruth Cissy Blackhorne ever had the upper hand over him.

———

"We could glue her locker door shut." Gavin tossed a soccer ball in the air and let it roll down his arm. He sat on the big boulder, determined not to let the ball drop again. Scrambling up and down was getting tiring.

"Nah. That's destroying school property. If we got caught, we'd really be in trouble. Too risky. What else you got?" Evan chewed his lower lip and absent-mindedly flicked pebbles into the water.

"We could pull down her pants when she leaves the cafeteria carrying a loaded tray."

"Ugh, Gavin! Gross!" Coolio shuddered and passed the bag of salt and vinegar chips back to Evan.

"Meggie, what have we ruled out?" Evan had to raise his voice to be heard. Meagan stood on the shore, skimming stones. She still couldn't get it to skip as many times as Gavin could, but she was getting better.

"We said no to duct-taping her and leaving her behind in the music room. We said no to posting nasty messages. Let's see." Meagan tilted her head and put her finger to her chin. "We said no to egging her house and putting a steaming pile of dog poo in her desk."

"Remind me why we said no to all of those. 'Cause honestly, they work for me." Coolio took the chip bag back from Evan.

"Because we are mature, not that mean, and know that if we got caught we would never see outside our bedroom walls again." Meagan angled her arm and threw a flat stone at the smooth surface of the water. She was rewarded with six bounces. She whirled around and pointed at Gavin. "In your face! Ha! Enjoy your title, Gavin. It's mine next summer."

Evan did not join in the laughter. "She's an animal. Pure and simple. She'd a rotten dirty animal." Evan spoke to no one in particular.

"I may have to take offence to that." Carolynn flew out of nowhere and landed on the boulder between Gavin and Coolio. She looked up at Evan and winked. "Mind you, if half of what you say about this Ruth girl is true, I would support the notion that she is a shark. A nasty, indiscriminate predator who deserves to learn a valuable lesson. How can I help?"

Evan perked up. Carolynn had a way of calming him despite his moods. If anyone could figure out a fair yet appropriate form of revenge, it was Carolynn.

"You can help us plot against our arch rival. Meggie, tell Carolynn what Ruth did to you in Grade 3."

"My mom, in her loving yet clueless wisdom, decided that I should not exclude any of the girls from my birthday party sleepover. Now, eleven nine-year-old girls at a sleepover is one thing, but eleven nine-year-olds with Ruth slithering around us was a really bad idea. I kept my eyes open as long as I could. I fell asleep between the twins, thinking I was safe. When I woke up in the morning, my hair—that used to reach the middle of my back—was cut to the base of my neck. I didn't know until I lifted my head and saw long locks of hair on my pillow. My mother cried for weeks, and it took forever to grow back."

"Wicked child! In the animal kingdom, such a child would be eaten by her mother." Carolynn puffed her wings and shook her massive head in indignation. "Evan, Meagan." Carolynn looked from one child to the other. "Tell me her weaknesses."

They spent the rest of the cool afternoon telling their defender about Ruth's obsession with chocolate, her phobia of spiders and her dislike of freckles. They told Carolynn about her complete disregard for authority figures and how she took obscene delight in tormenting smaller children.

Carolynn sat quietly as they recounted Ruth's evil deeds—all seven years of them. She only interrupted once or twice to ask for clarifications: Was a wedgie a fruit or mineral? How did Earl get the bubble gum off his steering wheel? How was it that no one saw her fill Miss McGrade's desk with slugs? When she stole so many lunches, what did the children eat instead? Did they go hungry?

By the time the kids were finished telling Carolynn Ruth's long history of destructive, abusive and devilish behaviour, they were exhausted and defeated. How could they ever neutralize someone as evil as Ruth? Were they destined to another five years of anxiety at her hands?

"Absolutely not," said Carolynn. "She just needs to learn that there is a greater force than her. She thinks she is the centre of her universe and everyone else's. It is time that Ruth learned differently." Carolynn looked peaceful for the first time since she'd flown in. "Time to call in the creative thinkers…"

Her hoots were loud and unexpected. The Shimmies arrived from all directions.

"My friends, our children are under attack. I need you to listen to them, and we need to help them find a way to defeat a bottom feeder."

Evan and Meagan kept Coolio clued in to the discussion. He volunteered to go first, and offered the best description he could think of. "She likes to intimidate younger kids, she steals whatever she wants, she lies effortlessly, and she has a knack for zeroing in on someone's insecurities and making them feel even worse than they already do. She enjoys making people mad, and threats don't seem to affect her. Ev, did I miss anything?"

"No, my man. You nailed her."

Mr. Biggsy stepped up and cleared his throat. "Ruth sounds like she suffers from a classic case of Oppositional Defiant Disorder. Her need to blame others and be vindictive is consistent with this disorder."

The kids slowly nodded their heads. "What did I miss?" Coolio said. "Who said what?"

Gavin looked at Coolio. "Mr. Biggsy said she is bad to the core and likes to mess with people."

"As precise as that may be," Mr. Biggsy said, "Ruth must learn the consequences of her behaviour. Let's start with her gluttony. Eating not just her own lunch but her classmates' is a thinly disguised attempt to show off her social status. She sees herself at the top of the food chain—quite literally, I might add—and she likes to display her good fortune at having so much." Mr. Biggsy moved aside when Coolio, Gavin and Evan hopped down from the boulder.

"Okay, so she's a pig. We all know that. What do we do about her?" Gavin dropped the ball on the beach and sat on it.

Meagan crouched down beside him. "I think Barry might take objection to that statement."

"Fine, not a pig. She's a sloth." Gavin was getting irritated.

"Technically," said Mr. Biggsy, "that is not correct either. Sloths are slow-moving mammals that live in the trees of South America. They eat leaves and sleep upside down in trees." Mr. Biggsy was not cluing into Gavin's exasperation. "Of course, one could compare her behaviour to that of a spoiled, overindulged, twelve-year-old Homo sapiens female." He sat back and peered at Gavin with one eyebrow arched.

"Fine! I get it! Human. Not animal. Bad human. Now help us defeat her!"

Rad-knows-ways looked sly and mischievous as he moved into the centre of the circle. "I'd say you give her everything she wants and then some."

Razor licked his lips and laid down at the beaver's feet. "This oughta be good."

It took a few days to set the plan in motion. With the exception of those who could not be trusted, all students of North Cedar Intermediate were signed up.

Mission FRRD went into effect the following Monday. At first no one took notice of the subtle shift in the behaviour of the students. Ruth and her goons assumed the kids finally understood that the last two rows on the bus should always be kept empty for her and her friends. Kids crammed into the first three-quarters of the bus and didn't even look at them.

In the hallway, students kept a noticeable distance from Ruth's locker, and if she walked into the bathroom, all the girls left. In the playground, if Ruth and her friends tried to join a soccer or handball game, everyone dropped the ball and walked away. In class, if a teacher asked a question and Ruth put up her hand, all the other students put their hands down. By the third day, the teachers started to take random children aside and quietly ask them what was going on. Why was everyone avoiding Ruth Cissy Blackhorne? These students all knew the drill. They sighed, cast their eyes to the floor and said in low voices, "I don't know what you mean." If pressed, they said, "Nothing is going on," and then asked if they could go back to their classroom.

When the bell rang for lunch on Thursday, there was electricity in the air. Everyone could feel the tension that had been building all week. Kids milled outside the cafeteria, deliberately waiting for someone to arrive before they went in. Ruth, Thumper Jones and the crew showed up five minutes later. Everyone stopped chatting when they rounded the corner and saw the corridor lined with half the school. No one was entering the cafeteria line. They all stood back and let her go first.

"What? Did someone fart in there? Too stinky for your delicate noses?" She laughed an uneasy laugh and walked past the students, whose eyes were on anything and anyone but her.

The cafeteria staff shared nervous glances. Where were the screaming, laughing, starving children? With only forty minutes for lunch before the caf doors were closed, the quiet seemed unnatural and eerie.

"What are ya staring at?" Ruth could feel the gazes of the cafeteria staff following her through the line. "Ain't ya got something better to do?" She took her tray and walked out into the lunch room. She slapped her tray down loudly on her usual table and listened to the echo in the empty room.

"What did you do, Ruth?" Roy, Thumper's younger brother, took his seat two spots down, but he didn't dive into his fries like he usually did. He pulled at the neck of his sweater and took a long swig of his Coke.

Ruth noticed the caf monitors and a few teachers talking at the back of the room. They all looked at her strangely.

"Whatever. If those head cases want to stand out in the hall all lunch, it ain't my fault." She launched into her meatball sandwich with gusto and laughed when Thumper swiped a handful of fries from Roy's plate.

When Ginger and Tina Coppy entered the lunch room, Ruth didn't even notice them. When they walked up to her table, put their lunch bags down and quietly walked away, she just shrugged. Evan, Gavin, Meagan and Coolio did the same. When student after student walked up to her table and placed an item in front of her, she started to pay attention. Sandwiches, drinks, chips, burgers, Pop-Tarts, apples, boxes of raisins, bowls of soup, plates of fries, a Thermos of Alpha-Getti, a Tupperware filled with veggies and dip, bunches of grapes, cereal bars and animal crackers piled up high in front of her. Thumper and the boys stood back in horror as the table disappeared under the mountain of food. Ruth's lunch was lost behind it all, and even after the food started to spill off the table, the lineup of kids didn't stop. Grade after grade came in, dumping their food around Ruth. She was speechless.

The students filed past the equally speechless monitors and teachers. Miss LeBoof joined the teachers and watched the odd scene. The students walked straight out the double doors and marched, single file, to the office. Miss Dickson, the school receptionist, had just sat down at her desk to enjoy a hot cup of chicken noodle soup and a romance novel when she peered through the glass partition and saw a sea of kids. She dropped her book and dialled the extension to the teacher's lounge. "Mrs. Rosaline come to the office immediately."

"What's the meaning of this?" Technically, there was no reason for the principal to be alarmed. Not one child spoke. They were lined up against the wall in an orderly fashion. They stood with their eyes cast down.

Evan stepped forward and cleared his throat.

"Mrs. Rosaline, may I please have a cereal bar from the snack basket?" The school kept a basket on the counter for kids who found themselves with a light lunch and were still hungry. It was only used in an emergency, and some days not one child needed to supplement their meal.

"Of course you can, Evan."

She turned to Tina and asked why she was not outside playing.

"Mrs. Rosaline, I'm hungry. I was hoping I could take an apple from the snack basket. May I?"

Tina walked in behind Evan and took a bright red apple. The wise old principal looked over the heads of what looked like her entire school of children. "Let me guess. You are all here to get something from the snack basket."

In unison, they all said, "Yes!"—although a mopier mob was never seen before, Mrs. Rosaline was sure. Before she could ask any more questions, one of the lunch monitors ran up to her, breathless.

"You'd better come see this, Mrs. Rosaline!"

The principal cast her eyes to the ceiling and counted to ten in her head. She ran off, wondering what she would encounter.

In her thirty years as an educator, she had never seen such a sight. Almost two hundred lunches sat piled high in front of Ruth Cissy Blackhorne's table in the cafeteria. There was so much food that the girl was trapped on all sides. Ruth was demanding that someone get her out of there, but her large foot soldiers were not moving.

"No way. I'm not touching any of that food. Ruth, you're on your own." Thumper and his friends ran past the teachers and disappeared outside.

"Miss Blackhorne, you had better have a good explanation for this!"

"I don't know why everyone put their food on my table. I want out of here! Where are the stupid teachers?"

"Watch your manners, young lady. It appears you are in enough trouble as it is." Mrs. Rosaline tried to get a clear view of the girl, but there was too much food in the way. "Why would every student in the school give you their food?"

"I told you, I don't know! I usually just swipe from five or six of them. They know I don't want their fruit or vegetables. Why would I? Now, come on! Help me!" Ruth's wails were pitiful. She tried to push her chair out, but when she did, a plate of poutine fell from the top of the pile and landed in her lap.

"I think not. I think it best that your father assist you. You can sit right there while I go and call him. Miss LeBoof, please make sure that Ruth does not go anywhere."

Miss LeBoof crossed her arms over her chest and leaned back against the wall. She nodded her head and smiled sweetly at Mrs. Rosaline. "I would be *delighted* to. Take your time. We're not going anywhere."

After Ruth was pulled free from the mountain of food and carted off by her exasperated father, Mrs. Rosaline uncovered the whole story. She had been too busy writing Ruth's notice of expulsion to witness the transformation within her school. But eventually whispers of FRRD's success floated through the corridor. Children danced merrily from class to class, and the whole school seemed ready to burst with joy.

A little fourth-grader was gulping water from the fountain outside the office when Mrs. Rosaline eyed her. "My dear, you look like a clever girl. Can you tell me what *FRRD* stands for?"

Without a moment of hesitation, the angel-faced girl blurted out, "*Finally Ruth Revenge Day!*" She laughed and ran off to her class.

Mrs. Rosaline cast her eyes to the ceiling and started to counted to ten. Then she stopped, shrugged and walked back to the teacher's lounge to finish her half-eaten sandwich.

14

IMMY-SHAY

MARCH ROLLED INTO APRIL, and April rolled into May. The children juggled their studies, sports and treasure hunting as best they could. The last of the season's rain blew out with the shift of the winds. Wet, muddy days were replaced with sunny, dry days. The birds' loud chirping woke the residents of the island by 6:00 a.m., and the temperature hit fifteen degrees Celsius by noon.

Evan, Gavin, Meagan and Coolio met every Sunday morning to discuss a plan for the week. After months of fruitless searching for Donkey's weeping willow, the children started to lose faith that it even existed. For so long they'd shared an enthusiasm for locating Brother Twelve's lost gold. It was the pursuit of that common goal that brought them even closer together and added intrigue to their week. But as weeks turned into months, and as each hunt turned into a goose chase, they wondered if the whole adventure was a complete waste of time.

It was Meagan who suggested they enlist the help of some adults. The trick was to do it without drawing attention to the real reason they needed assistance. Then there might be a chance they'd find the elusive tree. While the boys debated the pros and cons of that idea, Meagan decided to test her theory on Evan's mom. MJ had just come out on the patio to arrange some hanging baskets and add topsoil to the containers when Meagan approached her.

"Those baskets are beautiful. Do you need any help with them?" Meagan steadied the ladder MJ was positioning under some hooks high up in the wall.

"Thanks, honey. You can hand me that basket over there—the one with the trailing ivy." Meagan did as she was told and watched while MJ hung each of the six baskets artfully.

"You sure have a wide variety of flowers. What is that one?" Meagan pointed to a bunch of pretty pink flowers.

"That's trailing sweet pea. I grew all of these annuals from seed in our glass house this winter. First time I ever did that. It was quite satisfying to see how they grew and how it all came together when I made up the baskets. Want to hang the last one?"

Meagan traded places with MJ. She was surprised at how heavy the basket was, but with some help from MJ, she managed to get it on the hook. When she jumped down, she stood back and admired the arrangement.

"You did a great job. You must know so much about British Columbia flowers, bushes... trees and stuff, right?"

MJ barked with laughter. "Oh, I wouldn't say that." She pulled off her gardening gloves and picked up the lemonade she had left on the hot tub cover. "Growing a few seeds is one thing. Knowing all the flora of the region is quite another."

"Oh yeah, sure. That would be a lot to know. What I mean is, if you wanted to find a particular flower—or, say, a tree—and it was somewhere on the island, you would probably know where to go looking for it, right?" Meagan suddenly got very nervous. It didn't feel natural to drill MJ like this. But the boy's mom was busy taking pictures of her baskets and didn't seem to notice her flushed cheeks.

"Joe would be the expert in that area, or better yet, one of his pals from the Tree Society of Arborists. They could answer any questions you have. Probably the most knowledgeable is Davey Golding."

"Really? Old Davey?"

"Uh-huh. In his day he was a tree faller, a tugboat captain, a teacher and, just before he went blind, a honey farmer. That man has such a rich background, and because his mind is a steel trap, he seems to remember everything."

"Thanks, MJ! This really helps."

Meagan didn't notice the odd look that came over MJ's face. She watched as Meagan ran over to the boys and indicated for them to follow her. Something she'd said had excited the girl. She replayed their conversation in her mind, but of the little she'd shared about Davey, she couldn't figure out what would have triggered such a response. She took one last look at the kids as they headed around to the front of the house. It wasn't worth worrying about, she decided. She picked up her gardening tools and tackled the overgrown clematis bush that was creeping in every direction.

"Meggie, hold up. Where are you taking us?" Evan always marvelled at how long Meagan's strides were. She could cover more distance than anyone he knew.

Meagan stopped abruptly in the open area at the top of the property and sat down on a dry patch of grass. She patted the ground so they would join her.

"Old Davey is a tree expert, even better than your dad. I bet you he'll know where to look." She went on to explain her conversation with MJ. It had never occurred to any of them to ask what he had done all those years ago. No wonder he loved to talk to Mortimer. They could talk about plants all day long. Boring!

"Let's go visit him. He only lives down the road. We could ride our bikes there." Meagan jumped up as inspiration hit her. "My mom and Davey's daughter have been exchanging recipes for organic baking. We just made a batch of gluten-free cinnamon yam cookies. I say we ride over there and bring them a tin. What do you say?"

"I say I like Davey too much to do that to him. Meggie, couldn't you have at least added some chocolate chips or marshmallows? I mean seriously." Gavin's disgust was comical, but it had absolutely no effect on Meagan. She was running up the driveway at light speed.

"Be at my house in twenty minutes!" She disappeared around the bend and was gone.

The bike ride to Davey's was not quite "around the corner." It took them almost twenty minutes to get to the off-the-beaten-track farmhouse. Davey lived there with his daughter Anne. At sixty-four, she was tall and willowy with the same intriguing facial features as her father. Where Davey had deep blue eyes, hers were icy blue. When the kids pulled up on their bikes, Anne was in the garden, weeding.

"What a lovely surprise. What brings you to our neck of the woods?" Anne pulled off her gardening gloves and pulled herself up to her full size.

The kids jumped off their bikes and walked over. "My mom sent you these homemade organic cookies. She knows you've been looking for unique recipes that will allow you to feed Davey wholesome food he might like. The recipe is written on the bottom of the cookie tin."

"Claire is such a dear! How sweet of her to think of us. Her last recipe for bean curd with black bean sauce was amazing!"

Gavin coughed into his fist, "Poor, poor Davey."

Evan and Coolio giggled but wiped the smirks off their faces when they saw Meagan's scowl.

"Is your dad here, Anne?" Meagan walked past her and started toward the front door.

"He sure is. He'll be thrilled to have a visit from you kids. Give me a minute to put these gardening tools away, and then I'll join you." She picked up her gloves, clippers and hand spade and walked toward the shed at the back of the property.

Meagan had been to the Golding house a few times and knew her way around. The boys hesitated at the door but quickly took off their shoes and rushed in when Meagan headed up the wide wooden stairs.

"Where's she going?" Coolio tried to keep his voice low, but he was distracted by the birdcages in the front room. No less than four large cages stood near the front bay window. In each one were two birds. In the first cage, there were two rainbow lorikeet parrots. In the second and largest cage, there were two huge scarlet macaws. In the third cage were orange-winged Amazon parrots, and the fourth cage held peach-faced lovebirds. Coolio immediately stopped in his tracks and walked toward the domed cages.

"Wow. Look at these birds. They're beautiful! I wonder why Davey and Anne only have two birds in each cage."

"Because each set of parrots is bonded. One male with one female. They only want to be with each other. That is the only way to create a peaceful environment. If only humans would learn from these clever creatures."

Davey sat quietly in the corner of the room with a plate of half-eaten cheese and crackers on his lap. Taffy slept quietly at his feet.

"Oh! I didn't see you there, Davey." Coolio walked over to the old man and knelt down in front of him. "We came over to surprise you."

"Well, you certainly did. Was that Meagan who flew up the stairs? She often finds me in the front room banging away on the piano or playing my guitar."

Gavin stepped over to the staircase and screamed, "Meagan! Come downstairs! Davey is hiding out here. He's sitting in a ratty old chair—" Evan punched his arm. "I mean, he is talking to Coolio in the living room." Gavin was grateful Davey couldn't see him blush ten shades of red.

Meagan flew down the stairs and joined Evan and Gavin when they walked into the parlour.

"Meagan, I didn't expect you until next week. Your mom was going to show Anne how to bake cherry tarts."

"The boys and I rode our bikes over to give you this tin of cookies."

"You are the best children on the island! Tell me they have chocolate chips in them."

"Ha! What did I tell you?" Gavin smirked and crossed his arms across his chest.

Meagan didn't even bother acknowledging his statement. "Not quite. Here, try one." She took the lid off and held them within reach. Coolio guided his hand to the tin and looked on in wonder as Davey zoned in on the biggest cookie.

"Like parrots, cookies and milk must be paired together. Meagan, can you run into the kitchen and pour me a tall glass?"

"Happy to." She quite literally skipped off, humming a show tune under her breath.

"Okay, youngest Edmund boy," Davey whispered. "You've got exactly two seconds to tell me: Will this cookie have me gagging up my noon meal, or will I beg for more?"

Gavin didn't bat an eye. "Say you have a dodgy stomach and that you need to take your medication first. That'll buy you a day or two." When Davey cocked an eyebrow, he added, "And say your doctor advised you to stay away from experimental foods. Chips Ahoy! and Nestlé Toll House are the only doctor-recommended cookies you can eat. Protect yourself, Davey."

Gavin walked over to one of the cages as Meagan walked in with a large glass of milk.

"Here you go, Davey. A tall glass of organic, lactose-free goat's milk. Bottoms up!"

Davey grunted and took the glass with much hesitation. "What a good girl you are. At my age, I forget everything. My doctor cautioned me against cookies and milk at this time of day. Maybe I could save these for later…"

At that moment, Anne walked in. "What are you talking about, Dad? Doctor Kelly said you were fit as a fiddle. Go ahead and show Meagan how much you like her cookies."

With no way out, Davey dunked the cookie into the milk and shoved a corner of it into his mouth.

"Hmm, great. Lovely. Wonderful. Thank you." He mumbled and used a tissue to wipe the milk—and most of the cookie—away from the corner of this mouth.

Coolio leaned in and said as quietly as he could, "Spit it into the milk. No one will see it when it sinks to the bottom."

To distract everyone from Davey, Evan walked over to the first cage and pointed to the parrots. "These two are amazing. Look at the colour of their feathers. What are their names?"

"Claudette and Claudio."

"Cute. What about the two in the big cage?"

"My macaw beauties are Lucy and Lou."

"Davey, we are seeing a pattern here. Okay, what about cage number three?"

"If you are looking at the white-domed wrought-iron cage, that would be my orange-winged Amazon pair. Aren't they lovely? I call them Sonny and Cher."

He smiled huge and swept the room as if he knew where everyone stood. "Notice the blue and yellow feathers on their heads. See the orange feathers in their wings and tails? I've had them since I was a teenager. Isn't that something?"

"No way. But Davey, you're ninety!"

"Yup, they're old like me. They still sing and talk to me like they did when they were little more than a year old. Sonny and Cher never fail to entertain me."

"What about these three lovebirds?" Evan looked into the cage and thought he recognized the pretty little rosy-faced bird. "I particularly like the one that is glowing emerald green with a silvery halo around its head. I think it looks like…"

Evan stopped talking. He looked meaningfully at Meagan and Gavin and cocked his head toward the third lovebird that was sitting by itself on the top wood perch.

"Is that what I think it is?" Meagan tried to conceal her mouth behind her hand as she leaned in and peered at the beautiful bird.

"If you mean an immy-Shay, then yes." Gavin did nothing to keep his voice down.

"Ah! Immy-Shay: pig Latin for *Shimmy*. What is that? Anyway, you must be going blind too, Evan. We only have two lovebirds." Davey groped for his cane and tried to find Coolio's shoulder so he could launch his tall frame out of the armchair.

"A Shimmy! Here? Where?" Coolio spun around just as Davey grabbed his shoulder. Both stood up at the same time, and for a moment, they swayed like a great logging tree about to crash to the ground.

"Oh, we're just goofing around. Tell us about your lovebirds,

Davey." Meagan took a step back from the cage, but didn't take her eyes from the third bird.

"Well, let's see. What can I tell you about my sweet darling lovebirds?" Davey leaned his weight on Coolio and took a few steps toward the cage. "The male is boring and does nothing but eat his fruits and vegetables. His name is Tobias. Useless, really. Quite a disappointment. But the female, ah… She is my little sweetheart. She sings like Vera Lynn. I call her Little Theresa."

"Who is Vera Lynn?" Gavin stepped up to the cage and delighted in how the Shimmy stared back at him with her jewelled eyes. The little bird bobbled her head as if encouraging Gavin to listen to the old man.

"She was long before your time. She was a popular singer in England during World War II. When I was posted to Burma, I saw her perform at an outdoor concert she gave for the soldiers stationed there. I still cry every time I hear 'The White Cliffs of Dover.'" Davey surprised the children by sniffing and wiping his eyes on his sleeve.

"Oh, never mind weepy eyes over there. He joined the Royal Air Force when he was only eighteen years old. He hardly had any hair on his chin." Anne looked at the bird. "I agree, though. Little Theresa is a remarkable parrot. She only sings for Dad. I've never even heard her."

Anne walked up to the cage, and Evan could see that she was looking at the smaller female perched beside Tobias on the lower railing. She didn't seem to see the Shimmy in the upper left-hand corner of the cage.

"She sits dopey all day long, and the minute we turn our back on her, she sings and talks away. Dad says some of the things she says are hilarious. I wouldn't know. She doesn't seem to want to perform for me."

Anne opened the cage and extended her finger to the smaller peach-faced parrot. Before she took the bird out and closed the door, Little Theresa—*Shimmy* Little Theresa—flew out and landed on top of Davey's head.

"Hello."

The word came out of nowhere. Anne had been so busy locking the cage door that she didn't notice that the sound actually came from across the room.

"Clever girl." She reached out and patted the parrot's head.

"See! Isn't my Little Theresa a chatty girl? On her first day meeting you, too." Davey put his arm out so Anne could place his beloved bird there. Meanwhile the children looked intently at the lovebird sitting on his head.

"'We'll Meet Again' is her favourite song. She sings it late at night when the lights go out. She sounds just like the 'Angel of the Trenches.' If someone had told me, back when I was a young lad hiding scared in the Burmese jungle during the war, that I would one day own a parrot that sang like the iconic Vera Lynn, I would have told them they suffered from jungle fever!"

Evan, Gavin and Meagan surrounded Old Davey. Coolio glanced at Evan, who glanced at Davey and nodded ever so slightly in the direction of his head. Anne announced that she would put the kettle on and disappeared to the back of the house.

"How long have you had Little Theresa?" Meagan reached out and patted the female on his arm but never took her eyes off the peach-faced lovebird that was now clawing at Davey's hair and rustling her feathers prettily.

"Oh, not long, only five odd years or so. When Tobias's old mate died, we bought her to ease his broken heart. I'll never forget the day. I had just retired from being a honey farmer. My sight was gone, and I retreated more and more to the house. At eighty-five years of age, I still had a hard time accepting my blindness. Anne announced one morning it was time for me to stop moping. She took me to the local pet shop to pick out a new lovebird. While she and the shopkeeper were busy at the front of the store, I stood in the back, surrounded by cages of chirping birds. I could make out the call of each type of bird, and was lost in memories of how they looked, when I heard her. The sweet sounds of the famous British singer Vera Lynn drifted out from one of the lovebird cages. I was in disbelief. How could a parrot mimic so perfectly the singing style of a venerable singer like Vera Lynn?"

Davey adjusted the bird on his arm.

"Well, I bought her, didn't I? Right on the spot. I've never had another mopey day since. I swear on my beloved wife Victoria's grave. If I ever get down, this little bird seems to know it, and she just sings her little parrot heart out. Imagine that."

Shimmy Little Theresa hopped onto Davey's shoulder and winked at the children. She opened her beak and let out a shrill call.

"Now, now, Theresa. Something pretty, if you will." Davey patted the head of the impostor and turned his head away as if to will her to sing.

Little Theresa moved further down his arm. She positioned herself beside the other female and took a moment to compose her feathers.

What came out of her white beak was a shock to say the least. She sang quietly.

Davey smiled brightly, but his eyes teared up again. He swayed and joined in with her, and they ended on a unified note.

"Clever girl, clever girl." He kissed the parrot's head and asked Coolio to lead him back to his overstuffed chair.

Meagan put out her arm to see if Shimmy Little Theresa would come to her, but instead the parrot leapt back up onto Old Davey's shoulder and nestled under his shirt collar.

"Davey, MJ was telling us about all the jobs you've had over the years, and how you are a founding member of the Tree Society of Arborists. The boys and I are budding tree enthusiasts, and we were wondering if you could set us straight on a few things."

"Ask away. Nothing gets this old heart pumping like a good old yak about trees. Which species do you want to start with? Palm trees are my specialty, but it's safe to say I can yammer on about any tree."

"How about weeping willow trees?" Gavin could hardly contain his excitement.

"Oh yes, the shade tree. Genus is Salix, often found in moist soil. Thrives in our northern region. There are a few varieties on the island, of course. Any one in particular?" Davey settled back into his chair and lightly stroked his lovebird's feathers.

"The kind that is big, grows near the shore, and has knotty roots sticking out of the ground."

"Oh my. A description, not a species. No worries. I can play this game." He rubbed his stubbled beard and closed his eyes. "Is this a tree you've seen?"

"No!" everyone but Meagan responded. She was too busy watching the little Shimmy. Little Theresa had made a little nest for herself under Davey's collar and had tucked her beak under her right wing. She appeared to have fallen asleep.

"Okay. Do you know if it is on the mainland or on one of the islands?"

"The island!"

"Alrighty, then. Lower, middle or upper coast?"

"Davey, around here. It is somewhere around here!" Gavin was getting impatient, but when all three shot him a severe look, he toned it down. "We think it's south of Nanaimo, north of Ladysmith, near the shore, and up a hill. You can reach it by boat. Does that help?"

"It does, in fact. That stretch is only twenty-three kilometres long. Around twenty-five percent of that shoreline is sheer rock face, and you certainly couldn't pull a boat up onto it. Another twenty-five percent is exposed to high winds, and the willow wouldn't be able to take hold in the rocky, shallow soil. If I had to guess, your mysterious weeping willow is south of Dodd Narrows and north of Yellow Point. Now what's that?" Davey seemed to be doing some calculations in his head. "I'd say you've got around ten to twelve kilometres of shore to search."

"We can't do that!" Gavin ignored the looks of the other kids and paced the room. "Most of that is private property. Evan, how are we going to find it?"

"If I may inquire as to the significance of the search, I might be able to narrow that down for you a bit." Davey's face gave nothing away. He didn't seemed the least bit bothered by Gavin's outburst nor particularly intrigued by the fact that four children were on a quest to find a tree. And not just any old tree. A weeping willow tree with distinctive characteristics, one that stood somewhere near the shores of Georgia Strait.

Meagan's eyes swept their faces, and she decided to go out on a limb.

"A friend of ours told us about the tree. He stood under this tree a very, very long time ago. He can't remember exactly where it is, but he is certain we are not that far away from it. He knows he sailed west from Valdes Island, and when the boat was beached, he was led up a steep hill to flat, high ground. He cut through some blackberry bushes, and that is where the enormous weeping willow tree was found."

Davey tapped the arm of his chair. "How many years ago was this?"

Meagan didn't like to mislead him, but she certainly couldn't tell him a hundred-year-old albino donkey had told them the story.

"He is around your age and was just a boy when it happened. It was late at night, and there were no houses, no humans, for miles around." That was as much as she dared to say.

"Coolio, you're a tall lad. Go over to the bookshelf in the corner and reach your hand up to the top shelf. Bring me that long wooden box." He turned to Meagan. "Meagan, be a good girl and put my Little Theresa back in her cage." After the lovebird was back beside her mate and Coolio had brought the box to Davey, he indicated for all of them to sit on the large Asian rug.

Nestled in a cedar box were nautical maps. They were rolled up with elastic bands. Many were quite old and stained with coffee splatters. The fact that Davey was completely blind didn't stop him from sorting out the map he wanted. He pulled off the elastic bands and unravelled the map.

"Evan, locate Dodd Narrows for me. "He held out his left index finger for the boy to place on the map.

"Now, Gavin, place my right finger on the tip of Yellow Point. You'll know it because it should show the lodge located at that very spot. Blue Heron Park will be next to it."

"Yeah, here it is, Davey." Gavin firmly put his friend's finger down on the point, just where the coast cut into a narrow bay.

"The distance between my two fingers is where you will find this tree. No point trying to find it by foot. You need to search by boat. If I'm right, you will find it within one hour. You will see the top of the tree while you're bobbing out in the water. Bring some binoculars." He rolled up the map and handed it to Evan.

"I don't need it anymore. Put it to good use. I've marked it with all my favourite fishing and crabbing spots. Surprise your dad, and let him think you've got the luck of the Irish flowing through your veins. It's time your dad had that boat in the water anyway. Weather couldn't get any better than this."

"It just so happens that is exactly what he's doing. The hull got a fresh coat of paint, and he went to pick it up today." Evan tucked the map away safely in his backpack. He checked his watch and wondered if his dad was considering a quick trip out before the light faded.

Anne came back in with a tray loaded down with a teapot, cups and saucers, and Meagan's yam cookies.

"Here you go. One lump or two?"

They spent another hour enjoying Davey and Anne's company. Both of them had lived all their lives on the island, but throughout the years they'd travelled almost every corner of the globe. Throughout the spacious home was evidence of their travels: tribal masks, ceremonial swords, World War II memorabilia and silk rugs. In Davey's study, there were pictures of him from his days in Burma. He had been quite a handsome man. The framed black-and-white photo on his desk showed a fighter pilot inspecting the underside of a wing. He looked focused and ready for battle. Others on the wall showed his squadron engaging in various acts of leisure. One was of Davey suntanning on the side of a hill, while another showed him playing cards on large wooden box filled with ammunition. He enjoyed telling the children about his mates and how he kept in touch with the few lucky ones who made it out of the war.

After a tour of the garden, Evan looked at his watch. It was time to ride back. "Anne, we'll just say goodbye to Davey."

They found him in the armchair with his head resting against the back. His eyes were closed and silent tears streaked his cheeks, but he had a smile on his face. Shimmy Little Theresa sang quietly in the cage.

Meagan whispered into Evan's ear. "She must be singing 'The White Cliffs of Dover.'" The singing stopped.

"She is indeed. The voice of an angel." Davey opened his sightless eyes and used the back of his sleeve to dry his face.

"If it makes you so sad, why do you like it when she sings?" Evan looked at the petite glowing parrot and wondered if she would ever seek them out at their house.

"At my age, it is a gift to feel so much joy, even if it is bittersweet. My Little Theresa always seems to know what I need. She exists to take care of me, and her songs bring me back to a time when I was strong and felt invincible. You're still young, so this might not make sense to you now. Life should be a grand adventure. Go out and live yours. I hope you find your tree."

The Shimmy hopped to the edge of the cage and chirped once. When the children were all looking at her, she said, "Thank you for coming, knowing children."

Davey hooted and slapped his knee. "What did I tell you? A rarer bird you will never find."

The boys said goodbye, and Meagan ran over to give the dear old man a peck on the cheek. "See you soon, Davey. Next time I *will* make you some chocolate chip cookies."

⸺

"Wow. Where's the fire?" Joe looked up from his laptop at his breathless and flushed son.

"Dad, are we going out in the boat today?" Evan huffed and bent over to catch his breath. He glanced at the clock on the wall. It was past three o'clock.

"Sorry, monkey man, but no. I'll take you guys out next weekend."

Gavin, Coolio and Meagan ran in just in time to hear what Joe said.

"Oh, please, Dad!"

"Pretty please?"

"Just a quick trip out, *please!*"

The kids talked over each other. Joe sat back in the kitchen chair and looked at them curiously.

"Why the rush? We're in for a long, hot summer. We can go after school and on the weekends. Besides, don't you have homework?"

"All done. Dad, we've been looking forward to getting back on the boat since November. We only got out a few times before you had to put it away for the winter. Come on, it's mid-May. What are we waiting for?"

Joe's resolve started to waver. Coolio saw this sudden flicker of indecision and stepped in for the kill.

"It sure would be a great birthday gift. I'm thirteen on Tuesday. Isn't that a big deal? Shouldn't I have my manhood tested or something? I could catch a fish with my bare hands or maybe dive for crabs. I'm not big on the idea of harpooning a whale, but I might be open to lassoing it and going for a ride."

"And if you fail this test of manhood?" Joe asked gravely. "According to ritual rites, I am allowed to toss you overboard. If you swim back to shore safely, you get to stay in the tribe. If not, we never speak your name again." Joe tried to keep a straight face, but he burst into laughter. "All right. I'll call your parents to see if you're allowed to go. Evan, go see if Mom wants to come. Gavin, we'll need some snacks, juice boxes and the fishing gear. I'll check the latest marine conditions on Environment Canada's website. It was pretty calm this morning, but who knows what awaits us now."

Evan loved the way his dad never needed much arm-twisting.

Meagan and Coolio were expected home for dinner, so they went out only for a short ride. They untied quickly and made their way out of the protected cove. The conditions hadn't changed, and the sun on their face felt good. They were grateful for their wind jackets, though, as the breeze was just cool enough to chill bare skin. Meagan waved at the kayakers hugging the shoreline and called to the fisherman who had killed their engines and bobbed in their boats.

When they reached the opening of the harbour, MJ turned to Coolio. "Which way, birthday boy?"

"Due north, my fair lady. Hard to port! Watch for jetsam! Talk of mutiny will get you tossed overboard!" He added, "Forward ho!"

"This isn't a wagon train, but I get your drift. Hang on, kids. I'm opening her up!"

"Aye, aye, Captain!"

They all squealed when Joe slammed the throttle forward and, for a moment, the bow of the boat rode high. The two engines reached full thrust, and Joe trimmed the motor so they levelled off.

They flew past rocks and white beaches. Further out in the Stuart Channel, they could see sailboats flying in the wind. Joe pointed the bow north. He stayed in the middle of the channel between Vancouver Island and the outer islands.

"Dad, is that Yellow Point Lodge?" Gavin adjusted the binoculars, and suddenly a tall, wooden log building came into view.

"Sure is."

"Um, Dad, can you slow down?" Evan had to yell so his father could hear him.

"Sure. Let's crack open the root beer and divvy up the salt and vinegar chips."

Gavin passed the binoculars to Coolio, who scanned the shoreline for the elusive weeping willow. He swept the area until he was certain there was no tree that matched the willow's description.

Evan passed the bag of chips to Coolio, and in exchange he took the binoculars and searched the same area his friend had just inspected.

"We can rule out this area, he said casually into Meagan's ear. "It has to be somewhere further up the shore."

They meandered up the coast another twenty minutes, but then Joe announced it was time to head back.

When they pulled into Coolio's driveway, Evan hopped out of the truck and followed his friend to his door. "At least we've ruled out half of the area where the willow tree might have been. Next time we'll ask Dad to take us up to Dodd Narrows. We'll then head south toward the search area we covered today. I *know* we're going to find it. I can just feel it."

Coolio laughed and shook his head at his friend.

"You and your feelings. The last time you said that, you announced we were going to win a pair of Canucks season tickets. Before that, you said our punk video would be selected for television."

"All true. But I also predicted we'd win the jelly bean jar at Giuseppe's Eatery. No one even came close to the number we guessed. We were only off by four from the 937 in there!"

"Yeah, and they almost cracked my teeth in half they were so hard. They should have told us the jar had been sitting in that window for five years."

───

Like all good Canadians, the Edmunds spent the week planning for the upcoming Victoria Day celebration. From Newfoundland to British Columbia, people started their preparations by midweek. They aired out camping gear on front lawns, hosed down trailers, pulled boxed fireworks from garage rafters, and packed their freezers with burgers, sausages, steaks and chicken wings.

Joe made a few trips to the marina to drop off supplies for the boat. It was decided that they would camp on DeCourcy Island. Usually, the boys left all the planning to MJ and Joe, but this long weekend they expressed an intense interest in camping at Pirates Cove Marine Provincial Park. It was amusing to think that from the island, they would be able to look across the channel and see their little beach. If they ran out of ketchup, they could jump on the boat and be home in less than fifteen minutes.

On the ride over to the campground, Evan and Gavin tested their parents' knowledge of the island's history. Did they know it was named after Michael de Courcy, captain of the HMS *Pylades*, who originally surveyed the area in 1857?

Did they know the Aquarian Foundation, a religious cult with a leader named Brother Twelve, owned the island in the 1920s?

Did they know that the crazy leader stole from members of his foundation and made off with crates and crates of gold coins sealed in jam jars?

MJ and Joe were impressed by their questions. Who knew their little gamers were such history buffs?

They navigated into Pirates Cove and pulled the boat up on the shore so they could offload their gear easily. They tied the boat to one of the mooring rings and quickly located the Cove trail to their campsite. By noon their tents were pitched, their coolers were safely suspended from the closest trees, and they had located the solar washroom. They were now ready to explore the island.

They headed south on Pylades trail, which hugged the coastline. As it turned northward, they saw two harbour seals playing out in the water. Black-tailed deer were everywhere, and when they reached the opening of Pirates Cove, they saw two otters sunbathing. They ignored Red's barking and carried on as if they didn't hear him.

The sun was high in the blue sky. For a while they watched boaters and kayakers arrive from all directions.

"Can we go explore on our own?" Evan was itching to walk the Brother Twelve trail, and he wanted to do it without his parents.

"Sure. Take Red with you. Remember not to touch anything that looks remotely like poison oak, and don't disturb any piles of seashells. Much of what you see is protected."

"Okay, Dad. See you in a while."

The boys took off and followed the wooden sign that pointed them to where they could pick up the Brother Twelve trail. Neither boy was surprised when they were suddenly surrounded by their Shimmy friends.

"This is a lovely island for camping, boys." Carolynn flew onto one of the Garry Oak branches that sat at eye level.

"This would have been a fine place to live." Mr. and Mrs. Biggsy surveyed the area and noted the campers hauling coolers filled with tasty food. "Yes, we would have eaten like kings." Biggsy was tempted to follow the fellow who had a hot dog hanging from his mouth.

"Do you think the weeping willow could be on this island?" Rad-knows-ways was looking around keenly and went up on his hind legs when he heard more hikers making their way up the trail.

"It could be, but I doubt it. We think it's over there." Evan pointed across Stuart Channel and to the area where he guessed his street ended.

"So close yet so far." Gavin picked up a pine cone and balanced it on the tip of his finger. "We're going to take the boat back out and head up to Dodd Narrows. Dad thinks we're only going fishing, but we brought along Davey's map and plan to look for the willow the whole time."

"And if you find it? Then what?" Madeline had quietly joined them and was sitting, partially hidden, in an old-growth Douglas fir.

"We haven't figured that out yet. We're taking one day at a time right now."

The Shimmies stayed with the boys as they explored the trail and made their way back to the campsite. After a few chores they changed into their swimming trunks.

"Are you sure you don't want to join us, Mom?" MJ had stored the last of the leftovers and was hauling the cooler back up into the tree to keep it off the ground and away from bears.

"I sure am. An afternoon with Red, soaking up sun on a sandy point with a good book, beats an afternoon of fishing any day of the week. Have fun, and don't let your dad catch too many fish."

Joe and the boys headed north out of Pirates Cove. They rounded the top of DeCourcy Island and slipped past the south tip of Mudge Island. There was already a line of boats ready to pass through the Narrows. The tide was coming in again, and everyone was patiently waiting their turn. The rush of water was southbound, and when it was Joe's turn, he got on the radio and said, "All boaters, vessel *Carpe Diem* northbound in Dodd Narrows." Joe pegged the throttle and kept his speed up to sail over the whirlpools and rips.

The boys admired all the beautiful sailboats that were lined up to head in the way they had just come. They settled on a fishing spot just on the other side of the Narrows and threw anchor. While Gavin was busy putting worms on their hooks, Evan searched the tree line for any sign of a willow. It seemed to him that the surrounding coastline and winding trails featured every imaginable tree *but* a willow. So Evan settled back in his bucket seat. He decided to live in the moment and enjoy fishing with his dad and brother.

An hour later, with three ling cod in the cooler, the boys asked their dad if they could head back into the Narrows and cruise close to the shoreline to check out the neighbours' houses.

"Nosy little guys, aren't you? It's okay. I'm interested too."

They came out of the narrows and cruised slowly past Cedar-by-the-Sea. Knowing that Brother Twelve had lived there so many years ago, and had sailed these same waters to transport his gold and ammunition to his compounds on DeCourcy and Valdes islands, was a bit thrilling. Evan and Gavin took turns using the binoculars to search the coast. On a couple of occasions, they asked their dad to stop, look through the binoculars and tell them what kind of trees he could see. Joe was delighted that his boys were finally taking an interest in his hobby as an arborist.

"See any weeping willow trees?" Gavin was starting to get bored with the whole business, and thought turning it all over to their dad made a lot of sense.

"Nope, but here: look at that spectacular arbutus. Look how far it's hanging over the water." Joe handed the binoculars back to Evan, who promptly handed them to Gavin.

Joe took a look at their bored faces. "I think we're done for today. Let's go see what your mom is up to. Tomorrow we'll do some tubing. What do you think, guys?"

Joe didn't even wait for an answer. He cut across the channel and entered Pirates Cove just as four very loud sea lions exited. They seemed to be barking at everyone, but most of all at the blue heron that taunted them by flying low and then suddenly soaring high in the air as if to say, *Look at what I can do, you stinky, waterlogged mammals!*

They found MJ at the campsite, prepping for dinner.

"Are we eating Schneider's all-beef dogs, or am I pan-frying some tasty fish?"

In response to their mom's question, Evan and Gavin held up the bag filled with the freshly caught ling cod.

"Oh, my heart be still. They may be ugly, but they taste fine! Bring them here, boys. You gut, and I'll wash them."

In the end it was Joe who gutted and cleaned the fish. For all her talk, MJ was squeamish around anything that had once breathed— or in a fish's case, blew bubbles. They ate their dinner while the sun settled behind Mount Benson. One of the campers strummed away on a guitar and hummed a tune. Without putting up an argument, the boys climbed into their sleeping bags and fell fast asleep within minutes.

Sunday was even warmer than the day before. The sun rose early, and by breakfast everyone had stripped down to shorts and T-shirts. They took turns pumping water into the pots they brought and helped their mom do the dishes before they were allowed to take off and explore the island again. Reddy Bun-Buns and Ever-Ready Freddy took charge. They darted under bushes and beckoned the boys follow them. Going off the trails was breaking MJ's first rule, but the baby bunnies insisted they knew where they were going. On one occasion they brought them to a rabbit den. Nestled under a log, and partially hidden by tall grass and weeds, were two newborn cottontails. They had no fur, and their eyes were sealed shut. Ever-Ready Freddy explained that the mother was out foraging and would return at nightfall to feed her babies. The boys took a few pictures but didn't venture too close for fear they might disturb the sleeping bunnies.

Next, the Burrow bunnies took them up a hill overlooking a crop of trees. Balanced between three branches was an eagle's nest. Two bald eagle chicks squawked loudly for food. They seemed oblivious to the humans as they searched the skies for their parents. The eaglets crawled around the nest and bumped into each other repeatedly. At one point they played tug-of-war with a stick, and the smaller one seemed to win the battle.

Reddy Bun-Buns refused to let the children watch the eagles for too long. He wanted to show them something most people never see in a lifetime. He led them further up the hill. They climbed up a particularly steep incline, and at one point, Evan had to grab Gavin's arm before he slid back down the rocky slope. The bunny finally stopped in front of a shallow, wide cave. The bunnies hopped in and stopped beside a large mound.

"Do you know what those are?" For the first time since he had come into their lives, Reddy Bun-Buns seemed serious and solemn. When they didn't answer, he sat up on his hind feet and twitched his little nose.

"They're dinosaur bones!" Freddy burst with excitement and ran around in circles.

"No way. Are you sure?" Gavin went to touch one of the large bones, but Evan grabbed his hand.

"Not a good idea, Gav. If Freddy and Reddy Bun-Buns are right, we've got to tell someone. This is huge." He thought for a moment. "This could make us famous!"

"What kind of dinosaur was it?" Gavin got closer but didn't disturb the bones lying buried under a layer of dust.

"How should I know? I'm just a baby bunny."

"If you lived back when it did, would it have eaten you?"

"Um, no."

"It only ate leaves?"

"Uh-huh."

"Four legs or two?"

"Two, and two really small arms. He was kinda cute."

"Right. So we have a herbivore dino who was bipedal, and I see the hip bones are narrow—so maybe an ornithopod. Do you see a duck bill anywhere in that mess of bones?" Gavin looked up. Ever-Ready Freddy was staring at him.

"I see you're impressed with my dino knowledge." Gavin smiled smugly.

"No. You've got something stuck between your teeth."

Gavin swung around to Evan. "What is it?"

"Two poppy seeds from this morning's bagel."

"Great." Gavin dug his nail between his teeth and tried to pry them loose.

While he was busy with that, Evan looked more closely at the bones. "I've never seen dinosaur bones before. Wait till we tell Mom and Dad!"

"If we're grounded for life, we'll miss the grand opening of the exhibit," Gavin said. "Mom only gave us one rule: don't go off the trail. Can you see a trail up here?" He wiped the sweat from his brow. "Let's find the gold for Mom and Dad, and then an extra party gift will be the dinosaur bones, okay?"

They headed back to the campsite. They found their parents and Red cooling off at the beach. Most of the campers had found a shady spot and were complaining to one another about the unseasonably hot weather. The sky was overcast despite the heat, and in the distance, the cloud coverage was getting darker.

"There you are, boys. Do you still want to get some tubing in today?"

All temptation to tell their parents about the dinosaur bones went out the window. Neither boy had ever felt the thrill of speeding across the ocean water while hanging on to an inner tube for dear life. After the boys suited up in their life jackets and helmets and lathered themselves in sunscreen, they all headed out to the channel. For hours, the boys took turns being towed behind the boat. They flew up in the air over the boat's wake and screamed with delight when the boat made a wide turn, fiercely whipping them across the waves.

At noon they took a break from the water sports. Gavin asked if they could go back to where they had been yesterday just before they'd called it quits for the day. They nibbled on sandwiches while they cruised up the shoreline. The boys took turns looking through the binoculars and referenced the map.

While their parents admired the oceanfront houses, the boys chatted on the bow of the boat.

"We can now rule out this whole section. That leaves us only this small area between our beach and Robert Memorial Park." Evan refolded the map and stuffed it beneath his life jacket. "Who knew it could be so hot in May? This is a smoking day."

Gavin smeared more sunscreen on his face and took a swig of his water. "I never thought I would envy Coolio for being inside an ice rink on a long weekend. Do you think they're winning the tournament?"

"Do you hear screaming and sobbing coming from his house over there? No. So I'd say they're winning. Meagan said she was going to camp up in Parksville. Maybe she'll get home early enough tomorrow to come tubing with us."

Joe was concerned about Red being too exposed to the sun, so he decided to head back to the cove. They were much quieter on the walk back to the campsite. Each of them found a shady spot for their beach towels, and within minutes they settled down for a nap. The sounds of the tide crashing on the shore, the warm breeze blowing over them, and the soft music drifting down from another site created a perfect environment for an afternoon siesta.

Red's slobbering licks woke Evan up. The sun was sitting low in the sky, and the smell of barbecued chicken and grilling steaks was mouthwatering.

"Hungry, boy?"

"Woof! Woof!" Red's barking woke up the rest of the Edmund clan, but it took an hour for the drowsiness to wear off. The sun set, and the sky turned a murky bluish grey. The heat hardly cooled when the sun went down, so after dinner everyone went for a dip in the frigid water surrounding the tip of the island. It wasn't long before all the campers joined them.

Joe built a small fire on the beach, and MJ made s'mores. Everyone shared tidbits about themselves. A young couple from Germany was on their honeymoon. Vancouver Island was their last stop on a five-province road trip. Three twenty-something girls had driven all the way from Spokane, Washington, just so they could spend the weekend. They had left their homes at 4:30 a.m. on Saturday and had to leave the next morning at the crack of dawn so they could make it to work on time Tuesday morning. A family of four from Glasgow was busy snapping pictures of every tree, bird and seal in sight. The couple's teenage boys were amused by Evan and Gavin and soon had them playing a game of soccer on the sandy beach.

"So, where are you from?" Hamish bounced the ball on the inset of his right foot and then bounced it up in the air to Evan.

"We're from right over there." Evan pointed to the shore across the channel. "Ten minutes by boat, a ten-minute walk up the road, and I'm home."

"Wow. Let's house swap! You can take the three plane rides back to Scotland and then the forty-five-minute drive northwest to our quaint village. We'll happily trade our drafty century-old house for your house in the forest."

Brody kicked the ball away from Evan and passed it to Gavin. "We younger brothers have to stick together. These two have been hoggin' it all night. Gavin, show me some freestyle."

Gavin found a nice-sized boulder and started to bounce the ball against the rock. Each time it came back, he bounced the ball off his knee or chest and sometimes even off his head. He had a nice rhythm going and managed to impress the older boys.

"When do you leave tomorrow?" Gavin passed the ball back to Brody, who then deked it away from Evan. Evan did some quick footwork and managed to take it back again.

"The water taxi will come for us at eleven, and then we'll take the ferry to the mainland. We'll have a few days in Vancouver, and then we'll be off home. I've begged my mother for a horse-size tranquiller for the flights! Ya wouldn't let me move in, would ya?"

At midnight, Joe stomped out the fire and announced it was time for his boys to call it a night. The winds had picked up and were starting to howl through the trees.

It was only after Evan slipped into his sleeping bag that he thought about the dinosaur bones hidden out of sight in the rocky cave. He wanted to talk with Gavin about what they had seen, but the even breathing from the other side of the tent told him his brother was fast asleep.

In the morning, they woke to the exact opposite of what had been announced on the weather channel. The winds did *not* die down. The clouds did *not* blow away to leave bright, sunny skies. And the predicted one- to two-foot swells were in fact four-foot swells, with the west coast swell at ten feet.

"Sorry, boys, but we have to cut short our camping trip. There is now a small-craft advisory in effect. We'll pack up, and then help everyone else get their gear to the cove so they'll be ready when their water taxis arrive."

Despite the wind, the air was still hot. Once addresses were exchanged and their fellow campers were safely on board the water taxi, Joe slowly exited the cove out into the channel. The winds had whipped up even more since the morning, and out in the strait, their little boat rode the waves up and down. It did well, but Joe aimed for Ladysmith harbour and took the shortest route.

Evan had difficulty holding the binoculars steady while he searched the shoreline. He knew his starting point was their beach. When he wiped the lens dry and focused in, he was shocked to see Meagan standing on the shore and looking out to sea. Standing beside her was Claire.

"Meagan and Claire must have come home early. Look, there they are." He held the binoculars out to Gavin, who quickly handed them to their mother.

"Huh. They must be out for a walk. Honey, can you get a little closer to shore so we can wave to them?"

Joe swung the boat to the right and got as close as he dared in the high winds. Meagan waved back and jumped up and down. The boys dramatically pointed to their watches and then held up all ten fingers three times to communicate that they wanted her to come over in half an hour. When she nodded her head enthusiastically, they gave her two thumbs up.

Absently, Evan raised the binoculars and scanned the shoreline one more time. They were approaching the spot where they had looked the day Coolio was out with them. Even hadn't even bothered to focus the lens when he suddenly saw it.

High up on a steep hill, partially hidden behind blackberry bushes, was a massive weeping willow. The enormous ornamental tree's branches extended in all directions and blew gracefully in the high winds. Evan took one more look to ensure he was not dreaming and then nonchalantly handed the binoculars to Gavin.

"Look up there, directly across from us."

Gavin sucked in a breath. When the boys locked bright, shining eyes, they knew it was real.

They had found Donkey's tree.

15

FOR YOUR TROUBLE

BY THE TIME they got home, the winds were howling. The sky turned an odd orange colour, and sheets of slate-grey clouds rushed across the sky.

"I'm going to have to take some pictures of this storm," Joe remarked. "This is sizing up to be a weird one. Not a drop of rain in sight, yet the sky looks like it's about to explode."

"I'm glad we decided to leave DeCourcy Island when we did," said MJ. "I wouldn't want to be racing back in the boat against this storm." She had just started to unpack the cooler when the phone rang. She looked at the display and smiled at the boys. "Do you and Meagan have your watches synchronized?"

Into the phone she said, "Hello, Meagan," but then she paused. "Oh, Claire. Sorry. I thought it was Meagan."

MJ stopped what she was doing and focused on a spot on the kitchen floor. "Oh my God. Did Anne call 911?"

The boy's heads snapped up.

"Of course Joe and I will come with you. Just bring Meagan here, and she can stay with the boys."

"What happened?" Joe had walked in just when the phone rang.

"Davey took a nasty fall down the stairs," MJ said. "He refuses to let Anne call for an ambulance. She got him into the recliner, but she's terrified that he's broken something or has internal injuries. Claire just happened to call to see if Anne and Davey wanted to join us tonight for fireworks. The accident had just happened."

Joe grabbed the phone.

"Hi, Betty. It's Joe Edmund. Is Doctor Kelly available? Sure, I'll wait."

MJ quickly made sandwiches. "How did you know Doc Kelly would be in the clinic today?"

Joe put his hand over the receiver. "I ran into him at the country market on Friday, and he said he drew the short straw for this long weekend. I know he'll want Davey to go straight to Emergency. But maybe the old boy will take the news better if he hears it from the doc."

When Doc Kelly came on the line, Joe said, "Hi, Peter. It's Joe Edmund. Listen, we just found out that Davey Golding took a fall down the stairs. Anne wanted to call an ambulance, but you know old Davey—he wouldn't hear of it. Claire Richards, MJ and I are going over there to see what we can do to help. Should we bring him to you or just go straight to Emerge?"

Joe listened and nodded his head. "That's what I thought. See you there in twenty minutes."

He turned to his wife and snatched one of the sandwiches off the platter. "We'off. Boys, I need you to finish unloading the truck, and be sure to hang the life jackets up in the carport to dry. We'll call you when we know more about Davey's situation."

"Eat up these sandwiches and be sure to save some for Meagan," MJ said. Just as she was about to walk away, she stopped and took a closer look at her boys.

"Oh, sweethearts. I know you're upset about Davey, but he is a tough old bird. Say a little prayer for him, and I'm sure he'll be okay. Right now I'm almost more concerned about Anne. She must be out of her mind with worry." She kissed the top of their heads. "Be good, and we'll call you shortly."

They heard Claire pull down the driveway. MJ gave Meagan a quick hug and jumped into Claire's car.

Meagan's eyes were swollen and red, and as soon as her mom's car was out of sight, she called for Carolynn.

At once, she appeared.

"My dear, what's wrong?" Carolynn landed on the back of Joe's truck and cocked her head from one child to the other.

"Davey may be really hurt, and I'm worried about him. Can you go see what is going on?" Meagan's eyed filled with tears again.

"Of course." She took a closer look at them all. "You needn't worry, children. No matter what happens to Davey, he will be perfectly okay. He has had more time on Earth than most humans. He's had a rich life filled with purpose and meaning."

Carolynn spread her wings and soared into the air.

Evan led Meagan into the house. He pulled the milk out of the fridge.

Before Meagan could start crying again, Gavin jumped up and grabbed glasses from the cupboard. "We have something to tell you that will help take your mind off Davey. You won't believe what we found!"

Meagan took the cookie that was offered but put it down on the table in front of her.

"Meggie, we found the weeping willow tree!" Evan sat in front of her and grabbed her hands. "Truly, I'm not kidding you. Right after we waved to you on the beach, I looked up on the high point— just down from where the beach meets the sheer cliff—and there it was, high up on the hill behind blackberry bushes, just like Donkey said."

Meagan stared at Evan and then at Gavin. "But how did we miss it? We combed that beach for days."

"We never went as far as the cliff. You can't access it from the beach. In fact, the only way I think we can get there is to hike the deer path that runs through the conservation land that borders our property." Evan took a cookie and sat down on the kitchen chair. "To think it has been in our backyard all this time."

"To think that Donkey was right, and we doubted him." Gavin scooped two cookies and dunked them into his milk.

"How long will it take to get there?" Meagan picked up her glass of milk and took a sip.

"Not long. Fifteen to twenty minutes, top. We've only done the path a couple of times, but it winds down toward the ocean and comes out near the opening of the lagoon."

"Of course! So if we had walked the beach as far as we could and swum around the point to the lagoon, we would have seen it. Amazing." Meagan's tears had dried up, and she was starting to feel the same excitement the boys were feeling.

"When do we go with the metal detector?" Evan looked from one to the other, hoping he was reading their expressions properly.

"We go now." Gavin popped the last bit of cookie into his mouth. "Our parents will be gone for at least a couple of hours. We can get there and be back within that time, and no one will be the wiser that we were gone."

"Yeah, let's go. I can't stay here and stew about Davey anyway. Let's finally solve the mystery of what happened to Brother Twelve's gold." Meagan jumped up and grabbed her hat. "It's time to make some history."

"I'm calling Coolio to see if he's home yet." Evan dialled the number, but a look of disappointment came across his face when the machine picked up.

"Look, let's just go," Gavin said. "The winds are getting a little crazy out there, and I want to be back before Mom and Dad. I can't wait to tell them what we've found!" Gavin made sure that the stove was turned off and headed for the door.

"Wow, this could really be it. I can't believe it." Meagan laced up her sneakers and despite the intense heat, zipped up her hoodie.

Red barked madly when they locked him up in his pen. "Sorry, boy. But we can't be worrying about you when we're digging for gold. Just stay here and protect the house." Evan took the shovel Gavin handed him.

"Okay, we have a flashlight, the metal detector and two shovels. Did we forget anything?"

"A camera! We should have a camera to record this momentous event!" Meagan clapped her hands together and jumped.

Evan ran to the truck and pulled one of the duffel bags from the back seat. He rummaged through it until he found the camera bag.

"Got it! Let's go. The wind is getting worse. Be back soon, Red."

But as they walked to the back of the property, Red continued to bark and howl. "I guess he doesn't like being cooped up while the storm is coming in. Maybe we should have brought him?" Gavin hesitated and looked back.

"Do *you* want to chase after him? Forget it. We'll be back soon, and then we can take him into the house." Evan noticed the fort ropes were swinging wildly, so he grabbed them and tied them to a tree. As he stepped back, a branch crashed down and narrowly missed him.

"We'd better run. Gavin, take the lead. Keep to the deer path."

Evan had to yell to be heard over the howl of the wind. They kept their heads low and used the shovel and metal detector to push brush out of their way. When they finally reached the back of their property, Gavin stopped running. He bent over and took deep breaths. When his breathing was even again, he stood up.

"I forget the way from here. You'd better lead."

Evan took a quick look around and located the marker he was looking for. He pointed to the left.

"The ocean is that way. The only time we went to the ocean this way, Dad followed the orange tags that were tied to the trees. They're widely spaced, so keep an eye out for them. He said that when the land was donated, the new owners had it surveyed."

They picked up the deer path again but found it slower going because of the fallen trees and thick brush blocking their way. At one point they had to push a log across a creek, which was still high with winter runoff.

"I don't remember this creek." Gavin looked back up the way they had come and noticed that they had been walking alongside the creek the whole time. It was hidden behind a line of bushes.

"Yeah, it was dry when Dad brought us. We walked right

through it then. Be careful when you put your weight on this log. I'm not certain it won't break."

When they had made it to the other side, they resumed their pace.

"Evan, slow up! Are you sure we're going the right way? I'm so disoriented." Meagan tried to keep her hair from blowing across her face, but the wind had whipped it into a fury, and it tangled in every direction.

"Just follow me. I know where I'm going."

Evan took off again, and when he reached a ridge, he grabbed some long, ropy tree roots and pulled himself up. When he reached the top, he turned around and extended his arm.

"Grab hold!"

Meagan took a run at the ridge and just barely caught Evan's hand. She used her other hand to reach the highest root. Gavin scrambled up a little further down, and by the time Meagan had wiped the dirt off her jeans, he had joined them.

"We're really close now. Come on!"

Evan veered off to the left. The ground started to slope downward. What little sky had been visible through the canopy of trees was now almost gone. It had grown very dark and eerie as the wind whistled around them. Evan grabbed Meagan's hand, and she instinctively reached back and grabbed Gavin's.

Suddenly they emerged from the forest to stand in a small clearing that looked down over the lagoon. Beyond the sheltered water, the channel was black and churning. The waves sloshed back and forth, battling for a position on the surface. When they collided, they created whitecaps that sprayed in every direction.

"Oh crap! Imagine being out there in our little boat." Gavin took out the camera and snapped a few shots.

"Look at how creepy the sky is. I've never seen it so orange and purple." Evan was mesmerized by the fierce sight.

"The tree must be over here near the point." Meagan ran along the cliff and suddenly pulled herself up short.

The massive tree stood, swaying in the wind. Blackberry bushes stood guard, tall and wide, hiding the lower part of the tree. Although still devoid of berries, they were covered in sweet-smelling little white flowers.

They found an opening in the wall of bushes and inserted their hands to part the long, greenish-yellow willow branches that flowed side to side like silky hair. Entering the dark interior was like stepping into another world. Large, knotty roots protruded from the earth, and the smell of dank soil wafted over them.

"It's huge in here! We should have brought more flashlights."

Evan balanced the flashlight between two of the branches and pointed it down toward the uneven ground.

"You're on, Gavin. Make that detector sing to us."

His brother turned it on and started to sweep the area closest to the trunk. He fidgeted with the sensitivity setting and then walked slowly around the base of the tree, taking his time to ensure that the scanner had time to pick up any signals. Each time he completed a circle he took one step further away and started another lap around the tree. He was on his third loop when the detector started to pulse and let out a high whine.

"You found it. Oh my God, you actually found it!" Meagan jumped up and down. She grabbed the flashlight from its perch in the branches and pointed it directly where Gavin held the metal detector over a soft mound of earth.

Evan looked at Gavin and Meagan. "Ready to dig?"

He marked the spot with the tip of the shovel. Meagan held the light steady and watched while the boys took turns scooping out the wet soil. At first they piled it beside the hole but they quickly realized that they were going to run out of room between the tree and hole. So they started to make piles all around the trunk.

"Here, let me take a turn."

Meagan handed the light to Gavin, who gratefully swapped it for the shovel. Soon they lost track of time. They were so engrossed with their work that they were unaware of how bad the storm had turned. The howling wind was just background noise to the sound of their heavy breathing.

After an hour of digging, the hole was big enough for Evan to jump into. He asked Gavin to pass the metal detector down to him so he could take another reading. Immediately the digital reading confirmed gold was buried in that spot.

"I wish we'd thought to bring some water. I'm really thirsty." Evan wiped the sweat from his brow with his sleeve.

"It can't be too much deeper. Brother Twelve was crafty, but he wouldn't make it too deep because he'd have to dig it all back up again." Gavin squeezed in beside Evan.

"How about we make it wider, just in case there are lots of wooden boxes down here?"

"Makes sense. Start on that wall, and I'll keep going down."

They worked in silence for a few more minutes. Suddenly the quiet was broken by a thud. They froze. They exchanged nervous looks. And slowly, they looked down at the top of a partially exposed wooden box.

"My heart is going to burst." Meagan's whisper was hardly audible.

Then Gavin and Evan snapped out of their shocked state and started to shovel out as much dirt as they could.

"Locate the corners. We've got to move off all the soil."

It felt like an eternity, but eventually they had the cover fully cleaned off.

"Can you make out what is stamped on the top?" Meagan slipped in beside them and held the flashlight directly over the image.

"It's a cross with a loop on top." She wiped the last of the dirt from below the symbol to see if there were any words. She found nothing.

"Gavin, we know this symbol! This was one of the images mom taught us a few years ago. It's an ankh. What does it mean again?"

"Life or sun or something like that. Maybe it means gold!" Gavin tried to pull up the lid, but it wouldn't budge. "It's sealed shut."

Evan wedged the tip of the shovel under one side. "Do the same on the other side. Okay, good. Now on the count of three. Ready? One... two... *three!*"

Both boys used all their strength to pop the lid off. It creaked loudly against the force but didn't come off.

"Again! Try it again!" Meagan added her weight to Gavin's shovel, and on the count of three, they tried again. This time there was a loud splintering sound. Rusty nails hung out from the bottom of the lid.

"Careful. Let's put the lid over there. It was heavier than they thought it would be, and it took the three of them to move it.

They climbed back into the hole again. A dark cloth covered whatever lay beneath.

"Who's going to move the blanket?" Evan whispered.

"You do it, Evan." Gavin's eyes were shining in the dark, confined space. Like Meagan's, his heart was pounding, and he wasn't sure if they even heard him. All he could hear was the loud pulse in his ears.

"Okay, here goes!" Evan grabbed the blanket with both hands. He whipped it off and threw it to one side. Thick dust flew up in all directions. They all started to cough and choke.

"Sorry about that." Evan's eyes watered, and he tried to wipe the tears away without touching his eyes.

They peered in.

"What the heck is that?" Gavin stared down into the hole.

"Another wooden box? Are you kidding me?" Evan didn't even wait to see what was written on that lid. He grabbed the shovel tip and wedged it underneath. He gave it one good bash, and the lid splintered.

"This guy really loved his nails, didn't he?" Meagan carefully twisted the splintered pieces so she could pry off the lid.

Lying across the top of the box was an old newspaper. Meagan picked it up very carefully.

"It's dated May 29, 1940. The *British Columbia Gazette* headline reads, '*Prime Minister Mackenzie King announces the opening of Camp Nanaimo.*'" Her head snapped up. "Wait, this can't be right." She looked confusingly from boy to boy.

"What's wrong?" Evan said.

"According to all the research we did, Brother Twelve and Madame Z left sometime in 1933 or '34. This paper is from 1940."

Gavin looked into the box. There were twelve partitions, and in each one there was a jar.

"Look, jam jars. Isn't that what the books said? Didn't they say he buried the gold coins in jam jars?"

Gavin's hand trembled as he reached for one. He lifted it out gingerly. He held it up to the flashlight. A white note was coiled inside. They also heard the rattle of one coin.

"Read it." Evan never took his eyes off the white note.

Gavin took it out and handed the note to Meagan. He dropped the coin in Evan's hand.

She let out a gasp.

"What?" Both boys paled at the look of shock on her face.

"It says, '*For your trouble.*' Signed Edward Arthur Wilson and the number twelve."

Meagan pulled out another jar. It was empty. Gavin yanked out two more, and they were both empty. Evan pulled out as many as he could. Empty.

"He came back." Meagan fell back against the earth wall. "He came back." She handed the note to Evan. He took one look at it and shoved it into his pocket. "All those years, they didn't know where he was. They thought he died in Switzerland, but he obviously didn't. He came back for the gold." Meagan shook her head back and forth in disbelief.

"He left one lousy coin!" Gavin said, disgusted.

"He must have been one twisted guy to go to so much trouble. I can just see him writing that note. I bet you he laughed for years over that one! I hope he choked on one of those gold coins!" Evan hopped out of the hole. "We have to get home. We've been gone way longer than we thought we would be."

"Oh my God, you're right," Meagan said, coming back to reality. "My mom could be back by now. I wonder how Davey is doing." She grabbed one of the shovels and pushed her way through the branches that had been cocooning them for over an hour. Gavin swung the camera around his neck and picked up the metal detector.

What greeted them took their breath away. The sky had gone a fiery orange. Black clouds sat directly over their heads. White lightning bolts exploded in all directions. The kids couldn't tell if they were coming from the sky or the ground.

Gavin looked nervously from the lightning to the rod of his metal detector. "Oh, this isn't good."

"We've got to get out of here. We're too exposed." Evan yelled to be heard over the crash of thunder.

"Ya think? *Run!*" Meagan took off the way they'd come. She fell a couple of times over fallen logs and debris. Branches rained down on them as they tried to find the deer path to take them back home.

"I can't see anything! Meggie, are you sure you're going the right way?" Gavin tried to catch up with her, but she was too far ahead. "Evan, I don't think this is right way. "

"You're right. Meggie is going farther into the woods, above the cliff. "

"Where does it lead?"

"I think back toward the beach. I definitely don't want to be on the beach during this storm. Meagan, *stop!*"

Evan knew his voice was being carried off with the wind. They raced after her and had almost caught up when she fell hard over a log that was covered with moss.

"Are you all right?" They dropped what they were holding and got on either side of her. She was lying face down and moaning.

"My ankle. My ankle! It hurts so much." Meagan sobbed and tried to pull herself into a sitting position. She grabbed her right foot and doubled over in pain.

"Maybe you broke it. Evan, what are we going to do?"

"Can you stand?" Evan tried to pull Meagan up, but as soon as she put weight on her foot, she fell back down with a scream.

"Not good. Not good!" Gavin looked up just as an enormous thunderbolt struck a tree not far from where they sat. The tree went up in flames instantly. They all jumped and rolled in the opposite direction.

"We can't stay here. Meagan, you're going to have to hop. Put your arms around our necks, and we'll help you."

Tears ran down her face, but she nodded and let the boys pull her up. She yelped when she lost her balance and accidentally put weight on her right foot.

They had moved only four feet when they heard a growl above their heads.

16

EAT ME!

SITTING UP IN A TREE, directly in front of them, was a full-grown cougar. It dropped its head and hunched its powerful shoulders as if it were about to pounce. Another bolt of lightning showed the cougar's glowing yellow eyes. It was staring right at them.

Suddenly there was a flash of light, and a shimmer appeared at their side.

"Don't run. Stand tall and continue to stare at her. She is more afraid of you than you are of her. She only wants to protect her young." Lisa paced between them and the tree, where the cougar continued to crouch. For the first time, the children saw the two cubs behind their mother. The cubs cried out and clung to the branch they stood on.

"Lisa, what should we do?"

"Without looking away from her, slowly lean down and pick up those shovels."

Lisa growled threateningly at the real cougar, but it was obvious to the children that the fierce feline could not see the Shimmy.

"Gavin! Slower. Don't give her any reason to attack you."

Evan had reached back and managed to grab the end of one of

the shovel. Gavin used his foot to hook the metal detector and pulled it up so he could snatch it with his free hand.

"Hold it out in front of you, and all of you, start yelling. Make as much noise as you can."

The kids made themselves as big as they could and yelled at the cats.

"Go away!"

"Leave us alone!"

"Get lost! *Aggghhh!*"

Suddenly they were surrounded by all the Shimmies. Carolynn and Madeline flew straight at and through the cougar. They hooted and squawked as loud as they could. The lovebird, Little Theresa, darted and tried to peck the cougar's ears, but she kept evaporating into its head.

Mr. and Mrs. Biggsy, Rad-knows-ways and Razor stood in front of the children and yelled at everyone to make more noise.

"Eat me! Eat me!" Spotty jumped up and down and tried to get the real cougar to see him.

Abigail reared up and swung her legs wildly at the tree. "Go away! Leave the humans alone!" Abigail's usually calm voice was high-pitched and frantic.

The Burrow family came running from every direction. Reddy Bun-Buns, Ever-Ready Freddy and their brothers took running leaps at the tree and bounced off of it. Mama Bunny yelled up from the forest floor. "Come down here this minute, you oversized house cat! Leave these children alone. You've got enough trouble on your hands with those two scruffians!"

Mr. Burrow was yelling just as loudly, but at his wife. "She can't hear you, dear!" He kicked his hind legs out and aimed for the tree. "But maybe we can make her feel us. Formation, kids!"

All the bunnies gathered round and started to jackhammer on the tree.

In all the noise and excitement, no one saw Donkey, Barry or Duke Mortimer skid to a halt on the other side of the tree.

"Let 'er rip, Donkey!" The pig stood back while Donkey let out a deafening screech.

"Hee-haw! Hee-haw! *Heee-haaaw!*"

"You obnoxious animal! Go prey on some elk to feed your ugly offspring. Shoo!" Duke Mortimer quacked away, adding to the frenzy and noise.

When the cougar inched closer on the branch, Barry squealed loudly. "You wanna fight? You wanna piece of me?" Then he wagged his tail at her.

"Evan, I think I'm going to pass out." Meagan slid to the ground and fell backward. Both boys jumped in front of their vulnerable friend and started to scream even louder. They waved the shovel and metal detector as wildly as they could. Gavin felt the camera bang against his chest, and, without really thinking, he pointed it at the cougar and took a shot. The flash went off and startled the animal.

For one split second, it looked like the cougar was going to leap down on them, but she let out a threatening howl, turned and leapt away with her two cubs in tow.

The tree that had been hit by lightning was now smouldering. The boys took one look at it and decided it was time to get out of there.

Immediately, they dropped down beside Meagan and lifted her head off the ground.

"Is the cougar gone? Or am I dead?"

"You're alive but far from okay. Meagan, we've got to get out of this forest. If we took most of your weight, do you think you could try and move?"

She nodded her head and made a concerted effort to get up. The Shimmies' light glowed softly around them.

"Evan," said Carolynn, "follow Abigail and Spotty. They know the fastest and easiest way to get back to the road. You're going to cut through a property, but the owners are not at their cabin this time of year, so you won't be able to call for help until you reach Doctor Herb's house. We'll stay with you." She flew from tree to tree and kept a close eye on them.

"I am so proud of you," Madeline said as she flew around their heads. "You were brave and did everything Lisa told you to. You kept your heads." Madeline then flew ahead to perch on the branch beside Carolynn.

"How did you know we needed help, Lisa?"

The silver cat slowed to look back at them. "I was trying to find you. When Carolynn went back to the house to tell you about Davey, she couldn't find you there. Then your parents came home, and they quickly mounted a search. We were all out looking for you. I heard the howl of the female cougar and knew she was scared. I came to see what was alarming her. At first I thought it was just the storm, but then I saw the three of you."

"Good thing you did. I froze," Evan admitted. "I'm not sure I would have known what to do."

The adrenalin he had felt was quickly replaced by the dizzy realization of what had happened. The powerful stalk-and-ambush animal came flooding back into his mind. The memory of her powerful muscles, bare teeth and intense yellow eyes almost had him stumbling to his knees.

"You would have known. It was just the initial shock that had you hesitating. With or without us, you would have been fine." Rad-knows-ways was unusually serious. The beaver flapped his tail on the ground to emphasize his words.

Meagan moaned in pain and struggled to talk. "Is Davey okay?"

"Yes, the paramedics who came said his vitals were strong and he had full mobility. But they wanted to take him just in case." Carolynn flew around them anxiously. She did not like to see Meagan in pain.

It took a long time for the boys to help Meagan out of the forest. They stumbled out into the dark and found themselves at the dead end of Pacific Drive. It was easier to walk on the paved road. As they came up the hill, they noticed flashing police lights in front of Doctor Herb's house. There was a large crowd gathered around, and a fire truck and ambulance were parked further up the street.

Just as Evan was about to raise his arm and start yelling, someone saw them and started running. It was Coolio. He ran at a breakneck speed. He halted in front of them and took Meagan from Gavin, who was starting to fall under her weight. Right behind him was Claire. Even in the dark, she was deadly white, and tears were streaming down her face.

"Meagan! Oh my God. Are you all right?" She gathered her daughter into her arms and sobbed.

"Claire, we think her ankle might be broken." Evan turned just as his mother and father ran down the hill, followed by the paramedics.

"Claire, here. Let us help you with Meagan." Joe turned to his boys. "Are you hurt?"

"Not hurt, but maybe a little shaken." MJ fiercely hugged each of her boys.

One of the paramedics approached. "Meagan were going to put you on our stretcher and get you inside the ambulance. It'll be easier to examine you in there, okay?"

Meagan's tears were a mixture of joy—at seeing her mother—and excruciating pain. She let herself be lifted onto the stretcher, but she clung to her mother's hand.

While everyone was looking at Meagan, Coolio whispered to his friend,

"What happened to you guys?"

But before Evan could answer, a police officer approached his parents and spoke to them quietly. It was agreed that they would all go back to Doctor Herb's house. The boys turned around and saw all the Shimmies standing at the edge of the forest, watching.

Evan grabbed Coolio's arm when they got to the top of the road. The boys were shocked to see virtually every neighbour from the area standing against the wind. They held flashlights, and relief came over their faces when they saw the children.

MJ and Joe thanked everyone and said how much they appreciated their willingness to mount a search party. Doctor Herb had a few words with the paramedics and a few more with Meagan. He stood up and announced it was time to get the children indoors.

"What about Meagan? Is she going to be okay?" Evan didn't like the idea of being split up.

"The paramedics will take her to the hospital. Her ankle

doesn't appear to be broken, but they will do X-rays to rule out a fracture. She'll be in good hands, and her mother will stay with her."

They all walked into the house and took a seat. Candles flickered everywhere.

Mabel the housekeeper wheeled Joan, Doc Herb's wife, from the front living room into the kitchen, where the police, parents and boys all sat numbly. Joan reached out for the boys' hands and gave them a little squeeze. Mabel handed them each a bottle of water before she settled down on a bar stool.

"Boys, my name is Constable Douglas, and this is my partner, Constable Stephens. You're not in trouble. We're happy that you are reunited with your family, but we do need to ask you some questions, okay?"

The boys nodded, but they couldn't help but be intimated by the officers. Evan glanced at Coolio, who stood beside his mother. Isobel was busy making coffee and hot chocolate. She turned off the propane stove and handed the first cups to the officers. Constable Douglas took off his hat and ran his hand through his reddish-blonde hair. After a quick sip of his coffee, he smoothed down his trim moustache and turned his focus on the boys. "Can you tell us what happened after your parents left the house late this afternoon?"

Both constables looked at Evan. He was on the hook first.

"Well, we... um, we thought it would be a cool idea to take some pictures of the sky because it was such a weird colour. We didn't think the storm would get so bad, or else we wouldn't have gone."

"Did you make any calls before you left?"

"Yeah. We called Coolio but we got his answering machine."

"Did you call anyone else?"

"No."

"Then what happened?"

"We decided to take the deer trail that runs from the back of our property through the conservation land and down to the ocean. When we got down there, we saw how strange the sky had gone and thought maybe we should find shelter. We hid under a weeping willow tree."

Coolio gasped. Everyone looked at him.

"Sorry, my hot chocolate's too hot." He feigned a burnt tongue and waved his hand in front of it.

"Evan, whatever made you think to hide under a tree during a lightning storm? Haven't we talked about this a million times?" Joe was in complete disbelief. MJ gently laid her hand on her husband's arm.

Evan looked at Gavin to see if now was the time to share the truth about what they'd found. Gavin fiddled with the handle of his hot chocolate, and when he finally met his brother's eyes, he nodded once.

"Dad, I know it seemed stupid to hide under the willow, but it was huge, and the branches fell all the way to the ground. We had a flashlight, plus we had the metal detector and the shovel. We originally thought we might find something worth digging up."

MJ finally lost her cool. "Evan, we were scared out of our minds! When the power went out at Davey's house, we called home. It rang and rang. While your dad went with Anne to the hospital, Claire and I came home to see if you kids were okay. Instead of finding you, we found Constable Douglas and Constable Stephens, walking around the house. Red was locked in the pen, and there was no sign of you two or Meagan anywhere!"

Gavin looked at the officers accusingly. "Why were you at my house?"

"Someone from your residence called 911 at 3:52 p.m. We came to investigate."

"We never called for the police." Evan looked at his mom. "Promise."

"We found the cordless phone inside the pen with your shepherd. Your mother confirmed that you have 911 on speed-dial. The dog must have accidently stepped on it."

Evan looked at Gavin, and they both shrugged.

"I don't know how it got in there," Evan said. "It must have fallen out of my pocket. Are we in trouble for that?"

"No, but when your mother and Mrs. Richards couldn't locate you at either homes, and Mr. Gabriel confirmed that you had called but not come by, we mounted a search. With the power out and the storm directly overhead, it was very dangerous for you to be out, especially if you were anywhere near the water." Constable Douglas took another sip of his coffee and peered intently over the rim.

Evan chewed on that. "But how did you know we needed an ambulance for Meagan?"

"We didn't. Doctor Herb called 911 to report a fire at the point. Just as the dispatcher was starting to take details, the phone lines went down. It's standard protocol to send fire, police and paramedics."

"Mom, Dad, we're sorry we worried you. We thought we would only be gone for a little while. But once we got under the weeping willow tree, well, we sort of found something, so we lost all track of time and started to dig."

"What did you find?" Douglas pulled his chair closer to Evan.

"We found Brother Twelve's lost gold." Evan expected an explosion of questions, but no one said a word. Nothing.

He looked at Coolio, who was beaming from ear to ear. But Evan couldn't let his friend continue to think they were millionaires, so he finished the tale. "We found a wooden box with a case of empty jam jars. In one of the jars was a gold coin and a handwritten note from Brother Twelve. He went back many years later and dug it up again. All he left was this." He pushed the coin and note into the middle of the table.

Doctor Herb picked up both items and looked at them as closely as he could in the glow of one of the candles. He said nothing but handed it to his wife. Joan, a retired professor from Vancouver Island University, took one look at them and simply smiled. She turned her twinkling eyes on the boys and winked.

"Wait, you mean to tell me you think this is real?" Joe looked from Doc Herb to Joan and then back to the boys.

"It's real, Dad. All the evidence is there. A newspaper from 1940, the box stamped with an ankh, the jam jars, this coin from 1928, and a note signed by the Brother himself."

Joan clapped her hands and happily placed the note and coin back on the table.

Constable Douglas had been taking notes, but now he put down his notepad and stared at the boys.

"You may have solved one of the biggest unsolved mysteries on the island since the turn of the century. He was thought to have died in Switzerland in 1933."

"Actually, 1934," Gavin corrected him.

"Kid's right. I remember reading about it." Constable Stephens picked up the coin and examined it. "This is going to be huge. Wait till the press gets wind of it."

"How did Meagan get hurt?" Constable Douglas flipped his notebook back open.

"She fell over a log just before the cougar almost attacked us," said Gavin.

"*What?*" everyone screamed at once. Gavin just about jumped out of his chair.

"Did you say a cougar?" MJ was now visibly shaking.

"Yeah, and her two cubs."

Joe got up from his chair and knelt in front of his boys. "Gavin, I know you've had an exhilarating night, but it's time to settle down and tell the officers…" Joe's voice trailed off.

Gavin had removed the camera from his around his neck and located the last picture taken. Joe took one look at it and fell to his knees.

"I think I'm going to be sick."

17

CHILDREN OF MEN, MOST SACRED WONDER

THE LOCAL MORNING news led with reports about the extraordinary storm and power outages reported across the island. But by dinnertime, national news outlets were reporting that evidence had been found on Vancouver Island that Brother Twelve had *not only* buried gold in Mason jars, but that he had gone back many years after he was reported dead to dig it up. When it was leaked that the same children who found the wooden case also encountered a cougar and had a photo to prove it, the media went wild.

Experts were brought in to locate the cougar's paw prints. It alarmed the neighbours to learn how many prints there were circling their properties.

Joe and MJ kept the boys home from school and only took calls from family members or friends. The RCMP blocked their road to stop reporters from trying to gain access to their property.

The boys were bored all day, and were thrilled when Coolio showed up after school. He made loud remarks for MJ's benefit about the homework he'd brought Evan, and then he quickly closed the bedroom door. He dropped his bag on the bed and snatched the camera out of Gavin's hands.

Coolio couldn't stop looking at the photo of the cougar staring into the camera. It was like nothing he had ever seen before. Her entire face filled the frame. The fierce cat's eyes glowed yellow, and her teeth were bared.

"Man, I wish I had been home when you called. I missed all the fun."

Evan just grinned at his friend. "Yeah, laughs and giggles the whole time. We'll be sure to let you know the next time we decide to encounter wild predators in their natural habitat."

"So what's going to happen to the gold coin?" Coolio had been avoiding the question, but curiosity finally got the better of him.

"Dad and Mom says there's going to be a battle over it. The land trust that owns the property says it's rightfully theirs, the Nanaimo Museum says they should get first dibs, and some long-lost relative of the nutter came out of the woodwork to claim they should get it for sentimental reasons. But Gavin and I think our uncle from Toronto is right."

"What did he say?"

"He said we should tell everyone to stick it. And if they try to take it from us, we'll go and bury it again—right outside a bear cave! Ha!"

Coolio grinned wickedly and handed the camera back to Gavin.

"Why so glum?" Gav had said very little since Coolio had arrived.

Gavin let out a huff. "Well, if everyone is freaking out this much about one lousy coin and a note from a crazy old man, what's going to happen when we tell them about the dinosaur bones we found?"

"Gavin!" Evan jumped up and peered out the door. "Don't you think Mom and Dad have enough to worry about right now? Don't tell anyone about that. We'll tell them in good time, but not *now*."

"Are you freaking kidding me?" Coolio couldn't figure out if they were pulling his leg.

"No, we're not, but I'm not going to tell you here. Meagan got home from the hospital a few hours ago. Let's go see her, and we'll tell you then. She doesn't know either."

Joe and MJ insisted that they walk with the boys. They found

Claire sitting on the porch with a cup of tea in her hands. She looked worn out.

"How's Meagan?"

"She's more comfortable now. The painkillers are helping. Thank goodness it's only a sprain. She will have to stay off that foot for a week or two. Boys, she's inside watching a movie if you want to go in and say hi."

They found her lying on the couch with her right leg propped up on a pillow.

"Man, am I glad to see you guys!" She turned off the television and tried to pull herself up. Gavin pushed another pillow behind her back so she could sit up higher. "What happened after I left in the ambulance?"

"The RCMP interrogated us!" Gavin punched his fist into his hand.

Evan rolled his eyes. "They asked us a few questions."

"They confiscated my camera!"

Evan rolled his eyes again. "They just looked at the picture Gavin took of the cougar. My mom swooned. Yeah, I know, I never knew what that word meant. Now I do."

"Well, they did say we might have to go to the station for more questioning!"

"They did say that. We told them pretty much everything—except how we knew where to find the gold, how the dead Shimmies came to our rescue, and how we found dinosaur bones."

"What dinosaur bones?" Meagan wondered if the painkillers were messing with her hearing.

"Finally, I'm going to get some details." Coolio moved closer to the couch so he could hear the brothers' whispers.

They related the story as best as they could. Meagan got caught up and wanted more details about the baby bunnies, but Coolio begged her to stay focused. Baby cottontails and eagles were interesting, but nothing compared to dinosaur bones.

The kids had just shared the last of the details when the parents walked in to check on Meagan. MJ clucked like a chicken over the amount of bruising on her forehead and right cheek. Everyone pitched in to help Claire make dinner, and afterward they stuck around to wash the dishes.

"We should go," MJ said to Claire. "Meagan is fast asleep, and you look like you could fall flat on your face right where you're standing." She took the glass pitcher out of Claire's hand and led her to a chair. "Do you want Joe to carry Meagan to her bed?"

"No, I think she will be more comfortable out here. I'll just curl up on the other couch."

The boys walked Coolio home.

"Coming to school tomorrow?" Coolio lingered at the top of driveway. He was not ready to leave his friends.

"Yup. Dad spoke to Mrs. Rosaline, and she said she wouldn't tolerate anyone interrupting classes. Dad said, 'God help the first reporter who tries to put a foot on school property.'"

They walked to Coolio's front door and were greeted by Isobel and James. They answered their questions and promised to bring a copy of the cougar picture the next day.

As they made their way back up the street, Donkey and Barry appeared in front of Meagan's driveway.

"Well, hello, Donkey! Greetings, Barry."

The last time the boys had seen the odd pair, they were egging on a cougar. Today they were their usual placid, mild-mannered selves.

"Hi, Evan! Hi, Gavin! Good to see you in one piece. Close call yesterday. That kitty sure looked like she was going to feed you to her cubs." Barry circled around their legs and swished his little tail in excitement.

"But thanks to you and all the other Shimmies, we came out of that forest alive. The memory of you defending us will be forever branded into my brain." Evan looked at Donkey and Barry the way he looked at Red. His love for the mule and pig surprised him.

Donkey stopped walking and stared at Evan and Gavin for a long time.

"I've known humans who treated me real bad. But you humans,

you treat me different. You treat me like I'm special." He shook his head with the same puzzled expression. "Am I special?"

Evan wanted to hug him so badly. He got close and cleared his throat.

"You are an exceptional donkey, and you are my friend."

Barry sniffed and squealed at the same time.

Donkey nodded and started to walk up the hill toward the Edmunds house. He took a few slow paces and then he stopped again.

"So you didn't get the gold?"

"Nope. Not enough to make us rich, anyway. But that doesn't really matter. What matters is that we found out who cares about us." Gavin was lighthearted, and he realized he hadn't felt that way in a long time.

Barry and Donkey chose not to go down the driveway. They stood at the top of road and watched the boys until they were out of sight.

That night, as MJ listened to Evan say his prayers, she heard something new.

"And God, please watch out for our friends the way they watch out for us."

She kissed her boy good night and turned out the light, feeling very proud of her son.

The remaining days in May were sunny and bright. The gardens came to life, and the birds and bees appeared in droves.

Davey ignored his doctor's orders and discharged himself after four days in the hospital. He said Taffy needed him. And anyone who knew Davey knew he needed Taffy. When he got home, he went straight to his recliner. While his daughter made him his Sunday tea, he listened to Little Theresa sing "We'll Meet Again." She sang it sweetly in his ear and was rewarded when he laid back his head and fell into a deep, restful sleep.

MJ, Joe and Claire relented and let professors from Vancouver

Island University interview the children about their experience finding Brother Twelve's gold. The boys insisted Coolio also attend the interview, which was held at the weeping willow tree. In the end, Coolio asked more questions than the professors. Gavin re-enacted every scene, and Meagan enjoyed playing along as the injured heroine. The professors left the exercise wondering if the children had used it as an excuse to get off school for the afternoon.

The first weekend of June, Anne decided that Davey was finally up for visitors. He was embarrassed by the fuss everyone made. Anne pulled out her mother's best china and was busy making tea in the kitchen with MJ and Claire when Davey asked the question none of them expected.

"Do you hear them too?"

Meagan had chosen to sit in the rocker closest to Davey's recliner so she could prop her leg up on the ottoman. Evan, Gavin and Coolio sat on the floor directly in front of them.

"Pardon?" Meagan held her breath and tried not to fidget in her seat.

"Do birds talk to you too?"

The kids exchanged surprised looks.

"It's okay. You can talk to me about it. I never understood. Frankly, I thought I was losing my mind. But the day of my accident, I heard!"

"What did you hear, Davey?" Meagan leaned over and took his hand in hers. He grasped it and held it to his heart.

"I sat in this chair in great pain. My daughter was beside herself. She wanted to call for the ambulance. Well, at my age, that's not how you want to leave your home, let me tell you. Anne had just gone to answer Claire's phone call when I heard them talking." Davey stopped, afraid of what they would think.

"You can tell us, Davey." Meagan squeezed his hand.

"I heard a great whoosh of wings. I heard a voice I didn't recognize. She asked about me. I heard Little Theresa tell her I had fallen down the stairs. Little Theresa said that I was probably in shock and didn't know how much pain I was in. She said poor Anne needed someone with her. Then the other voice said, 'Help is on the

way. The children's parents are coming.' Then the phone rang
again. While Anne took instructions from my doctor, Little Theresa
sat near me and sang." Davey smiled a very perplexed smile. "But
you see, she couldn't have sung so near to me. She was in her cage
across the room. How could she have sung to me?"

"Davey," Evan said, leaning forward on his knees, "before you
lost your sight, did you ever see things that you thought seemed
odd? Did you ever see animals that were glowing and shimmering?"
He took Davey's other hand. To have an adult know their secret was
a wish he had kept close to his heart.

"Of course I did. For years, in fact. That's how I knew I had a
problem with my vision. I had the problem most of my life. I was in
Burma during the war when it started. I started to see things at
night."

"Like what, Davey? Tell us, please." Meagan felt just as anxious
as Evan. She wanted him to say it. She *needed* him to say it.

"Glowing snakes, birds, cows—you name it! I thought I was
going mad. I was so young. So far from home. I even thought they
were talking to me." He steeled himself. "Madness. It was all
madness. I told myself to ignore it and to focus on staying alive. It
was jungle warfare. What did I know about that? Never mind the
enemy. How would I protect myself from malaria? From the
predators of the jungle? I saw and heard things that terrified me."

Evan leaned forward and spoke as clearly as he could. "What
you saw, what you heard, was real. The day you fell down the stairs,
our friend Carolynn—a dead owl—came to visit your dead lovebird,
Little Theresa, to ask how you were doing. We were very upset
about the state you were in. They're real, Davey. You may be blind,
but you can hear them. Animals who die can be seen and heard by
a few of us. Gavin, Meagan and I can see and hear them too."

Coolio, expecting that Davey was struggling to buy it, chimed in.
"Your friend Mortimer down at the Boar's Moor is a duck, Davey.
You've been talking to a duck for years. Evan, Gavin and Meagan
know him. They think he is obnoxious. But Duke thinks you're okay
—for a human."

Davey laughed and rubbed his hand over his brow. He shook his head and gazed into the distance. Finally he raised his hand and extended his index finger.

"Little Theresa, will you come to me?"

The lovebird flew out of her cage and settled on his finger in an instant. "What they say is true. You were blessed to see and hear us, but you feared what you did not understand. You dismissed it as hallucinations, visions, failing eyesight. When your sight finally faded, you lost your anxiety, so you were able to hear us again." She settled onto his outstretched hand and started to hum a tune.

Coolio knew he wasn't seeing or hearing any of what they were experiencing, but he knew Davey's fear.

"Just trust, Davey. Just trust."

⌑

Claire was reluctant to let Meagan go down to the beach. They had just finished lunch with Doc Herb and Joan on the deck when the children said they were going down to skim stones. The sun shone bright, and there was hardly a cloud in the sky.

"Claire, she'll be okay," Joe assured her. "Just go down on your bottom on the steep steps. The boys can help you over the logs." Joe threw the sunscreen bottle to Gavin to grease up.

"I'll be careful. My leg isn't hurting near as bad as it did last weekend." She gave her mom a quick kiss on the cheek and put out her hand for a squirt of sunscreen. Evan picked up her crutches and held them out for her when she was done.

Red went headlong into the water and came up shaking. He swam out to the floating raft anchored in the bay and promptly laid down for a nap.

"One more log… Ready? Hop. There you go. Where do you want to sit?"

"Any chance I can get up on the boulder?"

The boys looked at her bruised ankle and then up at the huge boulder and decided it was a bad idea. They settled on a log near the water's edge.

"Here are some nice flat beauties. See how many bounces you get out of these."

Meagan tossed a few, but she was quickly lost in thought.

"Rock for your thought." Evan sat down beside her.

"I was just thinking that this is where it all started, on that awful day when we saw Spotty drown. Not a day goes by when I don't think about Carolynn flying out of the sky, landing on the boulder and greeting us with, 'Hello.'" She laughed. "If you two hadn't been with me, I would have thought I had gone mad. No wonder Davey questioned his sanity." She looked at her two friends. "I couldn't have done it on my own, you know."

"I know. Me neither." Evan looked at Gavin. His brother nodded in agreement and picked up another rock.

"It's very odd to count an owl, blue jay, beaver, whale, pig, donkey, cougar, lovebird, duck, dog, raccoons, bunnies and deer as some of your closest friends. But they are. They really are."

"Not sure if the duck ranks, but the rest hit the list." Gavin smiled his lopsided grin and checked to see if Red was still passed out cold. The huge shepherd was stretched out and clearly settling in for a long snooze.

Gavin looked across at DeCourcy Island and wondered about the dinosaur bones. He wanted to go back and examine them more closely. He wished he had thought to take pictures that morning.

He was just about to turn his gaze away when a ripple broke the flat surface of the bay. Suddenly, spouts of water erupted into the air.

"What's that?"

Evan jumped up and grabbed Meagan's arm to help her stand. "It's not…"

"It is!" said Gavin.

"Amazing."

The kids' screaming woke up Red. He ran madly from corner to corner of the raft, trying to figure out who or what to bark at.

"You kids okay?" MJ peered over the deck railing. She shaded her eyes and looked up and down the beach to figure out what had caused the disturbance.

"We're fine. Just admiring Gavin's rock skimming." Evan waved his mom off and dropped his voice to a hush. "They came! Marta said they would come!"

The pod of grey whales swam in unison. They came into the bay and slowed down as they approached the beach. Denise leapt high out of the water and landed on her back. She surfaced and swam straight up on the shore.

"You came!"

"Of course we came. I've been counting down the days!"

"It's so good to see you again." Evan leaned close to gaze into her hooded eye.

"It's wonderful to see you boys too. This must be Meagan."

"Yes, it is." Evan pulled Meagan closer so Denise could see her better.

"Meagan, what happened to you?"

"Oh dear, where do I start?" Meagan laughed and waved at Priscilla and Marta when they swam up behind Denise.

"Can you make room for us? We want to hear all about it."

For an hour, the kids told the whales about their adventures since March.

"And to think we just swam all that time."

The kids laughed. It felt so good to watch the miraculous, glowing mammals play in the bay and take turns spyhopping.

"You have to meet Carolynn and the others!"

The kids called for them. Carolynn flew down from high in the sky. Madeline arrived from the thick crop of trees, and the rest of the Shimmies stepped out from behind the bushes.

"Carolynn, meet Denise and her family." Evan was very proud of his enormous friend.

The children introduced all the animals, and in turn Denise introduced her extended family.

"I have to sit down," Meagan groaned. My leg is killing me." Evan helped her back to the log and decided to join her.

Denise looked at the Shimmies admiringly. "Thank you for taking such good care of my friends."

"Of course. We will always take care of them."

Gavin had been watching the interaction from a distance. "Why? Why do you want to take care of us?"

Suddenly the full realization of the Shimmies hit him. These animals, his friends, were evidence that when life seemed to stop, in fact it did quite the opposite. These animals loved, laughed and were as mischievous as when they were alive. The "great mystery" was not such a mystery after all. Evan looked from his brother to the owl and realized Gavin's simple question was an important one.

"Carolynn, why do you choose to be our friends?"

The Shimmies came together and faced the children.

"Because we love you."

Suddenly the Shimmies joined their voices to sing in one glorious, harmonized song.

> *Voices lifted high in song and in joy*
> *Gazes turned upon each girl and each boy*
> *Hearts filled full with the love and the light*
> *Burning and yearning in strength and in might*
>
> *On tides adrift with the ebb and the flow*
> *Burrowing along in field and meadow*
> *Soaring so high where clouds also roam*
> *These are the places each of us calls home*
>
> *Weaving for all time in the here and the now*
> *This commitment we pledge all our trust and we vow*
> *This unending bond kept with passion and thunder*
> *For the children of men, our most sacred wonder*

The song echoed off the surrounding rock. Their voices blended in perfect harmony, sending shivers up the children's backs. Their Shimmy light burned bright but didn't blind. Instead, the glow warmed the children to their core, and their hearts swelled with reciprocated love.

Meagan struggled to get up. Evan and Gavin each took an arm and helped her stand. Powerful emotions gripped the children.

These animals, these life forces, were their defenders, their confidants, their friends.

"I wish I could feel you. I wish I could hug you." Meagan took a step closer to Carolynn. Compulsively, she reached out—and was shocked to feel a solid form under her hand. Carolynn's feathers were soft and warm. Meagan ran her hand down the owl's wing, which was tucked close to her body.

"I can feel you!" Meagan's voice was filled with wonder. "And I can see through your eyes! Carolynn—how can this be?"

Evan supported Meagan's arm under her elbow and noticed how Meagan's hand moulded itself against the huge bird's body.

Before Carolynn could answer, Meagan gasped and stared into the twinkling eyes of the owl. Their gazes were locked, and they seemed oblivious to everyone around them.

"I can see everything. I can see here, I can see your memories of flying, I can see you when you were alive... a long time ago." She reached out her left hand and placed it on the other side of Carolynn. With intense purpose, she ran her hands over the top of the owl's head and down her long back.

"It's so beautiful. We're flying above treetops. I see a river, and salmon jumping. I hear the flow of the water and the buzz of bees." Meagan laughed in delight. "There are two bald eagles diving for fish!"

Evan and Gavin stared in wonder, and just as Gavin put out his hand to touch Carolynn too, the shimmering light around Carolynn started to swirl. A funnel of wind came out of nowhere. The wind blew debris all around them, and a thunderous sound erupted in front of them. In the centre of Carolynn's body, a hole opened wide. It was filled with shooting stars and ribbons of cascading lights.

Alarmed, Mr. Biggsy stepped forward. "Sever the connection. Meagan, take your hands off Carolynn now!"

"What's happening?" Evan tried to pull Meagan's arm back, but her grip on Carolynn was firm.

"They're joining as one. Evan, pull her away now!"

Over the deafening sound, Gavin and Evan heard their names

being called. They turned to see Coolio running as fast as he could and waving wildly at them. "I see them! I see them!"

Just as Coolio skidded to a halt behind them, the boys felt Meagan surge forward. When they looked back, they were terrified to see their friend disappear into the swirling hole in Carolynn's stomach.

Without a moment's hesitation, Evan dove in, followed by Gavin and Coolio. The owl—and the children—vanished.

A SHIMMY'S STORY

Keep reading for a sneak peek of Volume 2 of the Shimmy series!

PROLOGUE

EVAN TURNED JUST in time to see Meagan's feet disappear into the dark, swirling hole of Carolynn's stomach. The blood went cold in his veins. Without thinking, he jumped in after her. He tumbled in free fall for half a heartbeat, and then suddenly he felt like he had been strapped into a roller coaster seat that was speeding through a dark maze. Shooting stars whizzed past him, and dazzling lights of all colours exploded near his head. Just as a rolling wave of nausea came over him, he shot toward a blinding ball of yellow flame.

He hit the ground hard and came up gasping for air. It took a moment to realize that he was lying on a pebbled beach. He jumped when he heard a thud beside him. A second later, there was another thud. He looked around just in time to see Coolio vomit.

"*Now* what did we get ourselves into?" Gavin wiped the puke from the side of his mouth with the back of his sleeve—he'd thrown up too—and tried to sit up.

"I don't feel too good," Meagan moaned from the ground, trying to roll over onto her side.

"What just happened?" Coolio rocked back and forth on his knees and clutched his side. "Did I just jump into an owl's stomach?

I know I wanted to see the Shimmies, but did it have to come with a roller coaster ride from hell?"

Evan stood up on wobbly legs. "I don't know what happened, but I'm guessing Carolynn does."

He looked all around and up into the trees. He spotted her on a low branch. She looked whole again but a little dazed.

"Carolynn, where are we? How did we get here? He walked slowly toward her, but she wasn't her usual glittering self. Her light was not as bright or glistening.

"Evan, are you all right?" Her voice was thick with concern. "Where are the other children?" She peered around him and saw Gavin, Meagan and Coolio still on the ground.

"Did you hear my questions? Where are we, Carolynn?" Evan could see that she was shaken up, and he wanted to comfort her, but he was afraid to touch her.

"I'm so sorry. I don't know what happened. One minute I felt Meagan touching me, and I could feel her mind connecting with mine. It was like she was playing back all my memories. The last thing I saw in my mind's eye was this beach, and the eagles fishing for salmon." She looked around. "We're still in Cedar. We are near the mouth of the Nanaimo River. Look up."

They followed her gaze to the two high cliffs that framed the river on either side.

"That is where the Cedar Bridge will go one day," she said.

"What do you mean, 'one day'?" Coolio stood up and took a few steps toward Evan and the owl. "I recognize this beach now. Carolynn, where's the bridge? It should be right over our heads."

"It won't be built for another decade or two."

"What?" Evan sank to the ground again, trying to put together the pieces of the puzzle. "Carolynn, when was the bridge built?" he murmured.

"The year was 1881."

ABOUT THE AUTHOR

Anne Cateaux lives on Vancouver Island, British Columbia. Happily nestled in a forest, this mother of two sons and two German shepherds is an eco-warrior by day and a fiction writer by night. All things spiritual inspire and uplift Anne to follow her passion of writing.

Made in the USA
Columbia, SC
02 December 2021

50181775R00141